SOLOMON, MY SON!

By JOHN ERSKINE

FICTION

The Private Life of Helen of Troy
Galahad: Enough of His Life to Explain
    His Reputation
Adam and Eve: Though He Knew Better
Penelope's Man: The Homing Instinct
Sincerity: A Story of Our Time
Uncle Sam: In the Eyes of His Family
Cinderella's Daughter, and Other Sequels
    and Consequences
Unfinished Business
Tristan and Isolde: Restoring Palamede
Bachelor—of Arts
Forget If You Can
Solomon, My Son!

ESSAYS

The Moral Obligation to Be Intelligent
The Kinds of Poetry
The Literary Discipline
Prohibition and Christianity, and Other
    Paradoxes of the American Spirit
American Character and Other Essays
The Delight of Great Books

POETRY

Collected Poems, 1907-1922
Sonata, and Other Poems

DRAMA

Hearts Enduring

OPERA LIBRETTO

Jack and the Beanstalk
Helen Retires

SOLOMON,
MY SON!

BY

JOHN ERSKINE

ST. JOSEPH'S UNIVERSITY   STX

PS3509.E73S6
Solomon, my son]

3 9353 00149 4994

145145

PS
350
•E7
S6

The

BOBBS-MERRILL
COMPANY

Publishers

INDIANAPOLIS • NEW YORK

COPYRIGHT, 1935
BY JOHN ERSKINE

Printed in the United States of America

PRINTED AND BOUND BY
BRAUNWORTH & CO., INC.
BOOK MANUFACTURERS
BROOKLYN, NEW YORK

SOLOMON, MY SON!

SOLOMON, MY SON!

CHAPTER I

LOOK for no further scandals about the Queen of Sheba, and for no discussion of women in quantity. I hold that Sheba, the seven hundred wives and the three hundred concubines, are exaggerated. Wish-fulfilments. Solomon was not thwarted, but some of those who wrote about him were.

The industry which really occupied Solomon had to do with the temple of the Lord. This shall be my theme. In all reverence I refrain from comment on the religion of Solomon, or of his people, or of any other people. I would call attention rather to certain footnotes, clearly written down in the ancient Scriptures, but too seldom tarried over by the passionate reader.

These footnotes remind us that when Solomon built the temple he also had to pay for it. Or his people had to.

I invite you therefore to meet in the old story some friends of ours—tax, surtax, and income tax; barter, exchange, and the adjustment of international debts; overproduction, unemployment, and made work; the revolutionary aberrations of the laboring class, and the counterhope of the employers to weed out the foreigner, keep the race pure, and so prevent the generation of ideas. Of these elements came at least one section of Solomon's wisdom. Women of course he did run into, but he was always surprised.

To understand him, his part in the temple, his method of dealing with the consequent economic crisis, we must start with his home. I mean the amazing household which molded his childhood. He loved both his parents. This achievement alone would have made him a philosopher.

Neither parent, taken separately, would have been difficult to love, but you couldn't take David and Bathsheba separately. David was full of blood, flame, delight, and danger; Bathsheba, though her beauty was outstanding, passed for patient and demure. David, whom Solomon adored, was stormy, even volcanic. His poems cracked your heart with happiness, or smothered you with misery. He loved God so as to sweep you off your feet, yet at moments he would ask Jehovah pointed questions, why the world wasn't better made. In this same headlong fashion he loved men, or hated them. So also he loved women. At least, as Solomon knew, he loved Bathsheba.

Zest for living leads, of course, to an occasional mistake. As for Bathsheba, if you wished to portray her in a phrase, you might say she had a gift for getting in the path of a promising mistake.

Of Solomon's formal education we know nothing, but his real teachers were this overwhelming father, this serene and apparently docile mother.

On the positive side he wished to be a poet, like David, who blazed into music and love and grief and glory, composing songs which induced melancholy, or roused you, or chilled your spine, calling to mind the stars in their courses, the moon in her station, the sun rising and setting, the waters crashing on the shore. Solomon also wished to be, like his father, a man of action, in addition to the poetry, with a prompt yes or no to all questions. These ambitions were the keener because he had reason to fear he lacked the talent for them.

From his sixteenth year no day passed without some verses painfully meditated and revised, but when he had put the last polish on, they turned out to be not winged flights, but inscriptions, as for tombstones. Adonijah, who was practical, thought that nothing more cheerful would come unless you were in love, and in that case you would have no time for literature.

Solomon's other hopes were negative. He did not wish to be a king, sitting in judgment or perhaps going to war, and he did not wish to marry. The kingship he might avoid, unless something happened to Adonijah, his brother. Adonijah was the elder, therefore the heir. Adonijah was tall and muscular. They talked it out, as boys will, and agreed each to assume that area of David's genius which he was fitted to carry on, Adonijah taking over the throne and matrimony, Solomon cultivating the fine arts.

These wishes, both the courageous and the timid, dated, I think, from early influences, while Solomon was still small enough to be held on the lap, listening to his father's stories.

There was Goliath the Giant, whom David killed.

There were really five giants, closely related, but Goliath was the best known because he talked. The others were brought down under David's direction, but Goliath by David personally, with a slingshot. A home-made sling and a smooth pebble from the brook, in the middle of the forehead.

Solomon admired this tale, but not for the marksmanship. He envied the tribute which the giant had paid to unrecognized greatness. He had shaken his fist at the armies of Israel, and cried, "Give me a man!" And all the time there was David, a mere lad, waiting with the sling. Solomon repeated to himself Goliath's challenge. He hoped to be asked for, some day.

There was also the story of the bear, long ago when David was minding sheep, Solomon's grandfather's sheep. A big bear came out of the woods and carried off a lamb.

"What did you do *then,* Father?"

"Why, I went after the bear!"

The boy knew it was true. His father *would* go after the bear! In peril he would always be a sudden person. Solomon admired with a wrench of self-criticism. His own impulse would be to think it over.

As he grew older he tried to reconcile the bear with the temple. It was in David's mind to build a temple, but for once he did not carry out his purpose to the end. Something checked him. He said it was Jehovah's wish that the temple should be built in the next reign. He also said, in another apologetic moment, that he had too many wars on his hands, but he didn't mention the taxes, which Adoram, the chief collector, thought were already too high.

Solomon hoped that the next king, Adonijah or whoever it might be, would build a temple promptly, to take
away from his father's record this stain of a single hesitation.

Also, as he grew older, he learned why there were so
many women in the house. There had to be, because of his
brothers and sisters, and in a well-ordered home like his
father's, each child would have its individual mother.
Adonijah, the heir, was not Bathsheba's son.

All the women were beautiful, of course. His father
would not have it otherwise. His mother was the most
beautiful woman he had ever seen, and his father thought
so too, but the other wives held a minority opinion. Bathsheba was polite to them, and in her presence they bowed
almost to the floor.

Still later he heard, with a shock, about that handsome
brother Absolom, who had come to a bad end. He got the
story from Joab, the captain of the palace guard. Absolom
was so bad that he actually started a war against his father,
and when David ran away rather than fight his boy, a
patriot named Shimei openly cursed him for running, a rebuke which the king found it hard to forgive. But at last
some unknown person who loved God, killed Absolom.
Solomon asked who was the unknown person, and Joab
replied that he was unknown.

Solomon was glad his name meant Peaceful. Peace was
his mission, as Bathsheba frequently reminded him, pointing her finger at the fate of the rash. Peace with power,
she would add.

Unlike David, Bathsheba never told him stories about

her early life, and though he would have listened if she had insisted, it would have been through courtesy, because nothing important happens to a girl. But when the king grew old and at last took to his bed, the meaner sort whom he had trod upon paid themselves back by whispering, and Solomon at last heard how his parents first met.

Oddly enough, it was Adonijah who told him, in a friendly way, as though such things were to be expected, when the man is a king and the woman beautiful. Adonijah said you must look at life in the large.

The story was that Bathsheba once had another husband, and after she married David she bore another son. Solomon had always attributed his mother's devotion to the fact that he was her only child! Never had she mentioned that other boy! Never had his father mentioned that other husband!

The king, Adonijah said, was enjoying the evening on his housetop, and Bathsheba at that very moment went up to her own housetop, only an eye-glance away, and began to take a bath. Solomon would have been glad to blunt the coincidence, but he could not. Whatever his mother did, she aimed straight.

David, in that impulsive way of his, had sent for her, and after that brief visit, some time after, she said she would have a child. Somehow the unnecessary husband was removed, and David could marry her before it was too late, and the child came, but it died young, and then Solomon was born, and so long as David had his health, no one remembered the bathing incident.

"He was a true king," Adonijah commented, "even at his simplest."

"Simplest?" echoed Solomon.

"Well," said the handsome elder brother, "when she told him she carried a child, she was right, of course. Was it the first time she had been up on the roof?"

Solomon's friendship for Adonijah ended then and there. He turned from the courtyard, where they had been walking, and sought his mother, in her room.

He meant to ask whether the charge was true, but when she received him in the seclusion of her apartment and his gaze met hers, he decided not to. She was no longer young, but beautiful still, her skin ivory smooth, her black tresses faultless in their place, her fingers delicate, with pointed nails. Her body seemed that of a girl, and when she spoke it was like singing, a soft up-and-down of music, as though she never had been frightened or worried or even inconvenienced. He tried to imagine in what mood she had come from the roof when his father had sent for her, and what answer she had brought to that fierce love. He was sure it was fierce.

Now she was standing before a bowl of rose leaves, herself fragrant with a perfume from Egypt, David's gift, and her long robe flexing to her loveliness. One thing he saw clearly—whatever his father had done was right, and whatever she too did or thought of doing. Her beauty convinced him, and her obvious peace of mind. Besides, his father continued to adore her with the lavish idolatry of youth. If their companionship was sinful, would a good man like David keep on enjoying it?

Looking up from the rose bowl that momentous afternoon, Bathsheba read something of what was in his eyes.

"Solomon, my son!"

"My mother!"

She came slowly toward him, and lifted her white hands till they reached his shoulders.

"You have heard about your father?"

David would have had it out with her at once, but Solomon thought best to wait, looking steadily at the even teeth between the red lips.

"He is very ill. His blood no longer warms him."

David without his fiery heart!

"Then he will die?"

"Too soon."

His knees weakened. "No!" he cried. "They must do something——"

She led him to her couch, and sat stroking one of his hands, for comfort.

"The doctors have their temporary remedies, of course. I was at his side a moment ago. They have brought a young girl to lie in his arms. For the warmth," she added. "But I have no faith in these new medical ideas."

Solomon imagined his father, with the doctors grouped around the bed, and the young girl.

"If it were necessary," he protested, "if it really did any good, I should have thought they'd send for you."

"The treatment is rather public," said his mother drily, "and the desired temperature is found, I understand, only in extreme youth. Besides, I am better occupied, at the moment, with——"

On an impulse he blurted out more than he wished, as will happen to men who are silent through weakness.

"To wash on the housetop would be less discreet than this service in my father's deathroom!"

He checked himself, amazed at the indignation he had not known he felt, but except for a brightening of her eyes there was no sign he had spoken amiss.

"So he has told you!" she remarked quietly. "His mother envied me always. She would make him king."

"But that's decided!"

"I've been talking with your father," said Bathsheba slowly, "and we think the kingdom will be safer in your hands."

"But I don't want it!"

"Benaiah will be here in a few moments. Your father has appointed him captain of the guard—in fact, of all the armies."

Solomon perceived that his father, however chilled by age, could still make up his mind, and much had been happening while he walked along the wall with his elder brother.

"Joab," he reflected, "was captain of the guard this morning."

"Shortly before noon," said Bathsheba, "I asked your father what would become of you and me, if Adonijah and Joab seized the power."

"Why, I was talking with Adonijah just now, in the friendliest way——"

"And he began with that roof story! No, my son! When Joab found Absolom in the forest, hanging by the hair, he put an arrow through him. Don't look pale! A kingdom must have peace, even by purging. When your father came to power, he took the usual precautions, however unpleasant, and hanged those of Saul's relatives who might possibly fail to cooperate. If Adonijah now helps himself to the throne, Joab will protect him from differences of opinion by running a sword through you and me. I prefer to make you king, and let Benaiah preserve harmony."

Solomon stood up and took a deep breath. He had come to that room disturbed by a slight reflection upon his mother's sense of decorum, and here she was, unfolding in that pleasant voice of hers a program of domestic murder!

He would not be king! Never would he accept that uncomfortable honor if Benaiah must kill Joab and Adonijah, and as Bathsheba seemed to imply, Adonijah's mother!

There was a loud knock at the queen's door.

"That's Benaiah now," she said cheerfully.

"I won't have it!" he cried. "There'll be no killing! He can take his sword away with him!"

"He has brought your father's mule," said Bathsheba, answering the knock, and admitting one of her waiting women. "Tell Benaiah my son will be at the gate in a minute."

The woman bowed herself out, and Bathsheba closed the door firmly.

"The mule is easy to ride," she continued, "and Benaiah will lead it by the bridle through the city streets, and at every corner he will call, 'God save King Solomon,' or whatever the legal phrase is. The people will then know your father has chosen you to be his successor."

"I don't see that," objected Solomon. "What proves he chose me?"

"The mule. It's his property. They'll know it's symbolic."

The mule, as she said, was waiting at the palace gate, the magnificent white animal which had carried David about, in relaxed moments, when he didn't need a war-horse. They had put on the best saddle, the one with tassels, and the bridle carried a waving plume.

There was also an armed guard, ten stalwart youths shining in breastplates and helmets, each fitted out with a round shield and a glittering spear. Benaiah himself Solomon had always taken for granted, as part of the military equipment. Now for the first time he observed him carefully, since he would be charged, if Bathsheba's view of the future was correct, with the sad duty of preserving harmony. Benaiah had a heavy jaw, wide shoulders and thick fingers. His face was diplomatically inexpressive. Or perhaps it was not the kind of face in which expression could ever flourish, since his nose had been broken, and there was a heavy scar up his right cheek which compelled the eye on that side to stare.

He was the killer type. Once he slew a lion, single-handed, and at another time two Moabites who were as reluctant to be killed as the lion was, and on still another occasion he met an Egyptian who was carrying a spear, and though Benaiah had only a staff, he took away the Egyptian's spear, and thrust it into him. There was no war at the time. The lion was driven toward the settlements by an unusual fall of snow. The Moabites and the Egyptian just happened along.

Now Benaiah saluted Solomon with energetic precision, as though this ride were the order of an average day. Then he obligingly made a stirrup of his hands to help the prince get on the mule, and Solomon mounted.

He was sensitive to what the citizens along the streets might think of him. Their first response was a natural curiosity as he came around the corner, then a ripple of good-natured applause as the idea spread much faster than the mule could walk, and those who leaned from the windows or crowded against the walls to let him pass caught the idea that some day, when David was through with the kingdom, this thoughtful young man would take his place.

The loud announcement of his destiny at each cross-street gave Solomon no pleasure. He feared to be ridiculous, and he was inclined to blame his mother for haste. After all, David was still king, and these people who obediently smiled and applauded, were honoring the great monarch, not his son.

The mule was safe, but Solomon did not feel at ease, and he doubted if he looked dignified. It had not been his habit to estimate the effect of his appearance, but the question will come up if you find yourself parading through city streets, with the populace lined along the curb.

What the populace saw was a tall youth, with a silken, tentative beard, sitting the mule in a stiff angularity, knees gripping like iron, and eyes focused on the animal's ears. But he did not notice the ears. He was remembering that David won his kingdom, and perhaps kingship is endurable only if it comes from your own efforts.

It also occurred to him that he might be asleep. The ride had some qualities of a dream. Would he wake, unharmed and relieved? Or would it be necessary, on his return to ·the palace, to begin at once an imitation of his heroic father? Or his mother, who had so casually launched him on his difficult destiny, would she now suggest before supper, in her sweet voice, that he kill somebody?

If she was able to arrange this ride on the mule, she perhaps knew what she was talking about when she mentioned that plot of Adonijah's. One event was as improbable as the other. Now he must learn for himself whether Adonijah plotted anything at all, and if so, what. The first step in government, he realized as Benaiah steadied the mule, was to find out what was happening. The next step would be to do something about it. The rest of your life you would be accepting the consequences.

The mule had made almost the circuit of the town, and Benaiah's voice began to grow husky. Solomon compared the helmeted top of Benaiah's head, bobbing up and down, and the mule's head, bobbing also but in a different rhythm. So Benaiah had displaced old Joab! Was Joab really the unknown man who killed Absolom? Would David, knowing this, permit him to remain so long captain of the armies, or alive on any terms? Anyway, why was Benaiah promoted?

Solomon had never agreed with his mother about Benaiah. She found something to admire, but Solomon thought him stupid. Listen to him now, calling monotonously,

"God save King Solomon, God save King Solomon," as though he peddled vegetables on market day, or offered to remove your old clothes! Was it Bathsheba who had whispered in David's ear that Benaiah would make a good general?

To the palace gate he returned with spontaneous heartache. This ride, suddenly improvised, had softened the impact of the heaviest tidings, the warning of David's approaching death. For a whole month, of course, the old man had been failing. As often as the doctors would permit, Solomon had found his way to the sick room, for a minute or two, watching the great form stretched out there, the rich white beard, the noble forehead. If he was awake, Solomon would come near the bed and try to say something cheerful, and his father would acknowledge the affection by a gentle lifting of the wasted hand, a pathetic, relaxed gesture, as though he were glad of the good wishes but knew them vain. But you get used to sorrow, even to the threat of fate. After so many weeks Solomon had felt no extra grief when the doctors had forbidden all visitors except Bathsheba.

Still seated on the sedate mule, Solomon recalled a scene in that very room where his father was now lying, an exchange of ideas when he was but eight years old. He had asked a prophetic question.

"Is it easy to be a king when you learn how?"

David had laughed, and called him a quaint child, and had drawn him close, with an arm around his shoulder.

"You either are a king, or you aren't. But it's not easy."

Well then, Solomon now reflected, he either was or he

wasn't, and if he wasn't, what good would come of his mother's ambition?

At the portal he got off, thanked Benaiah for his excellent care, started up the steps, but under the first shadows of the hallway Adonijah was waiting for him, a quite new Adonijah, nervous, even frightened, speaking low, since the guards were within earshot.

"If I'd known you wanted it, I never would have consulted Joab! I thought it was understood! I was just protecting my rights—and my mother's!"

Solomon stared at him, first because the strong man's fear was incredible, then because of the reference to his mother.

"Against whom were you protecting yourself?"

Adonijah wrung his hands, and seemed about to burst into tears.

"Nobody in particular! I assure you, Solomon, nobody!"

The youth with the thin beard who had just descended from his father's mule, assumed the dignity of a king.

"I am to understand, then, you had no thought of putting me out of the way? You never hinted to Joab the advantage of removing Queen Bathsheba?"

The guards were listening. Adonijah turned very white.

"The thought horrifies me!"

"It should," agreed Solomon, pushing on down the hall. "I shall consider what you have said, and our friendship will depend upon your behavior."

When Adonijah bowed almost to the ground, Solomon wished to protest, but remembered in time that the circumstances demanded, perhaps, some ceremony. He walked down the corridor, not to his mother's room, but to his own, a sequestered chamber which he used for other exercises than sleep. At that desk near the window he had meditated his poems. Slender scrolls were pigeonholed in the opposite corner.

Now after the excitement of his momentous ride, he felt the need of ordering his thoughts. His couch was ready on the left side of the room, and ordinarily he would have stretched himself upon it with his hands behind his head, to gaze up toward the ceiling. Through boyhood this had been his posture when in the pursuit of ideas. But there was also a straight-backed chair at the center table, with curved arms ending in lion heads. Since he was occupied now with critical problems, he sat there, bolt upright, each hand resting on a carved lion.

It would be possible to conduct himself wisely if he were not interfered with. He would take advice, of course, even ask for it, but not orders.

No more rides on a mule!

He foresaw that his life would be lonely. No other man would talk to him again on even terms, and no woman, probably, would now approach him without a purpose. The old friendship with Adonijah had been spoiled; the next time they met, Adonijah would probably call him, "Your Majesty."

Very well. He would live with his books and with his thoughts. Most of all he would remember David. Before it was too late he would seize some conscious moment, to ask the old king one or two practical questions. How stupid not to have asked long ago, while David was still himself!

In the swift adjustment to his new station he was distinguishing sharply between his parents. He must shake himself free of Bathsheba, and attend more completely to his father's example. His father, of course, had been a great warrior, and had killed his enemies in battle, which was the place to kill them, but at all other times he was, you might say, poetic, the very opposite of bloody. Bathsheba, a woman, swayed by desires and dislikes, did not know where war ended and civil life began. He could no longer reject Adonijah's story about the rooftop, nor about that mysterious disposal of the first husband. Bathsheba rather than David must have been responsible for that ruthlessness. He would continue to love her, since she was his mother, but he would model his government upon those humane principles which his father illustrated; that is, when off the battle-field.

To protect himself in these high ideals, his loneliness should be permanent; he would never marry. The kingdom would be his bride. This self-denial would doubtless cost a pang, since the women of his people were frequently beautiful, and according to rumor, the outlying tribes of alien unbelievers often seemed to the eye more excellent than could be justified to the mind. Doubtless, since he was human, he would fall in love, but since he was king, he would mention it to no one. The consequent pressure on his heart might very well prove the inspiration of better poetry than he had yet been able to put together.

From these heroic thoughts his mother interrupted him

by knocking gently at the door. Thinking it was a servant, he said, "Come in," and to his surprise, she came. Her custom hitherto had been to send for him; now, as he observed, she sought him out. He recognized a tribute to his exalted position, and hesitated whether to rise and greet her as usual, or to sit still and let her stand. When she advanced across the room, he was poised half-way, neither sitting nor standing, with his hands clutching the lions' heads.

"Benaiah tells me," she began——

He interrupted. "The people received me well, and Benaiah is skilful at leading a mule. I am entirely satisfied."

She stared at him. "I was about to give you Benaiah's impression."

Solomon smiled. "I have not asked for it. I do not include Benaiah among my advisers."

Bathsheba fixed on him her lovely eyes. "May I crave the privilege, as a favor to myself, of telling you what Benaiah said?"

Solomon straightened back in the chair. "As a favor to yourself."

"He says you need practice in riding, and perhaps instruction. But the people forgave you because of your modest bearing. It was a happy beginning, my son. Remain modest!"

Solomon tapped on the chair with the fingers of his right hand. "I wish to talk for a moment with my father. Will the doctors permit it?"

His mother inclined her head. "It was really on that

errand I came. He is failing rapidly, but at moments his brain clears, and he would say to you a word of farewell. Go to him at once."

Solomon sprang to his feet. "Is my father waiting, are his minutes so few, and do you stop to talk about Benaiah and mule-riding?"

He strode from the room, leaving her, to say truth, with more to think about than he had hitherto provided.

In the sick room the doctors were ranged about the broad bed, in the middle of which the old king was lying, for the moment unconscious. The doctors watched him in silence, three on one side of the bed, two opposite, all with long beards and dark robes, and four of them with their hands folded over their stomachs. The fifth had his hands behind his back. Clearly the case puzzled them. They had agreed a fortnight earlier that David would die during the night, but David had declined to die, and the five ever since had been contemplating the miracle of their own mistake.

When Solomon entered, the five turned to see who it was, and immediately bowed low. They must have heard about the ride. He acknowledged the salute and stepped softly to the foot of the bed.

There lay his father, a grand frame of a man, more gaunt than when he had last seen him, but still of heroic build. The white beard spread over chest and shoulders, the deep-set eyes were closed.

Also upon his chest, balancing herself by her hands on the beard-covered shoulders, lay a very alluring young girl, white-skinned, dark-haired. It was with a sudden start, almost an exclamation, that Solomon realized her presence and remembered his mother's report of a new prescription for curing prolonged chill. Nothing that had happened to Solomon during this mad day was so sharp an overturn of destiny as the lovely creature displayed between his father's arms. He looked down at her, mouth open with amazement, and she glanced up at him. He thought she smiled a little, as though it were funny.

Between David's arms—but the arms stretched out limp on the bed. David did not know she was there. The pathos of extreme age gave Solomon a twinge of pity. His father had once been a great lover—not calculating and ambitious, like Bathsheba, but generous and reckless. To Solomon it seemed that life had played an ignominious trick, exposing his father in that room to the official gaze with this beauty nestled to his heart, unappreciated. Once in his childhood, when Solomon suffered an earache, Bathsheba had cured him with a hot onion to his face, wrapped in a piece of blanket.

The doctors kept an exclusive eye on the patient. To them the girl was only a mechanism, part of the treatment. Solomon found himself looking at her a second time for her own sake, and feeling repaid. The loneliness proper to a king might after all be insupportable. She was very beautiful—at least judging from the back, and from that one moment when her face had inquired toward his. Where had she come from? What would they do with her after the king was gone?

David, breathing quietly, so quietly that the doctors had to lean down from time to time to be sure, at last opened his eyes and stared with glassy intentness at the particular doctor who at the moment happened to be leaning. The learned physician straightened up and then folded over again in salute.

"Has the king slept well?"

David stared at each of them in turn, then last at Solomon, and recognized him. With a choke in his throat, Solomon bowed himself before this loving and tender spirit who contained the perfection of all he wished to be, and who was about to carry that perfection beyond reach. David turned his head feebly toward the larger group of doctors, the three on the left side.

"You may get out!" he said.

His voice was low but his intention plain. The three bent themselves in unison, and with dignity retired to the door. David for a second seemed about to relapse into unconsciousness, but with an effort roused, and turned toward the two on the right.

"Leave the room!"

Obediently they lowered their beards and left. David stared toward the foot of the bed.

"Is the door shut? Make sure."

Solomon tried all the knobs, then came back to where his father could see him. They three were alone, the tall prince gazing down on the withered body of the old king, and on the bloom of the young girl.

"Solomon, my son," David began in a mere whisper of his deep voice, "be strong! I wish to leave you many blessings, but this contains all—fear nothing and be yourself!"

He shut his eyes again as though to rest, and when he next looked up, his voice was firmer.

"I die at peace! I have sinned more than once, but Jehovah, I take it, has forgiven me, since I leave my people happy, with a son to reign over them, and myself the enemy of no man."

He shut his eyes again, but not to rest. This time he was trying to recall something. He lifted his right hand past the head of the young girl, and rubbed his forehead. His voice now showed that he was deeply moved.

"There was one man—just one man! Shimei—cursed me. He should not have done that! A kind of murder that was—to curse me there in the road—to curse the king before his people!"

For a moment he controlled his indignation. "Afterwards he was sorry, and I promised never to take vengeance on him. God knows I have kept my word!

"But when I am gone, Solomon——" The old voice rose to a battle call, and the broad shoulders propped themselves up suddenly, spilling the girl on the bed.

"When I am gone, Solomon, you'll know what to do to him!"

The eyes flamed so bright that Solomon quaked before them. Then they closed wearily, and David dropped to the pillow, dead.

Not a syllable about the temple!

So he was gathered to his fathers, and Solomon assumed the power, perplexed how to go on from where his parent had left off.

CHAPTER II

A WEEK or so after Solomon came to the throne, King Hiram of Tyre happened to be inspecting his water front, in a double mood of pride and perplexity. With good reason he doubted whether until that day any ruler had been so well equipped to dominate the commerce of the seas, by the quality of his exports and the speed with which he could ship them out. But what was the use, unless someone at the other end wished to buy?

For this dilemma King Hiram somewhat unfairly blamed David, of whose death he had recently heard. An interesting savage, King Hiram always said, who kept surprisingly good order among those eccentric and nervous people directly to the south.

But David, a few years before, had planned a temple to his tribal god, a small edifice yet much beyond his means, as any experienced builder could foresee, and he had placed with Hiram fabulous orders for cedar wood and nails and brass and gold and hewn stone. What the completed building would look like was a question, since David intended to be his own architect, working along as he got ideas.

Moreover, the basis of payment was not settled, not even mentioned, and King Hiram feared that this client, being both a soldier and a poet, would in all likelihood, lack the disposition or the mathematics to figure costs. At least, he had not gone very deep into geometry. To ornament his temple he had called for a circular vessel of brass, which should be exactly ten cubits from brim to brim and exactly thirty cubits in circumference.

Yet King Hiram had accepted all the orders, explaining to his counselors that the Tyrian artisans would have steady employment for the immediate future, whereas, if they were not employed, they must be supported in idleness, which is demoralizing, and this way the Tyrian products would be spread through the land of Judah, and perhaps a taste for them would be created.

As a matter of fact, King Hiram would have accepted an order from anyone just then, even if the bill could never be collected.

He had shifted his city from the mainland to a near island, he had built an aqueduct to bring fresh water from the coast, he had fortified a harbor on the south side for a fleet which should trade with Egypt and with his own Phoenician colony, Tarshish, among the remote Iberians, and another harbor on the north side, for a fleet which should trade with the barbarians in that direction, and he had constructed the aforesaid fleets, and provided them with sailors.

But such progress in the civilized arts, as he eventually learned, should make haste slowly. If once it speeds beyond your control, you find yourself dangling at the end of the reins. King Hiram now had on the royal payrolls an extraordinary number of workmen who could build ships in a world where no more ships were wanted. From

Tarshish the patriotic colonists did send iron and silver, lead and tin, which they wrung, not to say stole, from the natives, the natives refusing to accept the Tyrian products in legitimate exchange, since they were of a surly disposition and averse to compulsory comforts. The fleet which went to Egypt did bring back wheat and oil, but in parsimonious quantities, those clever Egyptians having discovered that the Tyrian wares competed with their own home products. As to the ships which visited the barbarians to the north, when King Hiram saw what *they* brought back, he gave up all hope of trade from that quarter, and maintained the route as a training cruise for young sailors.

When David ordered the temple, King Hiram had just played his last desperate card. His boldest men had sailed the length of the sea westward, past Tarshish, out through the straits to the edge of chaos, where a ship venturing too near is liable to drop off. Then northward, hugging that perilous margin, to islands with green shores or tall white cliffs, where dwell the Celts, the Gaels and the Picts.

But nothing came of it. The Celts, the Gaels and the Picts, if they have a little tin, have otherwise not even clothes, but wear in summer a dress of cranberry juice, in winter a coat of clay. King Hiram had sent bales of cloth, dipped in the noble Tyrian dyes, but cloth, as you can see, was out of place, and you can't dip a human skin while the owner is still wearing it.

Unless new markets could be found, something would have to be, as we would say, plowed under. The articles which now crowded King Hiram's storehouses would never be sold, not if his men went on making things. Why not burn them up, take the loss, and get it over with? The storehouses would then be empty. Why not burn the storehouses? The men who kept the storehouses would then have nothing to do. Why not——

No, he couldn't kill off his own people, not in peace, and the neighbors were as reluctant to take him on in a war as in a trade. He might tell his people to beget fewer children, but the results wouldn't show for some time, even if they followed his advice, which they wouldn't. He didn't blame them. It was an immoral idea, repugnant to the Phoenician temperament.

Then came David with that temple order! You can just put yourself in King Hiram's place——

But no sooner had he speeded up his workmen than David sent another message, explaining that his god wished the temple postponed, and the order would therefore have to stand over till the next generation, but King Hiram needn't worry about it, because some son of David's would eventually inherit the throne, and whenever that occurred he would let King Hiram know and the work could proceed.

At this communication King Hiram used a bristling Phoenician sound which meant that he didn't think David was well-born, and he asked about David's age, and when he heard, he was disappointed, but so many cedars were already cut down and so much brass melted, and his people were so grateful for the prosperity he had arranged for them, that he kept the bad news to himself, built storehouses, and hoped for the best.

He had almost abandoned hope, when the rumor came through, of David's end. Since it was only a whisper along the highway, he proceeded with caution, sending a smooth-talking courier to find out if it was true, and if it was, to present David's successor with King Hiram's compliments. If the successor had been friendly with David, the courier was to say that King Hiram was sorry, but old men like David and King Hiram himself must drop out, and youth is what the world needs today. King Hiram hoped this greeting might remind someone down there about the temple. But the courier hadn't yet returned.

Now, as he walked along his wharves, of a fine afternoon, he counted the ships tied up for the season, as they had been tied up for the seasons before, in slow decay. He could build no more sheds for superfluous products. He must send the workmen to their homes, and cut off their wages, and if they were disagreeable about it, he must call out the army. It might be wise to begin by enlisting some of the workmen, so that, if there should be a riot, the soldiers would outnumber the mob. But there again—he couldn't pay the soldiers already under arms.

Just in this crisis of bewilderment, he noticed his chief metal-worker coming toward him along the quay, a powerful youth with reddish hair, his mother's color, a prominent nose, a mouth full but firm, and dark eyes that glittered at you with a concentrated squint, acquired daily at the forge. Watching the confident swing of his long legs, King Hiram asked what kind of luck was this, which brought together all his troubles at once.

The youth had his confidence, and in a sense his admiration. He also had the king's name. Hiram the goldsmith. Gold or brass, according to the supply, and he could handle silver too. For skill and industry he had no equal in the world. The king had hoped to send this other Hiram into David's country, though when the temple was first mentioned he was only a boy. Storing the countermanded cedar was as nothing compared with the embarrassment of his growing up, in the eyes of the Tyrians, with his strong nature, and his name, and his looks.

He looked like the king, and the resemblance increased. His mother passed for a widow. She came originally from one of the tribes over whom David ruled, but the business which brought her across the Phoenician border was obscure. In any case, she had a gift for salesmanship. The father of her son was said to be a man of Tyre, and the king had reason to believe this rumor. The sight of young Hiram invariably roused gratifying memories, but it precipitated also a large uneasiness, since the older Hiram had committed himself publicly to the doctrine that the racial stock should be kept pure. He wished he knew what doctrine the youth would adopt. Already the spokesman for the guild of metal workers, he had a firm way of asking for what he wanted. It might be a bad moment to propose shutting down the industry.

"Well," he began cautiously, "what is it now?"

"The courier is back. He's waiting for you at the palace."

The king started off home, and his son stood on the wharf, watching him hurry. On second thoughts the king turned.

"Come here!"

Young Hiram approached, respectfully but without haste.

"What's the news?"

"He wants his temple, right away."

"Who?"

"Solomon."

"David's son?"

"He may be."

King Hiram resented that close stare.

"He wants it right away, does he?"

"And he'll pay any price."

King Hiram leaned against a mooring post on the wharf, and wiped his brow. "This comes at a convenient moment. We can send what we have ready."

"He wants more. He has enlarged his plans. He asks you to cut twice as much cedar."

"We can do that too," said King Hiram, faint with excitement. "That is, if he really can pay."

"Our men are tired of fish," said their spokesman. "Solomon has wheat."

"Oh, very well. Wheat will do. I'll send half the men to the hills, for more timber, and the other half to his country, to put it together for him, and you can go along with your best metal workers."

He slipped in this disposition of young Hiram, so it wouldn't seem personal or over-eager.

"One other matter," said his son. "He needs us, but he has workmen of his own, and they don't like foreigners coming in to take away the jobs. He stipulates that for each of us, there must be one of his people alongside."

"Why, they'll learn our skill!"

"That's what he says. And he wants it to apply to the cedar cutting. He'll match us, ax to ax."

"He's a fool!" exclaimed the elder Hiram.

"His workmen forced him to it," said the younger, "and they're right. I like their spirit. There's a fellow there named Jeroboam——"

King Hiram stroked his beard. "It will take some years," he reflected, "and it will be best for you to represent me in that land. When the temple is complete, he should have a proper palace. Suggest the idea gradually. Afterward he will need a fleet."

"You want other people to have boats?"

The king put an affectionate hand on his son's shoulders, as they strolled back to the palace. "These bottoms will have their cargoes now—wheat coming in, his temple going out. But he needs a fleet on the Red Sea."

The steady squint questioned him. "Where would he sail with it?"

"Leave something to his judgment," said King Hiram. "He is young. He'll have plans of his own."

In the palace at Jerusalem Bathsheba was visiting her only son, now her exalted master. Her entrance, unannounced, had interrupted the day's literary work. There was a manuscript on his desk and a slight frown on his brow.

"I shall delay you but a moment," she explained apologetically. "I understand you have ordered the temple?"

"The messenger is gone."

"Does Adoram approve?"

"He does not."

"And you made clear about the workmen, his and ours, two and two, as Jeroboam wished?"

Solomon tried to recall. "I think I said one and one."

"A much better formula," she conceded. "Now, have you thought of marrying?"

He recoiled. "Does that come next?"

"The daughter of the King of Egypt might do."

"Which daughter?"

"There are five. Any one."

When she mentioned a wife, he saw before him that white girl, Abishag, lying in his father's arms. In fact, the image had occurred to him before.

He cleared his throat.

"I probably shall not wed for some time."

"Your ancestors would be avenged rather neatly," she continued. "When we left Pharaoh, none of the royal family expected to marry any of us."

"They probably won't now!"

She shook her charming head. "Five daughters, and kings are scarce. They'd rather let one take you than keep her home unemployed."

Solomon was drawing absent-minded designs on the foot of his unfinished manuscript. His mother pulled a chair up to the desk, without asking his permission.

"I'm a little worried about Adonijah."

"What has happened to him?"

"My son, what will happen to *you?* He wished to be

king, remember, and though I applaud your gentle nature, you forgave too easily. He may try again."

"How, if I already have the throne? And why should I be the one to forgive? On him the disappointment fell."

Bathsheba smiled. "Your people will think you are king only if you act the part. Tolerate no rival!"

"At present," said Solomon, "I have none."

With the end of his pen he was drawing triangles and mountainous horizons, with a house-roof in the side of a hill.

"Coming back to your marriage," said his mother, "perhaps you would prefer to follow the ancient custom, and appropriate your father's wives. All except me, of course. Both the official and the less formal ones."

Solomon stopped drawing. "How ghastly!"

"Think twice," she urged, "before you criticize your own father, and many another good man! The idea is that when you take over the wives of the preceding king, there can no longer be question of your right to rule. The crowning and the anointing make the sacrament, of course, but the other ceremony is destiny itself."

"What's that about my father?"

"His son Absolom," replied Bathsheba, "that brother of yours, when he hoped to be king, married a number of David's wives, in an unsecluded place, and before invited witnesses."

Solomon gazed at her, horrified. "For a moment I thought you were saying that good men did this—that my father did it!"

Bathsheba rose gracefully. "I've interrupted your work

long enough. I quite agree that the King of Egypt's daughter is the better choice. Shall I inquire about her, or will you?"

He was studying the rug beneath her feet. "That girl of my father's, his last wife, Abishag——"

"Nonsense! She wasn't his wife! Just an extra blanket!"

Solomon looked reassured. "So I supposed. I saw her but once, and only for a moment."

Bathsheba's eyes closed slightly. "You have loved her? You have made her yours?"

"Me?" exclaimed Solomon. "Indeed I have not!"

"Then why haven't you!" she cried. "Are you a king? Have I borne a man or a walking question?"

"I didn't know," he protested, "you admired her so much!"

"Admire? She's good for what she was sent for, and that's all! But if you want the creature, don't be timid! One can applaud a grand, brave fool!"

She stopped in her vehemence and laughed. "Too much over too little! If I hadn't spoken, you'd have forgotten her. Now I'll send her in, if you'd like to discuss your poetry with her."

She laughed again, but he declined to join her mirth.

"Abishag will be here later in the day," he explained, in his new kingly tone. "I have already summoned her. We will discuss, as you suggest, poetry. I do not refer to her as a creature."

Bathsheba bowed low, and retreated toward the door. But in no state of panic. At the threshold she straightened up.

"I have the honor to be your mother. Shall I marvel if, now and then, we are much alike? I've already dispatched a greeting, on your behalf, to the King of Egypt's daughter, with him to choose which of the five. Benaiah told me a runner was starting south, and to save time I wrote out your proposal. She's not likely to arrive before another moon. You will be tired of that white girl before she comes."

When she was gone, Solomon put his hands to his head, and paced the floor.

However, the Egyptian wife was as yet too unreal to spoil the whole day. At the hour he had appointed for Abishag his manuscript was complete. No longer did absent-minded sketches, triangles, landscapes or experiments with the human form, disfigure the margin. He had made a fresh copy, supposing she might care to look at his verses as well as hear them. That is, in case she could read. The poems were not of length—few of them more than two lines. As he had inscribed them, they spotted the center of the roll, in an even and legible hand.

He was wearing the loose robe in which literary inspiration came most easily. Anything snug around the waist checked his ideas. The costume, as he happened to be aware, favored his handsome figure and his youthful beard. A voluminous grey robe with flowing sleeves, and a grey cap on the back of his head. If she liked the poems, he would know he and she were truly harmonious, and he could then proceed as his mother in irony had advised. People who belonged to each other should belong, and if everyone expected him to embark on romantic adventures, he might as well push off. On the other hand, if their tastes diverged, love would be inappropriate. Love, he held, was a sensitive adjustment, and your collaborator must be in tune. When she opened the door he tried to read at a glance how much in tune she was.

She struck him as even more effective with her clothes on than when she provided temperature for David, though you might say she was wearing now little beyond the essentials. She rather than her dress was modest. Her black eyes had the twinkle he had noticed when he had stood by his father's bedside and she had looked up at him. There was in her manner a confidence-building good humor, and a pervading eagerness, as though she expected something to happen and was prepared to like it.

He drew nearer to the desk the chair which Bathsheba had briefly used.

"Since you so kindly give me these valuable minutes," he began, "I should like to read you a few little things I've just been working on."

She leaned forward and put her elbows on the desk beside him.

"Did you really mean poetry?"

For the first time he heard her voice, a disturbing contralto. In that posture the whiteness took on a billowing vitality which went very well with her liquid syllables.

"Poetry is what I meant," he echoed firmly. "Shall I read?"

"Why not?" she inquired philosophically. He got the impression that she had expected less intimate entertainment, or perhaps he had arrived too abruptly at the pur-

pose of their meeting. Perhaps he should have built up
to a climax.

"As I say, they are only a few little things—I don't ex-
aggerate their importance."

"Do they hop into your mind," she asked, "or do you
have to work hard?"

The question though friendly missed the tone he would
have preferred. He rolled the manuscript, then unfolded
it again, allowing for her pardonable ignorance.

"A poet's ideas, to be worth anything," he explained,
"must be inspired, but there is usually a preparatory period
of meditation."

"I've always wanted to know." She was grateful. "Can
you feel when the inspiration is coming—like a sneeze?"

He looked her over, at first in astonishment, then with
a merciful understanding of her limited bringing up. The
doctors had not chosen her for intelligence, nor for literary
training. The poor thing had nothing but beauty. At that
moment, almost nothing. Her upper garment, put on care-
lessly, seemed about to fall. He cleared his throat and
began reading.

"If I explain the intention, you may follow with more
profit. In this kind of writing the charm is in the brevity
and the balance. For example,

> "A wise son maketh a glad father,
> But a foolish son is the distress of his mother."

He waited for her opinion.

"Is that all?"

He was a bit hurt. "I warned you of their brevity."

"It's very beautiful," she admitted, "and I can see it's better short. But why must his mother have the bad end of it? Wouldn't she be glad if her son had his wits? Wouldn't the father be put out if the boy was a fool?"

Solomon smiled, a magnificent patient smile. "The parents are divided for the poetic balance. In either case, as you observe, both are understood."

She was pleased. "I knew there was a trick somewhere. You're awfully clever. Read me another."

He looked down the scroll, to find an easy one.

> "Even a fool,
> When he holdeth his peace,
> Is counted wise."

She asked him to read it again, which he did, and for a broad interval she considered this theorem.

"It doesn't do much for silent men, does it! I've often thought that myself—if they won't talk, they've got you. But how do you know he *is* a fool, if he keeps quiet? And why don't you say it the other way——

> "Even the wise man,
> When he holdeth his peace,
> Is counted a fool?"

"That wouldn't be so true," explained Solomon.

"Why not?"

The poet-king's handsome brow puckered. "It's hard to explain, but that wouldn't be at all the same thing."

"I suppose it wouldn't," she agreed. In the press of her interest in poetry, her gown had slipped quite off, and she now gave up criticism temporarily to replace it. The process was deliberate and unabashed, and Solomon lifted his eyes from the manuscript to watch her. He discovered for the first time that she had beautiful hands.

"It's funny," she remarked, still looking down at herself, "you could say both those poems at the same time. Like this——

> "An eloquent son pleases his father,
> But a silent one worries his mother."

Solomon turned abruptly back to the scroll, and made ready to put it away.

"Oh, just one more!" she pleaded. "Something cheerful—not about fools."

Courteously he tamed his emotions, and chose what he hoped would escape mauling.

> "Whoso findeth a wife
> Findeth a good thing."

She laughed outright. "Absurd, isn't it!" she gurgled, as though he would share her opinion. "Almost everyone has a wife, and some are awful."

"In such a case," said the king drily, "I would not call her a wife."

She gave no sign that the distinction was clear, and with a pang of disappointment he walked majestically across the room, and restored the scroll to its proper shelf. When he faced her again she had forgotten his poetry.

"You know," she confided, "you're a wonderful man. You're really beautiful!"

That disturbing contralto voice! He came closer to her.

"Only one man in my family could claim beauty," he protested. "In his prime my father was incomparable."

She nodded. "He must have been an old dear, but that was before I was born. You're the best I've seen, so far."

He was tempted to analyze the causes of her cheerfulness, but her behavior disarmed mental effort. She drew him down to the wide chair where she filled only half the space, she kissed his nearest hand, then with her own fingers, the grace of which he had remarked, she explored his chest, under the literary gown, all the while laughing up at him with her eyes.

Solomon pulled himself together. Their intellectual harmony had not been sufficiently established, yet in itself her boldness was attractive.

"Let us remember who and what we are!"

She drew back as though he had called her a bad name.

"I am the king," he proceeded, "and you, if you wish, may be my wife."

Her eyes came together, he regretted to observe, in a vulgar grimace which suggested the streets.

"One of the good things, eh?"

He kept his dignity. "I ask you to marry me."

She was puzzled. "If you really mean it——"

"I do."

"Then I'm sorry. It's—it's impossible."

"So you hesitate because your family aren't quite——"

She interrupted. "Why don't you love me, and let it go at that?"

"Because I wish you for my wife."

She thought it through. "You mean, you refuse to love me unless I marry you first? You really are original, aren't you! With me it's the other way round. I'd be glad to love you, just as, when I came to your father—well, it wasn't his fault. But you and I couldn't marry. You're not my kind."

He rose from the chair and stood before her.

"You've no right to be angry," she told him. "It wasn't fair to send for me, and then read poems, and then ask me to be your wife. I wouldn't have come! Marriage is for always, and a man shouldn't talk so much, and he shouldn't be a fool either, and he shouldn't ask my opinion—he wouldn't need to—he'd just be there and I'd agree with him."

Solomon stroked his beard, to keep himself in countenance, and for further courage he stared at her, from the line on the top of her head where the black hair parted, down to the point of her sandal, where in the abandon of earnestness she wiggled a pink toe. Looking at the toe, he made a great decision, one of those kingly judgments he had dreamt of while riding on his father's mule.

"May I ask, have you yet found this man of yours?"

Her reply was unexpected. "I'm glad you're going to build a temple!"

"Oh, a temple is what you want, is it?"

She waved her hand as though brushing something

aside. "I want to see the Tyrians. Everyone says they are remarkable."

Solomon thrust out his beard at her. "In spite of the Tyrians, I shall offer my affection in my own way! I shall expect you here tomorrow. Unless you ask for poetry, there will be none. It is written in my fate that I am shortly to marry. If I may choose my wife, she will be you!"

Abishag was thinking. "When I said I hadn't found the man yet, did you believe me?"

He was startled.

"Is there a man?"

"Suppose there were?"

His jaw thickened. "There wouldn't be long! I'd kill him!"

She had her arms around his neck, as far up as she could reach. "You're queer, but I begin to like you! Of course I'll come tomorrow!"

The next day, after a busy morning with Benaiah about the huts to put King Hiram's men in, when they should arrive, he was setting his study in order for her return, and deciding upon the degree to which his passion for her might be disclosed. It was passion, he knew. She had caused him a wakeful night, full of wishes and doubts, which by dawn had congested into a steady pain in or near the heart. Today he must break down that girlish reluctance, in her own interest, since she would never find a better husband. But before she came, his mother knocked at the door.

More beautiful than usual, serene, composed. At sight

of her, Solomon bowed low, a boyhood habit which her loveliness made lasting.

"Let me kneel at your feet," she said. "I come with a petition."

He led her to the chair which sooner or later supported all his guests. "Whatever you desire," he promised, "so long as it isn't the King of Egypt's daughter."

She smiled. "Nothing for myself. Your brother Adonijah wishes to marry. He asked me to intercede with you. I bring you his request word for word, without prejudice. He wants your father's wife, Abishag."

She was prepared, perhaps, for the effect of her words. While Solomon was turning white, then purple, she sat there smiling innocently.

"He wants my father's wife, does he? Why didn't he ask it to my face? Absolom's business over again! First the king's wife, then the kingdom!"

Bathsheba lifted her soft hand. "Be calm, my son! The girl was not actually your father's wife. To do Adonijah justice, I think he loves her, and she probably loves him. I dare say she might as well marry him, by this time."

Solomon raised his voice. "It is not true! She cares nothing for him!"

Bathsheba raised an eyebrow. "That as it may be! In any case she is not *your* wife."

"She is! I have asked her to marry me!"

"Ah?"

He did not notice her smile. He was calling up an image of that broad-shouldered, easy-going Adonijah, and wondering whether the white girl would find there her perfect man. He decided she would not.

"In this room, only yesterday, I told her what would happen to my rival, if a rival should appear."

"What would?" asked Bathsheba. "That interests me."

Solomon drew a long breath. "He would die, of course."

"I'm glad you took strong ground," said his mother. "Sooner or later one has to."

"Meanwhile," Solomon continued, "there is as yet no occasion for violence."

"But there is! He wants her!"

He shook his head. "It will do him no good. He isn't her kind."

Bathsheba gazed into his face, and he watched those remarkable eyes of hers.

"More than once," she said quietly, "I have warned you that Adonijah is ambitious, and unfortunately he is not without charm. He writes no poetry. Much of the day he spends among the people. They might get the impression that he is your guardian or protector, since he has more years and a wider experience. Benaiah says many of the soldiers prefer him. Too many."

Solomon stroked his beard. "Well then, what should I do?"

She chose her words. "The message which I brought, about the girl, was at his request. I promised to convey it faithfully. But if you ask my opinion, which he didn't, I should have to say that he has, as you suspect, designs on your wife."

Solomon tried to be just. "He doesn't yet know I love her."

"True. The situation will grow worse, the deeper into it you go."

When he grasped her idea fully, he recoiled. "But I couldn't kill my own brother!"

In her face he saw a gentle pity. "I don't believe you could!"

"Let me measure this from every angle," he said, glad that he wasn't expected to do the killing at once. "I may have a talk with Adonijah."

Bathsheba didn't answer, and when he glanced toward her, she seemed to be thinking of far distant matters, until the silence roused her.

"By the way," she said, preparing to go, "I hope you will dine with me this evening."

He had been cherishing the idea of a supper there in his own studio with Abishag, but if his mother felt that state matters should come first——

Half an hour later, when Abishag arrived, he was pleased at a marked change in her attire. This time she was thoroughly covered in a long drape closely resembling his own studious robe. She walked in with a dignity all the sweeter because it seemed not quite at home on her pert little face. His heart leaped. She was fast acquiring the graces proper to a queen. The ideal which in recent day he had been projecting from the depths of his soul, and which he would, if he could, attach to her, now seemed likely to fit.

"Am I late?" she asked modestly.

"In point of truth," Solomon answered, "you are ten minutes early, but to me it seems late."

Her humility was striking. "Do you wish me to sit in any particular place?"

He held for her the chair Bathsheba had just relinquished.

"If you want to please me," she said, "you'll read some more of your poems."

"Not today!" he exclaimed. "Today *you* will be my poem!"

She looked straight at him, friendly but on her guard, as he put his elbows on the table and leaned toward her, as she had leaned toward him the day before.

"Do you know my brother Adonijah?"

The effort of memory wrinkled her forehead. "Not to speak to. Was he one of those visitors who used to come to your father's room?"

"Ah! Were there visitors?"

"All the time." She laughed as she spoke, and her lips moved forward to meet his. "You came only once," she complained.

He would have set forth his reasons for staying away, but she had not withdrawn her lips to any great distance. He put out his hand, just behind her neck, to adjust the lips.

After that he thought he had better bolt the door, and his judgment proved sound, for in a few minutes someone came knocking, when he had no mind to be disturbed. It was a terrified sort of knocking, and there seemed to be a scuffling of feet, but Solomon knew it did not concern him, and the noise drifted away down the hall. He could give his mind again to what he was doing.

Singularly, the white girl at the last moment made a great point of her personal liberty.

"You understand it's not for always," she warned him. "If either of us should meet someone else——"

When she left him in the early dusk, he sat down at his desk and felt the loneliness of the room, and reflected on the many things that had happened there, and made an estimate of human life in terms of his newly acquired knowledge. His thoughts were exalted rather than clear.

So long he sat there that the dinner hour stole upon him, and his dressing had to be hasty. In the corridor the guard saluted sharply as he came out, and there was in the man's face, Solomon thought, a suggestion of terror. He identified the same look in the other sentries, as he passed them one by one—something closer to fear than to affection. Near his mother's room he was reassured to meet Benaiah, on whose heavy countenance with the broken nose there was no fear at all. The young king attributed his fancies to the excitement of the afternoon.

And his mother was reassuring. The repast she had set for him was delicate, the flask of wine fragrant, she had come fresh from her bath, and her eyes were shining. Moreover, to his relief, she said nothing about Abishag nor about the daughter of the King of Egypt. She did refer to the temple, and to Adoram, the old tax-gatherer, who wasn't bringing in enough money for it, and she mentioned Jeroboam, the extremely young mason who was becoming the spokesman for the workers—but all this by way of small talk, to divert him.

At the end of the meal, while he was sipping the last drop from the golden cup, she recalled something which in the pleasure of eating she had almost overlooked.

"By the way, I meant to tell you Adonijah is dead."

Solomon's limp hand dropped the cup on the table. "How?"

"Benaiah arranged it," said Bathsheba. "You have now no rival."

He remembered the noise in the corridor, the knocking at the door. Was his brother pleading for mercy?

He rose to his feet. "You killed him!"

With a gracious gesture she motioned toward the couch again. "The orders," she said, "were given in your name."

He sat looking at her, at first stunned, then groping toward a strong wish. He wished he could reach his father David, and ask him a question.

CHAPTER III

BECAUSE King Hiram's workmen might arrive any day now, Solomon regretfully put aside his poetry and made some architectural sketches. In the cool of the day the guards were to admit no one but Abishag, but in the hours when he was concentrating on the temple Jeroboam frequently interrupted, to speak for the local laborers, who were assembled to help King Hiram's artisans and didn't enjoy waiting around. Or they complained of the food at the public tables. Solomon didn't like Jeroboam.

Adoram, the old tax-collector, also interrupted, to say once more that the people were not cooperating. There seemed to be a concerted effort among the rich to hoard. Before the king got too deep into this temple, he ought to acquaint himself with the future prospects of the treasury. Meanwhile Adoram would leave for the royal inspection the latest balance sheet. Solomon didn't like Adoram.

More often than anyone else Bathsheba interrupted. Solomon didn't like her either. Each time she knocked he thought of the possible wife she was fetching out of Egypt for him. Usually, however, she spoke of other things, with a tact which was ominous.

"My son, that young man Jeroboam is a trouble-maker."

Solomon groaned. "Well, what can I do about it?"

"Promote him! Give him a task beyond his powers, let

58

the people see their admiration for him is misplaced."

"I'll think about it."

He wished she would go, but she lingered to harp on Adoram and his taxes.

"You really ought to consult his opinion—your father always did."

Solomon permitted himself a mild irritation. "Who says I don't consult him? Look at that pile of figures he left with me this morning!"

"My son, the temple will cost more than you expect. Buildings always do."

"Didn't my father lay aside a round sum for just this purpose?"

"Your father also laid aside the temple. He hated debt."

Solomon quoted one of his own poems. "Better a small competence with an easy mind than large revenues unjustly collected."

She thought the quotation did not apply. "Whatever Adoram collects will be collected justly. Your father found him punctilious. But sooner or later these Phoenicians expect to be paid!"

"There is a time for everything," said he, quoting from himself again.

"I stopped in," she said, "to remind you that this is one of the times."

When she was gone he took from its pigeonhole a half-finished scroll and added a stanza to his new poem, about the perfect wife, which he intended as a tribute to Abishag, but parts of it glanced at his mother. The perfect wife would say nothing that was not welcome, and rather than talk at all, she would attend to the housework.

When Abishag appeared that afternoon, he resumed their daily debate about matrimony. "I am threatened with a foreign wife, and I prefer you!"

It was his customary overture, and as usual she laughed. "You don't have to marry one you don't like. Neither do I."

"You don't like me?" He had asked it a dozen times.

"As a lover." She never tired of saying it.

"But not as a husband?"

"How can I tell?"

"I offer you a throne," he urged, "a position in the world!"

"But everything changes. You might change. Even I."

"I will protect you, beloved!"

"My dear!" she exclaimed. "That's what I'm afraid of!"

So they hashed it back and forth until it was late, and he asked her to stay for supper. Her spirits were high.

"I expect to like the princess from Egypt," she told him.

"Why?"

"No reason—I just expect to."

"If I married her, we couldn't spend an hour like this!" He glanced sadly across the table.

"Why not? I can knock at your door once in a while, can't I?"

Later in the evening, in the hope that she might address herself more seriously to the problem of their fate, he took her up to the palace tower where they could look out together over the city, and inspect the stars in the glowing blue. In the tower wall was a sheltered balcony, for a sentinel if war should come, and a flight of steps reached down from the rampart top to this listening post. It had long been his habit to send up a rug and a cushion when he became thoughtful at night, and there feast on the privilege of solitude. The solitude was sweeter now that the girl shared it.

"Here," he told her, "I could remain forever!"

"So could I, but we shan't."

"Surely you are happy now?"

"That's just it! Now!"

A wistful slant to her voice, heard for the first time, gave him hope. "Would you not make it last, if you could?"

"Forever! If I could!"

From which he drew confidence that she would come around in a day or two.

Who knows? Perhaps—if those energetic Tyrians the next morning had not landed at Joppa, and come marching up from the coast, eager to get on with the temple. Solomon had the news first from Benaiah, when a runner reported the sighting of the ships.

"You and Adoram be ready at the gate, show them their quarters, and remember that one of our people must work beside each of theirs, and at the usual rate for such labor."

To these simple instructions Adoram replied next day in person, an old man, white-bearded, with a bald and shining dome, but his feelings at the moment gave him the sprightliness of youth.

"How much cedar did you order?" he asked, in a tone hasty rather than respectful.

"No amount was mentioned—I just said a temple."

"They've brought enough for two. Every ship is loaded, and each tows a float. And Hiram says they must go back for more, and you must fill them with wheat. He says it's payment on delivery."

"Ah, did King Hiram come with the wood? That's very friendly of him!"

"No, your majesty, it's a rough foreigner by the same name, a blacksmith or something, who gives orders. He says he's to put the work through for you, and we're not to delay him."

"A blacksmith?" repeated Solomon, indignant.

"Metal work in all kinds, if I understood him, and he has already constructed several temples, and we're to leave it to him. Also, he says he personally represents the King of Tyre."

"I don't like this!"

"Your father would have liked it still less!"

Solomon made rings of his beard around his fingers. "However, since he's here, we'll accept the cedar, if you approve the quality."

"That's what he said about the wheat, your majesty. He won't land a log till he sees the wheat."

"Well then, show it to him!"

"But we haven't enough!"

Solomon paced his study. "I thought my father set up a special fund——"

"Gold, not wheat. He says your contract calls for wheat."

Solomon was near the boiling point. "Bless my soul,

can't you take the treasure and buy what he wants?"

"In time we could," said Adoram, "but he wants it this afternoon."

"Well, he can't have it! You tell him so, from me! Show him the gold, not as though we were worried, but just to entertain him. Then show him a sample of our wheat. Then give him the dates when he can expect payment, and either he can unload the lumber cautiously, one log for every bushel, or he can get it ashore and trust us, or he can take his trees back where they came from! Be sure you repeat my precise words!"

"I'd rather not," pleaded Adoram.

"My precise words!"

"Would your majesty consider meeting the fellow?"

"Of course! Tomorrow morning, just before lunch."

"If your majesty could arrange to confer with him now——"

"Impossible! Tomorrow!"

That evening he was absent-minded, and when Abishag came in a special gown which she had borrowed from a friend, and in the mood to say yes if he asked again, he forgot to ask, and she went home from the tower and returned the gown without thanking the owner.

Next morning Hiram strode into the study as though he had only a moment, and perhaps this wasn't the right place to spend it.

"Every hour this fleet is held up, the men are drawing wages. If the cedar stays in the boats, my carpenters can't begin, but their pay is reckoned from the moment we cast anchor."

"Not so fast!" Solomon protested. "Who arranged these terms?"

"They're customary between builders and clients. You haven't done much building yet, have you?"

Adoram stood to one side, wringing his hands at the lack of etiquette, but Solomon smiled with quiet dignity. "We are a military people, with little experience in trade, or taste for it."

"That's why you're so hard to deal with," confided Hiram, man to man. "Now, I'll tell you how to straighten this out. Next time you order a temple, or anything else, get your plan first, and figure the amount of material and the cost. Since you didn't know how much wood you'd need, we sent all we had. In our place you'd have done the same. . . . And I don't want to take any of it back. If there's any left over, I'll tell you what else to build. . . . Now as to the payment. I'll send the boats home with the wheat, and you can piece out with some honey, and I hear you have a rosin which you call balm, good for weak stomachs if applied internally, and helpful for wounds on the outside. We can use a ship of two of balm. The rest of the account can wait, because of the friendship my country has for yours, but each day, of course, you'll add one bushel for every hundred you owe us."

"Your majesty," interrupted Adoram, "there'll be no more wheat till the next harvest, and meanwhile our own people and these visitors must live!"

"I'm coming to that," explained Hiram. "Better lay a special tribute on all the countries you rule. You rule more than this, don't you?"

"Far more!" admitted Solomon, with assumed calm.

"Well then, you send your tax-gatherer to collect the tribute, as an emergency sacrifice for the dignity of your religion. That's the usual ground when it's an expensive temple. Not money, of course—let them contribute fruits of the soil."

Adoram in agony foresaw his fate. "Your majesty, if I try to collect any more, they'll stone me! Even if they sent half their food, it wouldn't be enough!"

"I'm coming to that too," said Hiram. "You need a navy. Whether you wish it or not, a country like this, with projects on foot, needs trade with other countries. In the exchange you increase your wealth."

Adoram raised his hands to heaven.

"May I interrupt? They won't give us something for nothing, will they? And if it's an even exchange, we have to pay for the ships we build, don't we? So it's sure to be a loss, isn't it? Your majesty, if the temple must lead to trade, and so to ruin, let us continue to worship in the open air, and avoid the possibility of becoming a pest to our neighbors!"

"I was saying," continued Hiram, "we'll build you a fleet on the Red Sea, with a few ships of our own besides yours, to show good faith, and we'll give you some of our sailors, till your people know how to navigate, and we'll teach you how to trade with advantage in the best markets—Ophir, for instance."

Solomon remembered the name. "Which Ophir is that?"

"In Arabia."

"I've dreamt of it," said the poet king. "That's where you buy almug trees, whatever they are, and you bring home gold and silver, ivory, apes and peacocks."

"Almug is sandalwood," explained Hiram, "and the peacocks are usually parrots, but it's a rich market, and if you know how to buy, you make a profit."

Adoram was on his guard. "These sailors you would give us, would we pay their wages?"

"Naturally, while in your service."

The old tax-gatherer bowed to the floor. "Your majesty, I resign! Put a younger man in my place!"

Solomon rose, to end an awkward session. "For the present we are building a temple. Take what wheat we can spare, honey and balm, carry in the cedar, and tomorrow or the next day you shall have the plans in some practical form. After that you and Adoram may agree as to probable costs, and then he and I will decide what extra tribute need be raised. . . . One other thing—the introduction of foreign craftsmen, as you know, irritates the natives. May I count on you to treat my workers with some imagination? We've already agreed, you recall, there's to be one of mine for every one of yours."

"That's why I brought such a large force," said Hiram, moving toward the door. "Had we worked alone, I could have done with fewer men, but with unskilled labor tripping you up, you need a third as many again. It will cost you more, but we understand your point, you want them educated."

When he was gone, Solomon and Adoram stared at each other.

"Do you suppose," asked the king, "my father had his own reasons for not building this temple?"

The question disgusted Adoram so profoundly that he left the room with a minimum of manners, and Solomon went up on the palace roof to defy the midday sun and compose his mind.

When he heard a step behind him, he doubted if it could be Abishag at that hour. It wasn't. It was Benaiah, the broken-nosed captain of the guard.

"I don't want to hear about the Tyrians," said Solomon. "I've been all over that ground this morning."

There was no change on the leather-like face. "It isn't the Tyrians, it's Shimei, the man your father wished you to kill."

If there was killing to do, Solomon marveled that his mother had left anything to his discretion.

"Where is he?"

"Right here in Jerusalem. He counts on you to forget. Shall I attend to it?"

If Hiram, in the interview just closed, had not been so masterful, Shimei's fate might have been sealed, but Solomon was now disposed, by way of protest, to exercise independent judgment.

"Bring him to me this afternoon. Be gentle, until I direct otherwise."

He reflected that Shimei, who was older than David, must by this time be old indeed. There was something impious in a revenge which raced with natural death. On the other hand, it was his father's dying wish!

He spoke of it to his mother, in her queenly room, before

he returned from melons and dates to his afternoon appointments. To his relief, but also to his surprise, she saw no need for severe methods.

"Your dear father," she explained, "was a man of passion, and passion is a total gift. He was passionate in everything, in his hates as in his loves."

"I thought of that," said her son enviously. "It shows in his poetry."

"Admirably put," said Bathsheba. "He could express hate beautifully. Beyond question he disliked Shimei, but if he had had the leisure and the health, in these recent years, he would have blasted that offensive person in an inspired psalm, and once the poison had got into words, he would have been proud of the poem, and indifferent to the vermin-bite which precipitated it. To take his dying words, therefore, as a literal command, would betray ignorance of the literary workings. You had the privilege of hearing the last improvisations of a great poet."

For those humane sentences, saturated with light, Solomon forgave the treatment of Adonijah, or whatever else of ruthlessness he had imagined in her conduct. With admiring love he departed, and before the hour was gone he made a treaty of peace with Shimei.

David's enemy was indeed of a vast age, but sinewy and tenacious, disposed to die a martyr if the occasion were sure to attract attention—backbone gone sour, a hoary nuisance, too busy with his own rights to keep off the next man's toes. Benaiah, standing at the door, did not like him, nor indeed did Solomon.

"You did my father wrong."

"I told him the truth, as was my duty!"

"As you say, but he charged me to kill you for it."

Shimei embraced what he thought was a crisis. He lifted, very deliberately, a bony finger to heaven. "In the sight of Jehovah, I swear——"

"You will now go back to your house," Solomon continued, "and you will stay there. It was on the public highway that you insulted my father. Your punishment will be to lead an inconspicuous life in your immediate precinct. You know the boundaries. Live within them, and fear nothing. Step once beyond them, and I'll do what my father asked."

"I plead for justice, O King!" clamored Shimei.

"At home you may plead for what you choose. Benaiah will escort you thither."

That evening he told Abishag about it. "Lucky for him I didn't do what my father asked."

"Why didn't you?"

He was horrified. "Why, you wouldn't have me kill him, would you?"

"I wasn't thinking of that, I was wondering whether you'll ever be firm unless you are angry."

He took refuge in sensitive dignity. "When I do the magnanimous thing, you don't understand!"

"Tell me this," she asked abruptly, "what kind of dress did I have on last night? Three guesses!"

He thought hard. "Blue."

"There goes one!"

"I remember now—green."

She shook her head. "Uh—uh!"

A faint flush colored his brow. "I always liked that black gown with spangles!"

She laughed in his face. "Wasn't I right about the Tyrians? I *knew* they'd be fascinating!"

A week later Adoram tried to insinuate that these fascinating Tyrians were upsetting the country, that their coming had spread unrest not only among the craftsmen but among the domestic servants, and that the emergency tribute would more than ever be impossible to collect. Solomon refused to hear the details.

But he heard them from Hiram. That brass-hammerer got himself listened to, in full.

"You wanted one of your people to each of ours, wasn't that it? Well, if it works both ways, if we're to keep one of our men to each of yours, I'd better send home for more hands. Your folk seem to like this public work. If I turn my back, another hundred or so join up."

To this new problem Solomon offered his courteous attention. "Experienced builders like yourself can doubtless tell to a man how many workers you need."

"Not with your people! You'd save a fortune by sending them back to whatever they did before we came."

Solomon met this criticism of his subjects with inscrutable patience. "In any event, I pay the wages of my own workmen, as well as of you who have kindly come to our aid."

"Even so," persisted Hiram, "your people have a way of getting under foot. There are too many of them, and they talk while they work. In some instances they shout. They are of a supremely expressive temperament, the slightest emotion becomes with them an earthquake, and the noise is terrible. You said you wanted to hear none of our hammering, no blows of our axes, while the frame was going up. Well, I didn't understand you intended to drown us out."

Solomon continued patient. "My people are eager to learn. Adoram will advise them to work in silence."

Hiram snapped his fingers in contempt. "Silence won't make them useful! They are farmers or shepherds, and the latest comers seem to have been cooks or tailors. I can't make carpenters of them overnight!"

"What would you advise?" asked the king. "They wish employment, and I want to keep them happy."

"How would it be if we started another building? There'll be enough material left over for a good palace. Don't you need a palace?"

"I hadn't thought of it," said Solomon, a little bewildered, "but anyway I couldn't afford so fine a palace as you would probably achieve."

"When you start to improve a town," urged Hiram, "you rebuild it all before you get through. One thing brings on another. As for the expense, Adoram and I have agreed on an annual tribute."

"Tribute?" exclaimed David's son. "You don't own this country, you know!"

"I used a commercial term. It's a device to spread the payment over a long period. Each year you will send us twenty thousand measures of wheat and twenty measures of pure oil."

"For how long?"

"That depends on what the bill comes to. Meanwhile you might as well have the use of a new palace."

"Let me think it over," said the king. "This house was good enough for my father."

"I'll bring plans for a better one tomorrow," said Hiram, "a rough sketch. We'll shift some of your people on to the new job!"

When he was gone, Solomon passed a dark hour, gazing vacantly across at the scrolls in their racks on the wall, those manuscripts in which he inscribed wisdom, but to which he was in the vein to add nothing that afternoon. So his people all wished to work on the temple, did they? Was it from fervor of faith, or was it the lure of novelty? To be a cook or a tailor or even a shepherd might be a bore. His father hadn't stayed a shepherd. If one could only escape the desire of change!

As for that, why had he undertaken this expensive temple? In honor of Jehovah? Or of his father? Or of himself?

Bathsheba had reminded him that David used to say God should have a better house than the king, but what, from God's point of view, was a better house? Must the divine altar be put together by Tyrian hands, metal-pounders who privately worshiped by a different system but would do anything for pay?

At that moment Solomon regretted the throne, though it had been his for only a cluster of days. Could he then have followed his heart, he would have gone to Bethlehem, to the very spot where his father was feeding sheep when the giant appeared, to change his life. Perhaps David was at his best in the brief second while the pebble was traveling from the sling to the giant's forehead. Could one now go back, Solomon asked, as Hiram wished the workmen to do, and be once more a shepherd like David? If you began with sheep, would you learn how to care for men? Or with the sheep around you, grass under you, sun above, and water courses singing from the hills, could you lose your senses and become a king?

That evening Abishag did not join him in the tower balcony. He watched the stars alone, and stored up fresh reserves of melancholy, recalling the time when he had imagined that life was good.

But she came to his study the next afternoon, wearing a simple dress of her own, a stiff Egyptian linen which stood out but you could see through it. Solomon observed without pleasure the Egyptian influence.

But Abishag, in her Egyptian linen, was what you couldn't be angry with, and Solomon requested no report on what she had been doing the night before.

"You are my only happiness," he told her.

"I have much to thank you for," said she, "particularly for bringing us those men from Tyre! Have you seen any of them, or do you always stay in the palace?"

"A superior type of craftsmen. Thorough." The praise was a little stiff.

Abishag opened her eyes wide. "Then you haven't seen them! I mean, that's the least of it! When they talk to you, you feel—you feel——"

"They've talked to me," said Solomon. "I wonder if we felt the same thing."

"Oh," she cried, "they have strange eyes, and they're so persistent, and they say so little but it means so much!"

"Just what did they say to you?"

"There you are! I can't remember a thing, to repeat, but their voices haunt me, and they look at you, and their hands are so broad and flat! Did you notice their hands?"

"They come from a distance," he reminded her, "and you see them for the first time. What enchants you is your own ignorance."

"But wasn't I right about not marrying?" she asked cheerfully.

"Ah! You will marry one of my hired workmen?"

She patted his cheek. "Don't be ridiculous! I shan't marry. You shouldn't either. Think of all the cities you haven't seen, and in each a beautiful woman. At least one. If I were king, I'd travel and admire."

Grieved though he was, Solomon could smile at her childlike enthusiasm. "If you are a king, you stay at your post, guarding your people."

She nodded sympathetically. "And queens stay at theirs, guarding the king. I shan't be a queen. Or if I had to be, I'd travel just the same."

Solomon shook his head. "They never do. Not the queens who deserve remembrance."

Saying the words, he knew he was surrendering the last hope of making a royal partner out of her, but facts were facts. His wife could not go exploring.

"I've a notion," said Abishag, "the women in Tyre are less attractive than the men. I judge so because the men

seem astonished, now they're here. In Egypt it's the other
way. The women are cleverer than the men."

He would have challenged this opinion, but they were
interrupted by a loud knock.

"Would you like to retire? That's a visitor."

She leaned upon his shoulder, in a corner of the divan.

"I'll stay, if you don't mind. I hope he'll be interesting."

It was Benaiah. If Abishag expected a Tyrian, Solomon
was glad she was disappointed.

"Your majesty," said the captain of the guard, "did I
understand that Shimei was to be a prisoner in his own
house?"

"In the precinct," corrected Solomon.

"And he was to consider himself in his own custody,
on his word of honor?"

"That was my will."

"And if he stepped out of bounds, he was to die?"

"That was my promise."

"Well, your majesty, he has been roaming at large
through the city, into the suburbs. Shall I clear the record
with him?"

In anger Solomon half rose, Abishag and all, and then
sank back again.

"If the fool defies me—— What excuse does he give?
I suppose you haven't examined him?"

"Your majesty, his servants ran away. He had but two,
a middle-aged fellow who cooked, made the beds, swept
the house, and a more active person who carried water,
chopped wood, and did the errands. They left together,

and Shimei, rather than clean the house himself, tried to catch and bring them back."

Solomon stroked his beard. "Those servants, I suppose, prefer to work for Hiram."

Benaiah nodded gravely. "There's a general drift, your majesty, toward the public payroll, where the discipline is light and the hours humane. Shimei kept his servants busy."

Abishag laughed quietly, and Solomon felt sudden embarrassment to be seen with a girl clinging to him in this unconventional posture. When he next spoke to Benaiah, it was in irritation.

"Usually you act without my advice. Why are you asking me now?"

Benaiah replied with some warmth. "Your majesty, I sympathize with the servants who ran away, and to some extent with the old man who ran after them! If ever the temple is finished, it will doubtless be for the glory of God, but first it will disrupt society. The lower class are seduced by this opportunity to work for the state. Shimei never gave his servants half what they'll get if Hiram lets them chip away at his cedar logs. Of course Shimei has thought it out—though he loses their aid, yet through extra taxes he will be providing them with double pay."

Abishag laughed again, so much at ease before Benaiah that Solomon wondered whether she expected the soldier's coming, and had heard his message in advance.

"If I grasp the argument, my building a temple is the cause of Shimei's disobedience?"

"In a manner of speaking."

"And therefore the disobedience should not be punished?"

"I'll kill him if you wish, but it's not a routine case."

Before Solomon could make up his mind, another loud knock interrupted.

"I will wait outside," said Benaiah, "for your orders, when you are free."

Solomon raised his hand. "Don't go! I have no appointments. I can't imagine who this is."

It was Bathsheba. He saw at once that she brought news which he would not like, because she had dressed with care, and her eyes shone with good nature. When she bowed to the king who was her son, he noticed again the amazing youthfulness of her figure. Her dress was not quite so transparent as Abishag's, but the reticence of her attire had a purpose rather than a cause. She had no need to hide; she wished to tantalize. At least, Solomon got this impression. So did Benaiah, standing off on one side. Abishag was sure of it.

Of course if she had removed herself from Solomon's arm, the king might have risen to greet his mother. The thoughtlessness of the girl could, however, be overlooked since her years were few, and her training imperfect. It did not occur to Solomon that she knew Bathsheba's dislike of her.

"My son," said the tall dark woman, "the messengers have returned from Egypt."

Egypt again! Solomon's heart sank.

"The king's daughter," she continued, "is conscious of the honor you propose. She replies in those terms of exaggerated humility which the Egyptians employ. I prefer to say simply that in the ironic patience of Jehovah those who tried to destroy our ancestors will now collaborate in producing our posterity. In short, the king's daughter will marry you. She is already on the way."

"What's this?" whispered Abishag, glancing up toward Solomon's troubled beard.

"How soon will she arrive?" he asked.

"The messenger said she would travel leisurely in order to look her best."

He rubbed the top of his head. "Do you know which one of the five it is?"

"Next to the youngest. Her name is Magsala."

"Did the messenger happen to say—but I suppose he didn't really see her himself."

Bathsheba understood. "His report makes her not beautiful in our sense, but even so, of a notable appearance. Her eyes have a slant, her nose, unfortunately, is straight, her lips are a trifle full and soft, and her neck is slender and long, but she is said to have a beautiful mind, and a taste for poetry."

"How am I to talk with her? I don't know Egyptian, or whatever it is she speaks!"

"She speaks our language," said Bathsheba. "The only one of the five daughters who possesses that accomplishment."

Solomon frowned. "Will an accident of that sort make her my wife?"

His mother smiled. "No accident, but the will of heaven, working through your own inspired choice."

Had he been dealing with her in privacy, he could have said something sharp about this trick of forcing a wife on a man, but in Benaiah's presence he felt compelled to support Bathsheba, as Bathsheba well knew. And with Abishag listening, it seemed appropriate for him to be choosing a princess and receiving the lady's thanks for the honor. Abishag might as well realize **that** an offer of marriage from him had current value abroad.

"Very well," he said, with the hint of a sigh, "when she comes, we'll marry her."

"Meanwhile," suggested Bathsheba, "shall I arrange her quarters?"

"Ah, yes!" said Solomon. "We'll have to put her somewhere. Why not in this wing of the palace with me?"

Bathsheba shook her head.

"Your apartment did well enough for your boyhood, but a princess needs space. I thought perhaps I might give up some of my rooms."

Again Abishag laughed, which to Solomon seemed inappropriate.

"I'd be sorry to disturb you——" he told his mother.

Another knock at the door, quite the loudest yet. He turned to Benaiah.

"Explain that I can see nobody."

Benaiah tried to explain, but Hiram, catching sight of the king on the divan, pushed in.

"I stopped just to leave you the plans for the new palace."

"Which palace is that?" asked Bathsheba.

Hiram paid no attention to her. "We've put in what a

king usually requires, providing for the normal expansion of the family."

For once Bathsheba showed unpremeditated satisfaction. "My son! Is this a gift for your bride?"

Solomon was following the direction of Hiram's eyes, which were making a swift appraisal of Abishag. The king flushed slightly and coughed. Hiram looked straight at the royal throat, and continued.

"As to the cost of the additional building, I have consulted your man, Adoram, and I bring what doubtless you will consider a fortunate solution. The Egyptians are selling linen in large quantities to your people, both the finished article and the yarn. They also provide you with horses. Why don't you insist that such articles be delivered to you personally, or to your agents at a fixed price?"

"How would that help?" asked Solomon mournfully.

"Why, you'd then dispose of them to your people at a slight advance. You guarantee the quality, and for the guarantee you make an infinitesimal charge. The total would be magnificent."

The words struck a shiver into the king's heart. He was to become a tradesman, was he? Had the temple brought him to this? Was he to rob his people that he might build himself a house? Shame covered him.

All the more because Hiram was looking at Abishag again. The tall brass-expert was gazing down at the girl, who with her head in comfort on Solomon's chest was cheerfully gazing back. He remembered another day, when looking down at his helpless father he had noticed the twinkle in those same eyes. Was he now, like David then, helpless? He stood up so suddenly that Abishag tumbled over.

"The revenues of my kingdom," he announced, "I will provide as I think best! Where my future wife shall live is for her husband to say. Since I give commands only after prolonged study, I expect them to be obeyed!" He looked at Hiram. "You may go!"

He bowed to his mother. "My gratitude and my respect!"

Hiram went through the door first, being without breeding, and Bathsheba, allowing a fair distance between them, followed. Solomon gave a hand to Abishag, and lifted her off the divan.

"Your services to my family will never be forgotten."

"Shan't I see you again?" she asked.

He turned his back on her, and she went down the hall, humming a tune.

"Your commands are to be obeyed?" asked Benaiah.

"They are!"

"That applies to Shimei?"

Solomon bowed his head.

Benaiah went out too.

Chapter IV

When Bathsheba came knocking respectfully at the door, the princess Magsala was occupied with the two maids she had brought along from Egypt. Bathsheba had decorated the room with special care, but the princess liked neither the location nor the furnishings.

She disliked something else too. Her handsome brow was puckered.

"Ano, find out who makes that noise at the door!" Ano was the tall one, with the philosophic expression.

"Tii, bring my best wig!" Tii was stout, more cheerful.

"If my daughter the princess would grant me a precious moment," murmured Bathsheba. Ano left her on the threshold, to see if the princess would.

The princess was fast losing her temper. She had just taken the mirror from Tii's hand, to make sure the wig hung right.

"What extraordinary people! I arrive in the middle of the morning, and does he meet me? He does not! Not a sight of him! His mother sends word that doubtless I need a bath!"

"We *were* dusty," said Tii, "and the water was cool."

The princess put down the mirror. "Am I to be married, or am I not? Have they lost the bridegroom, or has he run away?"

The jewels circling her brow, holding the wig on, were less brilliant than her dark eyes, and her body made you think of a rush swaying by the river bank, even when as now she stood straight and still.

"Madam," pleaded Ano, "his mother is here."

"Now really," exclaimed the princess, "that's no substitute at all!"

She throned herself in a deep chair, at the foot of the bed, with Tii fanning her, both of them gazing hard at the mature but lovely mother of Solomon, now brought in by Ano. Bathsheba bowed to the ground.

"My son will be covered with shame as soon as he returns."

"Then you do expect him back?"

"He's building a temple," explained his mother, "and this forenoon there was a crisis."

The princess raised ever so slightly her eagle-like nose. "Temple-building in this country? Is his motive religious or architectural?"

"It was piety at the beginning," said Bathsheba, "then it was architecture, now it's labor trouble. The workmen chose this, of all days, to demand few hours and a high wage."

The princess, coming of an old dynasty, was on familiar ground. "In such cases there is usually a leader."

"It's Jeroboam. Every time the tax goes up, he says the men should have more, but that way, of course, we'd never get ahead."

"Jeroboam," said the princess, "should be promoted or killed. Which policy does my future husband favor?"

"At the moment I believe he's arguing with him."

The princess had an eccentric humor. She could always cease from anger if she found an excuse to laugh. She laughed now.

"I may hope, then, that when he's finished his argument with a plumber, he will drop in and marry me?"

Bathsheba flushed, not having practice in being laughed at. "He adores you! Your image accompanies his going out and his coming in!"

"The letter he sent," said the waiting bride, "was flowery. Why didn't he choose someone nearer home?"

"Sentiment," said Bathsheba. "Our people once dwelt in your land."

"Did you? I never heard of it."

"Oh, it was an episode in our history!"

The princess accepted a compliment. "Kind of you to say so. Egypt is really too extended. Most of the time we hardly know what's going on, and of course the border families are always moving back and forth."

Bathsheba gasped, but a footstep at the threshold changed the subject.

"That's my son now!"

The princess, recognizing the tall young man with the tentative beard, of which report had spoken, would have prostrated herself, as a matter of form, but he held out his hand.

"My beloved," said he. "Rise up, my love!"

It was a great relief to Bathsheba that he took his betrothal so well. He and the princess were gazing at each other, he soulful, she smiling.

"My husband!"

"My bride!"

"Did you kill Jeroboam?"

Solomon's jaw dropped. "Why should I?"

"I am making your acquaintance," she answered quietly. "Your answer is equal to ten years."

At the words Bathsheba's heart sank, but Solomon thought Magsala must be tangled in the language, as will happen to a foreigner, and tactfully he moved on toward gracious themes.

"Shall we marry today?"

"I am in your hands."

"Hiram wished to see me this afternoon," reflected the ardent bridegroom, "but I put him off till tomorrow."

The princess gazed so intently that his thoughts came back to her.

"My beloved!" he remembered to exclaim.

They were married quietly. Indeed, the record says nothing of it, but doubtless it was in that room, since the temple was not complete, and there would have been an unfitness in Solomon's study, where Abishag had visited him.

We do know about the banquet, also in that room, with Bathsheba a thoughtful guest, listening to the wise talk of her son, and studying the poise of this tall girl who had such an infinite line of kings in her blood that she craved decisions and perhaps would make them for herself. Bathsheba, though she had planned the union, foresaw the wane of her own day.

She spoke to Solomon vaguely of her forebodings when

at Magsala's request mother and son left the banquet table
together.

"I meant to choose well," she said. "Is she the wife you
desired?"

The remembrance of Abishag came back with a pang.
"She is not," he answered, "but who knows? She also may
have thought of one who did not resemble me."

Bathsheba had no answer for that, and he retired to his
chair before the desk, and sat with his head on his hands,
and seizing his pen, he started a sad little poem which
asked how you can tell whether you're a wise man or a
fool, and then remembering it was his wedding night, he
went down the corridor again to his bride.

In his absence her maids had changed the room to a
bower or tent, with dark fabrics hung on the walls, golden-
patterned, and with blue silks for a ceiling. In the heaven
above the bed glittered a silver sun, a silver moon, a stream
of silver stars. She lay there waiting for him, bright-eyed,
and on her lips a little smile.

Her beauty was the beauty of a queen. At that moment
he preferred not to think, but the thoughts would come.
She had always been a queen, without effort or intrigue.
She had not needed to bathe, like his mother, on the housetop. She would have been regal even though she had not
married him. Solomon approached the sacrament of love
with a certain awe.

When he awoke in the morning he had for greeting that
attractive smile of hers. "You'll be wanted at the temple."

Solomon gazed up comfortably at the silver stars.
"There's no hurry."

In a white flash she was out of bed, and he saw he had one of those wives who like to get at the day. "Let's be there," she said, "before those difficult workmen have cleared their heads! The first hour they're always sleepy."

Thus it was that Solomon found himself on the building site while the dew was still in the air, and the laborers, stripped to the waist, were running about like ants. Ano and Tii walked behind the queen, with shades and fans, but Magsala was too energetic for sunlight to wilt.

"Now explain it all!" she commanded.

He pointed with his staff. "The general shape is discernible in the foundations. That further end, where the wall is rising, is the sacred part. I should say, the most sacred. We shall have there a vast room, thirty feet square. Next will come an outer hall, still more imposing, thirty by sixty, the whole edifice to be introduced, as it were, by the porch, just about where we are standing, a magnificent entry, thirty by fifteen. There will also be a series of chambers running around the sides and behind the sanctuary. The total ground plan, therefore, measures a hundred and twenty feet by sixty."

He paused, to see if she was impressed, but on the contrary, she looked worried.

"The walls, you'll notice, are three or four feet thick."

Because he hadn't seen how they build in Egypt, her silence puzzled him, and for courage he talked on.

"I still must decide about the roof, but there's plenty of time for that. With a large house like this you can go up indefinitely. Or I may keep it down and get the height by columns."

"It's for one of your minor gods, I suppose," she ventured.

He was startled. "We—we have but one, you know!"

"To be sure! How stupid! I was warned about that. Of course! This is your more intimate temple, for the palace, perhaps?"

He hoped his mortification wouldn't show under his beard. "We have no other. This is for all my people."

She hastened to put him at ease. "It's beautiful! I don't wonder you're proud of it!"

He was annoyed to see Hiram making his way inexorably through the mob of toilers.

"Who is that powerful youth with red hair?" asked Magsala.

"He represents the King of Tyre, an expert in brass," explained Solomon, courteous but weary.

"What a chest he has!" exclaimed the queen. "Have you ever seen such a chest, Ano?"

Ano never had.

The red-headed youth with the muscular shoulders stood before them, his bronzed skin gleaming with sweat. Shocking, Solomon thought, for the creature to intrude in that condition, but Magsala was entertained, far more than by the temple.

"We're moving along now," said Hiram, without wasting ceremony on the queen. Indeed, his etiquette even toward Solomon was of the briefest.

"The men," said the king, "appear contented today."

"They aren't," said Hiram. "They'd feel better if they had more to do."

"Why, Jeroboam thought them overworked!"

At the moment the temple was blotted out by swarming toilers.

"It would help," suggested Hiram, "if I could begin the new palace at once. They wouldn't get so much in each other's way."

Solomon turned to Magsala. "We contemplate a modern home."

Hiram turned to her also. "Four or five times as large as the temple. A real house."

The queen smiled. "A wedding gift for me, perhaps?"

"We'll build you a separate one," confided Hiram.

Solomon was beginning to discern the principles of Tyrian salesmanship. "Are you speaking now of two palaces?"

"It's customary," said Hiram. "The big one for you, the small one for your wife."

Magsala looked at him, and he looked back. "Do we need," said he, "to live apart?"

She laughed. "Later you may wish seclusion. It's not a bad idea."

To have your wife ordering palaces for you, playing into the hand of that insatiable Phoenician, who hawked buildings around like a peddler! With those two girls standing marble-still, but doubtless listening!

If his mother had been less ambitious, she might have mentioned his poverty when she proposed. Poverty, that is, in comparison with the extravagant resources of Egypt. He had intended one simple temple, nothing more, yet the people—Jeroboam, to be specific—groaned at the cost.

Now to add two palaces in one morning! In Magsala's family perhaps they gave palaces, like rings, as dinner souvenirs!

A dark thought—had Magsala and Hiram ever met before? Were they in league to ruin him, his neighbors on the north working pleasantly with his neighbors to the south? What did he know about his wife, anyway?

"This whole matter of the new palaces," he began, "needs careful planning. The city in my father's time enjoyed a haphazard development, but now we'll take a long view. I'll consider it at my leisure."

Magsala touched his arm with her lovely fingers. "You bring your leisure with you, you hold it in your hand!"

Gazing past the Phoenician metal-worker, he could see and to his regret could recognize a figure emerging from the mass of toilers, striding toward them, an unwelcome petitioner, as yesterday's encounter had taught. Solomon turned his back on the threatened interruption, and looked at his wife.

"Did you say leisure?"

"You mentioned it first."

"I know the word," he sighed, "but not the thing. There are moments when I dream of a small cottage in the wilderness——"

She laughed. "In my land a poet mentioned that four thousand years ago. The hallucination of the civilized! You want solitude, but with all the conveniences."

Solomon was compelled to notice, not Magsala, but Ano, standing beside her. The girl was evidently fascinated by something over his shoulder, by something in the distance—no, unluckily, by something not distant enough, by that oncoming pest which he had hoped to ignore.

"The burden of your people is still heavy!"

A deep succulent voice booming in his ear. Jeroboam was about to make another speech, and that voice always commanded an audience. The women were listening, even Hiram. Solomon swung around, resigned.

His most dreaded labor-leader was as tall as Hiram and if possible more naked, but his body was not muscular and there was no gleam of sweat on it. Since the day the temple-building began he had stripped for effect, to be one of the people, but his industry was oral.

He had a massive head, with thick black hair parted in the middle, thick eyebrows and a habitual frown, to indicate a crisis of thought, and when he spoke he pursed thick lips, sensual and soft. His style was rotund, suitable to prophecy, and he favored a moral tone.

"Will you never hearken to us?" he inquired. "Yesterday I spread our sorrows before you, yet today the task is no lighter, and we hear there is another weight to fall!"

With that he gave Hiram an accusing glance.

"Was this the one you told me about?" asked Magsala sociably, as though Solomon were exhibiting a rare animal in his zoo. He pretended not to hear her question, but Jeroboam had heard, and he worked himself into a sudden eloquence.

"Why have you brought strangers among us? Could we not build our temple with our own hands? Were there no daughters of our own race to bear you children?"

Solomon's wedding had been so precipitous that he had

thought little about his children, but now that the question was raised—if Magsala had a son, would it be just another Egyptian, or would it be something he could feel at home with? Could he talk to the boy about David, that true king? What would David in his grave say of all this?

Of course, if David were there in the flesh, Jeroboam wouldn't say anything!

"Get back to your task!" commanded Solomon. "It is not I that am heavy upon you, but the hand of God, since you are a fool! Before you retire, you may ask pardon of the queen!"

"Oh, don't make a martyr of him," said Magsala cheerfully. "I like to hear him talk!"

This was a taste which Hiram, apparently, did not share. He stepped forward, elbowing the orator slightly to one side. "We can start on those palaces tomorrow, if you say so."

"Why, I thought that was decided!" exclaimed the queen. "My sunshade, Ano!"

"You have heard the voice of your people!" warned Jeroboam, from guttural depths.

"I have heard you," replied Solomon.

"Will you not listen to Adoram?"

"That's the tax-collector, isn't it?" asked Magsala.

"When we saw this evil counselor approaching you," continued Jeroboam, indicating Hiram, "we sent for Adoram. He comes now. Your people wait upon your answer."

Sure enough, the work on the temple had suddenly

stopped, Tyrians as well as natives all watching Solomon. Up the road Adoram was hurrying, out of breath.

"I suppose we'll have to delay another minute," said Solomon apologetically to the queen.

The aged provider of income had inwardly no more patience than Jeroboam; in fact, he arrived in a storm of wrath. But good manners were with him such a habit that he bowed low before his sovereign and his sovereign's new wife, and even waited for an invitation to speak.

"Well?" exclaimed Solomon, all acid.

"I resign!" said Adoram. "I'm too old!"

Though he felt rather tossed about by the morning's series of nuisances, Solomon now roused himself and replied at large to impress Magsala.

"We went over this ground before, did we not? You understood that I'm satisfied, on the whole, with your performance of your present duties, to which you were assigned by my father, who had skill in the choice of servants?"

"If that man from Tyre," challenged the angry comptroller, "has persuaded you to build another temple or palace or what not, let someone else find the money!"

"It's two palaces now!" put in Jeroboam. "The Tyrian announced his plans before the king got here this morning!"

Solomon turned to Hiram, expecting a denial of so grave a charge, but the red-headed brass-worker adroitly deflected the line of thought.

"When we discussed the cost of your palace the other day, before you commanded a separate one for the queen——"

"I've commanded nothing yet," protested the hard-driven bridegroom.

"—speaking exclusively of *your* palace," Hiram continued, "we thought it would be a good idea for you personally to take over the trade in linen and horses from Egypt."

"We thought? Who's we?"

The shameless salesman pushed on. "You would of course vouch for the quality—you recall that point?—and the slight charge for this great public benefit would double your revenues."

Jeroboam glared at his king. "You intend to steal from your people?"

Adoram, shocked, raised a soothing hand. "That is not the word—you forget yourself!"

"I said steal!" repeated the champion of the working class, in a voice loud enough to reach the regiment of attentive masons and carpenters.

"The linen and horse business," shouted Solomon, hoping to be heard by the same audience, "does not attract me! We will fill the treasury from the natural sources, when it needs filling!"

"It needs filling now," groaned Adoram. "Your money goes like wine through a split skin."

Solomon glanced sideways to see what Magsala thought of what she had married into. Here he had taken her for a walk, the morning after his wedding night, to show off the kind of king he was, beginning inevitably with the temple, his first and perhaps his supreme achievement—and how far had he got?

He ought to have kept her in the house! She thought the

temple too small, and though you could pass over a difference of taste, and though no building, anyway, looks its
size till its up, still a wife ought to see the bright side and
encourage her husband in whatever he's doing.

Then Hiram had appeared, and if she were sensitive to
her husband's point of view she would have disliked Hiram. He feared she didn't.

That is, he was noticing faults in her in order to offset
Jeroboam and Adoram, who were his subjects. After their
abominable behavior she might believe his people did not
respect him. On the very threshold of their life-long companionship—he assumed it would be life-long—she might
doubt his talent for governing. He doubted it himself, but
a wife ought to keep her faith.

"The questions which you have laid before me," he announced, in the same far-reaching tone, "are to you hard
but to me simple. We shall build two new palaces, not
that I strictly need them, but they will furnish work for my
people. The wages on the first palace will be one-tenth
higher than on the temple, since this is a secular enter-
prise, unsupported by religious enthusiasm. The wages on
the second palace, when we get to it, will be one-tenth
higher than on the first palace, because the second palace
will be my gift to the queen, and the kingdom will naturally not wish to skimp on it."

The announcement of higher wages produced subdued
applause which Jeroboam did not like. Solomon was se-
ducing the workers.

"Deception!" he boomed. "One-tenth on the wage, but
double on the taxes!"

"As for the taxes," continued the king undisturbed, "if by misfortune they need to be increased, which I do not now admit, the increase should be sought among those outlying districts of the kingdom which do not share your manual labor. You who do the work will have higher pay. Those who merely enjoy the unearned benefits will have higher taxes."

Adoram was holding on to his head with both hands.

"I cannot ask my tax-collector to assume this new program. He needs an assistant. I therefore appoint one known and trusted by us all, your friend and mine, Jeroboam!"

"Not me!" exclaimed the spokesman for humanity. "I refuse!"

"This office," said Solomon calmly, "I can assign only to a patriot of humane disposition."

"But you'd expect me to bring in the money!"

"That certainly is the intention—you and Adoram together."

Jeroboam knotted his brow. Out of the knot emerged a sudden light, not reassuring to a keen face-reader. He assumed a tone of lugubrious resignation. "If I must, then——"

Solomon gathered his robe over his left arm, and turned to escort the queen. "You must indeed, since it is my command!"

He thought he had exhausted the evil chances of the day. "Very dull for you, all this," he apologized, as they strolled home.

"Quite the reverse." She smiled.

He was encouraged by her charm. "I handled those men fairly well, don't you think?"

"No, I don't." Her cheerfulness was undiminished.

"What's wrong?"

"That man Jeroboam is dangerous—you gave him power."

"Didn't you say I should kill or promote him?"

"I didn't advise promotion."

He walked by her side, in startled reflection. "Are all good women bloodthirsty?"

"Not bloodthirsty, but thorough. Half-measures bring grief."

He was still puzzling it out, not yet beyond sight of the temple, when a girl rose at his side, interrupting the procession.

"Will you present me to the queen?"

Abishag! The sight of her made him catch his breath. She was wearing that thin dress which had pleased him in their private encounters, but which he had not expected in the street. Magsala was looking at it too.

"This girl," he began awkwardly, "is a friend of my father."

For the first time Magsala lost control of her face and betrayed a primitive astonishment. "Your father must have——"

The pause was trying, and Abishag promptly made it worse. "I was prescribed by the doctors."

Magsala laughed outright. "Upon my word!"

"I can explain another time," interposed Solomon, in some irritation.

"Oh no, now!" urged his wife, recovering herself. "This charming girl—I didn't catch the name?"

"Abishag," said the charming girl.

"You were the old king's friend, and afterwards you were doubtless the friend of the new king?"

"Much better with the new king," agreed Abishag.

Magsala turned to her husband, without jealousy but with a certain relentless curiosity. "Was this too on the advice of physicians?"

Solomon was conscious of those two girls, Ano and Tii, holding graceful fans between the queen's head and the sun, and pretending not to listen. Their faces were immovable, but they had quick eyes.

"We will proceed," said he, stepping off to lead the way, but if he had not changed his mind he would have gone home alone.

"Abishag—Abishag," his wife was repeating, to fix her memory. "I like that name. So you were of benefit to the king! To two kings!"

Though her words had a possible edge, she was, so far as he could observe, in the best of humor. Abishag, equally content with the world, returned her smile.

"You came just in time. You are what he wanted. You make us all happy."

"This approval," said Magsala, a bit surprised, "gives me courage. I must talk with you at length. To me also you may be helpful."

Thereupon Abishag bowed herself to the dust, and mercifully permitted Solomon to escape. He strode several paces before he could command an easy voice.

Her price is far above rubies.
The heart of her husband doth safely trust in her.
She will do him good and not evil all the days of her life.

He would have elaborated this theme, but Benaiah interrupted with a thunder on the panel.

"Who's that?"

The captain of the guard thrust his broken nose across the threshold.

"It might be well," said the king, "if you respected the few secluded moments I now enjoy. The lack of discipline in this palace depresses me."

Benaiah closed the door carefully and came over to the desk, unabashed.

"Didn't you tell me to report an emergency, any hour, night or day?"

"Only if it were serious!"

"It's desperate," said the muscular warrior. "Your mother thought you ought to know."

"You told her first?"

"I did, but you're in charge now, she says, since the wedding, and you should begin to take responsibility."

The king rose from his chair. "You offend!"

"I'm explaining why I came! There isn't enough food for our own people, now the Tyrians are here. Great eaters, every one of them!"

"This," exclaimed Solomon in disgust, "might be Jeroboam speaking, or Adoram! They've pressed you into the service, eh?"

Benaiah, when in intellectual motion, kept to a straight path. "If another nation should visit us, one with an appetite, we'd starve."

"Content yourself," said the king, resuming his seat. "I was afraid you brought bad news. Your present worry is fantastic. I shall never again invite a foreigner, for any purpose."

"Some don't wait for an invitation," said Benaiah. "The Queen of Sheba is already on the way."

"Who?"

"Her first name is Balkis, and the runner assures me she's beautiful. A colored woman, but from every angle beautiful."

Solomon turned the idea in his mind. "An embassy of some sort, I suppose. These parleys among monarchs are an old institution. One guest won't eat us out of the house."

"But they're all coming with her!"

"Who? Who all?"

"Her people! So many, the runner says there must be none left at home."

Solomon drew triangular decorations on the edge of his manuscript.

"The black nations," continued Benaiah, "have a peculiar anatomy. The legs are more often parallel than shaped, and in other details they differ from us, but this woman, though dusky, is altogether what we admire. That is, what we haven't seen but hope to. Cast in bronze, so to speak."

The intimacy of the image which rose in Solomon's

thought seemed indelicate. "On this topic the runner can give no reliable testimony. A queen holds herself aloof, even sacred."

"Maybe someone had a glimpse of her before she was queen," suggested Benaiah with dangerous slyness. "Anyhow, the report has got around."

Solomon stared at his desk, appalled at his thoughts. Did Benaiah, by any chance, refer to his mother's roof-doings? No—Benaiah was high in Bathsheba's favor, and consequently would be discreet. Yet the incident was doubtless talked of still, among the ordinary folk!

To come back to this dark-hued visitor—if there was one things the palace didn't need, it was another woman. His mother on his hands—Magsala—Abishag! Particularly Abishag.

"Does the runner know her errand?" he asked.

"She intends to marry you," explained Benaiah. "She says so herself."

"But I've a wife already!"

"Your mother doesn't think that will stop her."

Solomon stared at the complacent soldier, who knew his mother better perhaps than he did. "She turned this problem over to me?"

For the first time Benaiah hesitated. "No exactly—but I thought you should hear of it."

"What do you mean, not exactly?"

Benaiah was ill at ease. "She said, let her come and we'll watch them fight it out."

"Me? Why should I fight?"

"She meant your wife and this dark woman. Your wife,

she said, hasn't been cordial to her anyway, and perhaps Sheba will be a retribution, like the plagues."

Solomon looked hard at the man, to see if he was lying. Would Bathsheba's favorite give her away?

"My mother and my wife," he announced at last, "have no quarrel. You must have misunderstood."

Benaiah, the strong assassin, showed unmistakable signs of fear. "Am I not your servant first of all? Will you not hold me to account if she——"

He couldn't go on.

"Well, if she what?"

Benaiah held out trembling hands. "Keep my words secret! She must not know! Grant me my life if I tell!"

"You've lost your wits," said the king. "Tell anything you like, and stop shaking."

"Your mother," whispered Benaiah, "expects Queen Magsala to die by an accident. I refused to arrange the accident for her. She considers she made a bad mistake, which should be mended promptly, before Balkis arrives from Sheba."

Solomon stared wide-eyed.

"Your mother," continued Benaiah, "is a friend of mine, but I'd be sorry if she did something you couldn't approve."

Solomon cleared his throat. "Ask the Queen of Sheba to travel slowly, if possible to delay her visit altogether. We'll need time to prepare suitable quarters, as you were saying a moment ago."

In another part of the palace belonging to this king

whose name meant peaceful, Magsala was looking at Abishag, and Abishag was returning the gaze with interest—the queen on her throne-like chair, Abishag on the floor, and both of them smiling.

"I sent for you," Magsala began.

Abishag nodded. "I thought you would."

"I sent for you," continued Magsala, "because you are my enemy."

"Of course," said the girl. "I wanted you to know I love him."

"I can easily forgive his errors," said the queen, "but I shall endure no rival."

"I," said Abishag, "have none."

The queen stared. "You are extraordinary!"

"So are you," said the girl. "I'm sorry we must share him!"

"Share him?"

"He married you, but he thinks of me. Or, if he begins not to, I'll remind him. But nothing stealthy. I'll always let you know about it."

Magsala watched her, and neither smiled.

"You are daring! I shall deal with you—in my own way!"

"So would I, in your place."

The queen rose, then changed her mind, and settled down again, relaxed and amused. "I wish I knew what has gone on between you two!"

"You'd like to hear?" Abishag drew her knees up to her chin, and clasped her hands around them. "Well, in the first place——"

Chapter V

King Hiram's dock hands shouted orders back and forth and got in each other's way as the ship rounded the hill where the lighthouse was, and bore down upon them.

Among his dock hands stood King Hiram himself, detached but impatient. Since the heavy trade with Solomon had set in, the coming or going of a boat was nothing to get excited about, and King Hiram usually permitted his sailors to manage the navy, but this one afternoon he wished to be there when they let down the gangplank. Hiram the brass-worker was on board.

His father had sent for him, reluctantly as we may suppose, since the energetic young man was needed to push the building operations in Jerusalem, and since, moreover, his presence in Tyre embarrassed the king, for reasons already stated. The tall youth had his elbows on the rail while the ship was warped in, and King Hiram could see even at that range a resemblance more striking than ever between them—the same tilt of the chin, the same resolution in the middle of the mouth. For the hundredth time he asked himself why he hadn't foreseen this awkward persistence of his own face before he had gone too far with that wayfaring woman, beautiful but imperfectly educated, from David's country.

He didn't want his son back, yet he had sent for him. The timber, the metal and the stone had poured out of

Tyre, according to contract, and Solomon's wheat, his oil and his few other odds and ends had served for ballast on the home trip, but nothing you could call payment for exports so vast. Therefore King Hiram forwarded a hint to the younger Hiram, his viceroy and business agent, to inaugurate conversation over this formidable debt, but the younger Hiram, being no letter writer, replied that you first had to find someone to converse with, and anyway, the debt was as nothing compared with what it would be later. At that point King Hiram insisted on a word with him, face to face.

On the dock he contented himself with hoping the voyage had been smooth, and young Hiram said it had not. As they rode up in the chariot together, hanging on to the sides, he asked whether the streets of Jerusalem were better than this, and young Hiram said they were even worse. With such small talk they reached the palace, and climbed to a room in the tower, where through a slit in the wall the king could keep an eye on the harbor. There were two benches, both hard, flanking a narrow table, and a jar of water between them because the tower room lacked ventilation and your throat got dry.

"Well, what's the latest? How's the temple?"

"We could finish it in a week," replied his son, "but he thinks it's more reverent to do it slowly, so I'm stringing it out. He wants it to take seven years."

King Hiram stood up, but his son raised a hand.

"Don't worry! He likes to say seven years, but we'll run it off in a month."

King Hiram sat down again, and his son continued.

"I'm putting up a new palace for him—that is, I started it, but he married, and I've shifted over to another palace for his wife—that is, I've dug the cellar, but he's expecting a visit from an Ethiopian queen, with her court and her guard of honor, and we're putting up barracks for them. There's plenty to keep us busy. Besides, I'm laying three keels for that fleet of his on the Red Sea, and in our spare moments——"

"When," asked King Hiram, "do I get paid?"

"If you ask me——" began his son deliberately.

"I do!" said the king sharply.

"You won't get paid at all. Not a chance."

King Hiram would have leaned back, faint, had there been anything on the bench to lean against. He caught the edge of the table just in time.

"Can't he raise more taxes?" he gasped.

"They're never going to pay that debt! They don't like it, and what they don't like they think is an affliction."

"But why then," exclaimed King Hiram, deeply moved, "why do they continue to accept our goods and services?"

"Oh, that end of it! They're used to that. That's different."

King Hiram took a turn around the room, then faced his son. "I'm not eager to fight—the army isn't in a reliable frame of mind. But——"

"He married a princess of Egypt," interposed the younger Hiram, "and if you attack her, the Egyptian chariots will get in motion. My advice would be——"

"I haven't asked it," snapped the king, then tamed his

voice to a more sociable tone. "He's a shrewd rascal! I'll say that for him!"

"Solomon? Not shrewd at all! They're pulling him to pieces. His mother wants to rule. She intrigues with the captain of the army——"

"Much of an army?"

"Haven't seen it! But his wife's a person! She wants to rule. Besides, there's Jeroboam—he loves the people and makes speeches. He wants to rule. Then there's the old tax-collector, who sees what they're coming to, and has a fit over it. And now the Queen of Sheba will pay them all a little visit."

"A madhouse, I'd say!"

"If I might suggest," urged the younger Hiram, "why not push on with the work and pile up the debt and see what happens?"

The king took a drink from the water-jar. "Wait till you talk with the workmen here!" he exclaimed. "Nothing will last, in times like these!"

"I was thinking of the Queen of Sheba," persisted the undiscouraged salesman. "If she should marry him——"

"You just said he *was* married!"

"Well, for the time being, but suppose she took over the government herself? Or even if she didn't, suppose she likes what she sees of our work?"

In his palace at Memphis the King of Egypt was reading a letter to his wife and his remaining four daughters. That is, he was picking out the parts he considered proper for them to hear. Since the moment was domestic and intimate, the great ruler was perched on a low stool, which brought his knees close to his cylindrical beard. The women sat on the floor.

"Her manners were always excellent," said the queen proudly. "In the novelty of marriage another girl would have forgotten to write home!"

The king handled the scroll with evident delight. Being far-sighted, he had it out in front of his knees.

"She keeps her sense of humor," he remarked. "It's as one monarch to another, with all the titles. She addresses me as The Sun, Divine Ruler of the Land of Red Mud."

"What," inquired the queen anxiously, "does she say about her husband?"

"Let's see," said the king, running a finger down the page, "there ought to be mention of him somewhere—ah, here it is. . . . Well, she thinks he's entirely possible—uneducated but naturally polite. That's the substance of it."

"Is he handsome?" asked the eldest daughter.

The king ran his finger up and down again. "She doesn't commit herself, but I get the impression she likes him. He is given to poetry but she hopes to interest him in the art of government. . . . Hitherto he has permitted his mother to manage. She doesn't like his mother."

The queen smiled. "Poor child, did she need to write us that?"

"She finds the climate healthful," continued the king, "and the food clean. They do their butchering, she considers, with more care than we. It's a little country, she adds, everything on a small scale, but the effect of miniature gives an exotic charm. . . . Well, that's a satisfying report, by and large!"

He rolled up the letter deftly, and tapped it on the floor to even the ends.

"I'm glad she's happy," sighed the queen. "We shall miss her."

The king stood up and stretched his right arm. "Since the marriage seems to be permanent, I must think about a wedding gift."

"No more jewelry!" exclaimed the second daughter. "She has three wigs now, four tiaras, and a tray of rings!"

"My gift," said the king, "will be in accord with her state. I shall give her a city."

The daughters laughed in chorus. "Father's darling! The land will be whittled away before *we* find a husband!"

"Not one of our own cities," he explained with affectionate good nature.

The queen looked worried. "Your neighbors resent capture," she pleaded, "and you promised me you wouldn't irritate them again!"

Filled with his new idea, he was moving toward the door, but he talked as he went. "I never promised not to give her a wedding present. Some city close by, so she can take possession without inconvenience. Gezer, perhaps—yes, why not? Gezer!"

"Where is that?" called the queen after him. "If you disturb someone of importance——!"

He turned at the threshold to reassure her. "There's a

right method for everything, my dear. I'll lead the chariots myself."

When he was gone the youngest daughter clapped her
hands. "Won't Magsala love it! A whole city!"

In his study, most unwilling, Solomon heard the complaints of Adoram, the tax-collector.

"What madness came upon you," wailed the old man,
"that you should give me Jeroboam for an assistant? He's
been working on the tribe of Ephraim!"

"Of course!" murmured the king wearily. "They're his
own people—it's a special justice to confine his oratory
to that district."

"But he tells them not to pay! He says the wealth of
the country, instead of going to foreigners, should be spent
at home, and he swears he could build two temples for
what you waste on one, and they wouldn't be in Jerusalem, either!"

Solomon took a livelier interest. "You've been misin-
formed. I asked him myself how much he had collected,
and the sum, as I remember, was considerable."

"But that came from Gezer, on the southern border! He
robs those Canaanites, and lets the sons of Ephraim go
free!"

"If this is true," said the king slowly——

"He's talking to the workmen at the temple this evening. He's spreading treason while Hiram is up there in
Tyre. If you'd just send Benaiah with a soldier or
two——"

"Treason is a large word," protested Solomon, roused

but still cautious. "The man has a terrible talent for sounding off, and most of what he says is foolish, but I can't hang him for that. His promise of more and cheaper temples will deceive nobody."

Adoram leaned over the desk, to whisper discreetly. "If you could creep up on him while he's charming your people away from you, you'd see at his elbow that tall girl your wife brought with her!"

"Ano?"

"She follows him everywhere, and I suspect she tells him what to say! It's an enemy we have among us, to divide the kingdom!"

Solomon rubbed his forehead. "When does Hiram return?"

Adoram turned out his hands, palms up. "Who knows?"

"It's this evening he's speaking? I mean Jeroboam."

"As soon as the palace is asleep. The rabble stay awake for it."

"You," said the king, "might attend, take notes, and report."

Adoram raised his eyes to heaven. "What a welcome, if I showed my face!"

"As soon as Hiram comes back," said the king, changing the subject, "send him here."

He dined alone that night, though Magsala had the table spread in her room. For his absence he sent her no excuse. If she, the daughter of an ancient enemy, had married him for his country's ruin, he preferred not to break bread with her. Nor see her, even. Not till he had tested this story of Adoram's.

With the first darkness he slipped out of the palace. That is, the guards recognized him, but he ignored their salute, and once beyond the main door he drew over his head a copious shawl, concealing the beard and other characteristic marks. Remembering how men walk who are not kings, he rounded his shoulders and fell forward on his feet along the uneven cobblestones which led to the temple.

There was no moon, but the heavens glowed, and the stars hung close to earth. In his errand Solomon was not alone. Clear shadows moved before and behind him along the narrow street, trying to be silent—along all the narrow streets, drawing in toward the open space from which he had explained the temple plan to Magsala.

Jeroboam was standing there now. Even in the half light his figure was unmistakable, still naked to the waist, though the working hours were long past, and the crowd, most of whom had really spent the day in toil, were now washed and clad.

Solomon found a prudent spot on the edge of the gathering, fifty feet or more from the impending eloquence, but that deep and oily voice would reach.

Perhaps Ano was there too, as Adoram had foretold, but in the somber light it was hard to distinguish women from men. Solomon resolved to watch after the speech was over. If the girl loved the trouble-maker, she would perhaps go up to him, certainly if the audience were pleased with what he said. A woman, unless she has a rare stock of brains, likes to advertise her intimacy with a popular hero.

Now a heavy person pushed alongside, brushed Solomon's elbow, and asked pardon, by way of automatic civility. An official, well-bred voice, which Solomon imagined he had heard before. The man wore a long beard, and carried his head at a meditative angle. To follow Jeroboam he would have to look up from under his eyebrows. He planted his feet firmly, as though settled to endure, and his hands were clasped behind his back. Solomon tried to recall where he had seen that posture.

But Jeroboam was about to start. He folded his arms across his chest and took a deep breath. "My people!"

Woe moaned in the syllables. He waited for his people to digest the emotion.

"You have suffered too long! Your misery has broken your spirit! Be patient no more!"

Again he paused, and Solomon wondered if the crowd were either patient or miserable. They seemed introspective, as though examining the break in their spirit.

"We work, but we earn nothing. Our reward for toil is another assessment. In our own land we are slaves!"

Solomon tried to remember what work Jeroboam had done. Also, he made a mental note to ask Adoram whether Jeroboam paid a tax.

"Were this sacrifice necessary to build a temple, who would grudge it? But we are squeezed dry to profit a race of strangers, who despise our blood and our faith. We are not permitted to build a shrine for our own God! The heathen are our masters, they clutter our city, they lead astray our youth, they beguile our daughters!"

The crowd stirred uneasily, and Solomon himself was shocked at the blackness of the picture, which now that

Jeroboam spoke it, was self-evident. Abishag had praised the Phoenician men. . . . On the other hand, if Jeroboam was for segregating the race and keeping it pure, why did he permit Ano to admire him?

"This young king of ours, this verse-maker, who has fought no battle for us, risked no hardship, who lives on what he takes from us—he goes to the heathen for a wife. No daughter of yours would do. How could he marry the child of a slave? A princess for him!"

From the sullen murmur Solomon judged that every man there had a disappointed daughter. Unwillingly he admitted justice in Jeroboam's point. Abishag would have made the right wife, if Bathsheba hadn't set her mind on Egypt.

"Now the Tyrian is to build another palace, larger than the temple, with strong walls for our king to hide in, and another house for his bride, with cool gardens where she can walk without the inconvenience of meeting you and me. For these luxurious insults we must pay."

It occurred to Solomon that Ano could hardly approve of the attack on Magsala, nor could Magsala be urging her on to support Jeroboam. Or was treachery in Egypt so complicated an art?

"You have not yet heard—to my grief I must bring the news—we are no longer free to buy where we will, in the best market, a horse or a piece of linen. These useful objects will be sold to you exclusively by your king, who will get them cheap from his wife's country, and pass them on to you at a higher price."

The crowd were surprised, but not more than Solomon.

He had forgotten this advice of Hiram's. What ground had Jeroboam for saying——

"Moreover, we are to entertain among us shortly, at your expense, another queen, a dark woman from Ethiopia. One wife is not enough for our ambitious monarch. The dark woman will share him with the red-skinned one. Our children will bear the yoke of a half-heathen, of an unpredictable color."

When someone in the crowd laughed, Jeroboam spoke louder, to hold his audience.

"But the day of rescue is nearer than you think! Manhood will spring up in us! We shall cast out the strangers! We shall establish justice and put an end to inequality! Those we have toiled for, will toil for us, and we shall sit at ease with our foot on their necks!"

This climax pleased everyone except the bearded man with the hands behind his back. He turned to Solomon.

"That fellow's an actor!"

"I should like to ask him," said the king, "on whose neck he intends to put his foot. His words seem to convey a threat. His audacity surprises me!"

"Well," said the man, turning away in disgust, "we'll have opportunity enough to get used to it! This couldn't have happened in David's time."

The people were pressing around Jeroboam, praising or telling him how to do it better next time, and he was raising his hand for order. It looked as though he might make another speech. But Solomon decided not to stay. He thought he saw a tall girl, about Ano's height, but his curiosity was satisfied for the evening.

He remembered now where he had seen that man with his hands behind his back. At his father's death-bed! One of the doctors! The other four always folded their hands on their stomach.

And this doctor thought David would have put a stop to Jeroboam. Solomon thought so too.

He walked swiftly home to his palace, conscience-stricken. Now he must act! He would kill Jeroboam, of course, but first he would ask Magsala what Ano meant by consorting with an enemy, and if there really were a plot, he would invite his wife to demonstrate her own innocence. They would realize that at last he was the sort of king his father would have approved.

Yet, to tell all, shame sapped his firmness. Jeroboam had spoken too publicly, but in a measure he had got the facts straight.

When Solomon found his wife in her room, therefore, it came about by natural steps that he deferred the critical challenge to another season. She was lying on her bed, already half asleep, but only too happy to be roused.

"I have waited!" she exclaimed, stretching out her arms. "Such a busy man! Hour after hour, and I have no word from you!"

Melted by this affection, he sat down on the side of the bed and reflected upon her admirable qualities, several of which were visible. A great tragedy, if so much charm were devoted to double-dealing! He wouldn't believe it unless he had to.

She reached up and began to remove the long cloak he had worn in the streets.

"You work late," she whispered sympathetically. "So late and so hard!"

The idea of his industry was flattering, the more because he wasn't used to it. Jeroboam thought he didn't work at all. He permitted her to unfasten the garment next under the cloak.

"Were you far away from me tonight?" she asked. "I never felt so lonely! Remember, you are all my people now. I've no one else to trust—or love!"

He stroked the hand that was steadily disrobing him. "A disturbance in the city took me abroad," he began, nervous. "I stopped in to ask you——"

She put her hands one on each cheek, alongside the beard, and drew his head toward her lips. "You came to me only to discuss a crisis of state?"

In the morning he woke first, as he thought, and employed the freshness of his mind in planning the domestic inquisition he would start as soon as that still form beside him should stir. It might be best to report the speech of Jeroboam in full, as an exhibit of the man's depravity, meanwhile keeping an alert eye for any telltale flush of guilt as she listened.

Then he would bring in Ano, casually, and guilty or not, she would surely express astonishment that the girl was neglecting palace duties.

Then he would press the question home, whether she knew of Ano's revolutionary occupations, and whether she had abetted them.

To be certain of the right order, he went over the topics again on his fingers.

"Is that a game you're playing?"

Magsala was watching him, wide awake and amused.

"I feared you meant to sleep all day," she laughed, "till you began that cat's cradle!"

Because what he was about to say might hurt her, and because he hoped to perform the operation kindly, he leaned across the pillow to bestow a kiss, and when that was done he needed a detached second to recover the severity of his purpose, and meanwhile she took the words as it were out of his mouth.

"I'm glad you went to that meeting last night! I loved you for it!"

He gasped. "How do you know I went? What meeting?"

She sat up in bed and gazed down at him. "There was no other trouble, was there? Don't tell me you didn't go?"

"I went," he admitted, in a positive tone.

"You must be king!" she urged.

"But I am."

"Are you? Jeroboam seeks your life—Ano has told me things."

Now Solomon sat up too, to show that his disposition toward the kingdom was energetic. "I intended to ask you about that girl."

"She has lost her head," said Magsala. "By temperament she is given to improving the human race, and he seems to her a great improver. She ought to be married, that's all that's wrong with her, but I permit this present infatuation because I learn what Jeroboam is doing."

"She wants him to kill me, does she?"

"I doubt if she looks ahead to that conclusion," said Magsala, "but she has grasped one idea, against which I can't argue—unless you take charge of your kingdom, someone will."

"I'll dispose of Jeroboam," said Solomon with dignity.

"Even then."

He eyed her sharply. "Who else?"

She smiled. "I may have to save us, but I'd rather not. It's your work, and you should do it."

So her opinion agreed with Jeroboam's! He was deeply mortified.

"My people have a talent for reckless talk," he explained, reaching hastily for a defense. "I keep myself informed of what is brewing—would I have gone out last night otherwise?—and I know the right moment to strike."

She nodded her head slowly. "Do you by chance know that your mother wishes me out of the way?"

"That too."

"Well—what is your own wish?"

He flushed. "Need you ask?"

She laid her white hand on his arm. "I can protect my life even against her, but you should not leave me in this danger! Not if I'm to think well of my husband!"

He stared at the covers of the bed, as though the answer might be written there.

"Perhaps we are not important, neither of us," she went on, still leaning toward him. "After a thousand years who will care what end we had? There will always be kings enough. And kings take so many wives; who will remember my name? But for you and me, two creatures drawn from across the world, who have tried to put our hearts together—for us it does mean something, doesn't it?"

Her pleading wounded his pride. "I am married to one wife. I will——"

"Don't speak of *me!* Think of yourself! For me to be happy, you have only to be a man!"

When he stared, startled, she dropped the earnest manner and laughed softly. "You don't know what a woman wants, do you? My father used to say women require two things—to be loved and to be stepped on."

He felt there was a collapse of dignity in the expression she used, but he overlooked it in the whirl of his emotions. "You mean you'd love me more if I took a strong hand, beginning with Jeroboam?"

"And then on to your mother, and up to me!"

He got into his garments, thoughtfully deliberate, conscious that she was sitting there on the bed, watching each motion.

"What should I do about Ano?" he asked.

"Nothing."

"But if she aids him?"

"On the contrary. She is a millstone about his neck. No man was ever loved at a less appropriate time."

Before he left her, he thought of a parting kiss, but if she wished a ruthless husband, perhaps he should begin now, so he stalked to his room and demanded food. Having eaten, he called for Benaiah and Adoram.

"About the Egyptian horses and the linen," he thundered, "who dared attach my name to them?"

"That man from Tyre," began Adoram.

"But I said at once I wouldn't rob my people!"

"Yesterday morning," ventured the old tax-gatherer, "Jeroboam recalled the plan and urged me to try it."

Solomon paled at this uncovering of treachery. "*He* suggested it, eh? And laid the blame on me?"

He turned to Benaiah. "Find Jeroboam and kill him!"

Benaiah bowed, rather pleased at the commission, but Adoram raised a warning hand. "I like him as little as you do, but he has a powerful following."

"That's while he breathes," answered Solomon in a royal hardness of tone, "but the cowards will wilt when they see his head on the fence in front of the lumber yard. Last night he defied me; one of us must die."

"The tribe of Ephraim," persisted Adoram, "have a strong prejudice in his favor, and if they should decide to march up here——"

"Who is king in this country?" inquired Solomon, with a biting pretense of curiosity. "Benaiah, you may carry out my orders and report to me. I'll wait in this room till I hear from you! You too may go, Adoram!"

He was delighted to discover that authority, when you assume it, comes easy. Moreover, he understood for the first time the merits of Benaiah, who had departed cheerfully with a reassuring air of competence. If you must decide to execute a dangerous enemy, it is gratifying to have the necessary machinery ready at hand. Bathsheba was after all less bloody-minded than she had seemed—that is, from the point of view of a ruler who does actually rule and who must preserve discipline.

In this mood of enlightened exaltation Solomon spent the morning, with a fresh pen and a clean parchment on his desk, setting down hints for new poems, all welling up out of the peril he had successfully faced. These were but notes, optional versions of a single idea, which of course would need leisurely polishing. At the top he wrote, in clear letters,

The wrath of a king is as messengers of death.

A terrible thought, except when the king has right on his side. At that very moment Benaiah might have caught up with Jeroboam.

The king's wrath is as the roaring of a lion.

That on the whole would be a favorable way to put it, meaning no less, but with the grace of understatement. Solomon preferred this variation.

A wise king scattereth the wicked.

Better still, because the royal wrath here takes moral ground. The other formulas forgot to say what the king was angry at, but you could assume it was the wicked.

A king against whom there is no rising up.

Not a complete theme at present, but Solomon entered it in the manuscript to satisfy an ache in his heart. Later he would think of several other beautiful things, and for a climax he could mention the king who has no trouble with his own people—who, for example, never sends Benaiah to find Jeroboam.

Not that he wished to recall Benaiah from the pursuit, but after a few hours of verse-making he was in that civilized bliss which is the reward of poets, while they remain at work.

After several hours, in fact, since his method of composition was careful. He sent for his lunch. He intended to write till Benaiah came back.

But later his patience wore out, and he called to the guard at the end of the corridor.

"Find me the Captain!"

"He's on the way to Gezer," said the man, as though the news would be welcome.

"Overtake him and bring him here!"

Gezer! That would be half-way and more to Joppa, where Hiram landed his expensive wares. Why was Benaiah traveling around the landscape? Suppose now he was in league with Jeroboam, and would rather run off than arrest him? Or suppose he was fetching Jeroboam's friends? No, there would be none in Gezer—that was the town he had wrung taxes out of. Well, suppose Benaiah was looking for Hiram, who should be returning soon, and suppose Hiram chose to defend Jeroboam?

Solomon strode restlessly up and down the narrow room. It was no satisfaction, after all, to entrust great errands to others. He ought to go himself. Wouldn't his father have done his own fighting? Too often David had come to him that day, a reproachful ghost.

But you have to know how—to fight, that is, and even the most skilful warrior needs some kind of armor. Solomon considered the soft draperies which covered him when he wrote. In his strides from wall to window he faced his poverty—he had no stronger breastplate than this. There was a golden thing in the closet yonder, but he had never worn it in the open, and couldn't get into it without help. If someone gave him now a sling and a pebble, and showed him where Jeroboam was hiding—well, that pebble and Jeroboam would never meet. As for a sword or a spear, one would be too heavy, the other too long. And a war-horse, to mention the worst—that coronation mule, even with Benaiah leading it, had challenged his nerve.

To these thoughts he was not resigned. What he saw when he measured himself made him angry. He had become ripe for a storm when at last a dusty figure pushed in at the door.

"Have you killed him?"

"We haven't found him yet," said Benaiah, "but we think he's near Gezer."

"Why didn't you say so before you rode off? Here I've been waiting——"

"You didn't ask for reports of progress," argued the weary captain. "You just said kill him."

"Get out!" shouted the king. He remembered how his father had spoken to the doctors. "Go back where you came from, and let me see no more of you while he lives!"

The effort of vigorous speech always restores the spirits. By the time Benaiah was on his horse again and galloping down the stony street, Solomon was taking a firmer grasp of destiny. He was still young, he could master the crude arts upon which, in a cross of wills, a noble purpose may depend. He would learn to ride, to swing a sword—he would even solve the intricacies of that golden armor.

He was in fact just taking it out of the closet when Bathsheba knocked. He put away the shining inconvenience and peered around the edge of the door.

"I would speak to you a moment," said his mother.

"Not now!"

"It's about the Queen of Sheba."

"Never!"

With that he shut the door in her face, but she was not discouraged.

"She approaches the city!"

Her voice came through the wood very imperfectly, and he would have been glad to hear all, but she too must submit to his new strength. If he said never, then the Queen of Sheba would have to do her visiting elsewhere. One wife was enough.

He looked again at the armor, saw through the trick of the buckles, decided to try it on tomorrow, when he should be dressed for action. Now he would jot down a phrase about the ruler who rules diligently.

Another signal at the door suggested his mother, that persistent woman, but when he refused to answer, the latch lifted and Abishag came in.

"I thought it was bolted!" he exclaimed ungraciously.

"It wasn't," said she, quite pleased.

There she stood, after all these days. Her gown was careless, as he observed, but not for that reason less fetching, and an idea formed itself in his mind. He recalled what a true king like David would do if so beautiful a woman came before him, and if such thoughts stirred at sight of her.

"I didn't come to be loved!" she protested. "I just wanted to talk a little!"

"With whom?" said he, pursuing the idea. "The man you formerly talked with is outgrown. I have learned to live!"

Yet afterwards he had his old conscience. "Perhaps I shouldn't have done that, since I'm married. If I offended you——"

Abishag laughed. "Have you time for the talk? I'm glad you were at the meeting last night."

"Everyone's glad," he admitted, "except Jeroboam."

"He isn't entirely wrong," said the girl.

"Ah—not entirely?"

"Your people are wretched, and no one tells you. If you knew, you wouldn't permit it."

"My information is complete," said the strong king stiffly.

"Why, you don't know how your people live!"

"But I do."

"Then—by the way—where do I live?"

Of course he had never thought of it. When he sent for her, she came, and sometimes when he didn't send, but between those moments——

"Where *do* you live?" he commanded.

"With the doctor, of course—the one who carries his hands behind his back."

Solomon paled slightly. "You—live with him?"

"In his house—in case I should be needed—along with the other medicines."

He might have seen in her eyes that she enjoyed his torture, had he known how to read eyes.

"But that is one service you surely would not repeat!"

She lifted her shoulders. "Perhaps—if it were a king— an old one, I mean. Anyway, the doctor thinks I should stay."

Solomon forgot Jeroboam.

CHAPTER VI

WE ARE told that Balkis, Queen of Sheba, came to Solomon with some hard questions, and he answered them all. But in the most widely distributed account of her visit the questions are not given, and few readers have the curiosity to look them up elsewhere. Just as well; the conundrums, when you do get at them, are not what you'd expect of a lady.

We are further told that Balkis spent with Solomon an indefinite period—a day, a week, a year. There are no marks or signals to verify the chronology. We learn that she went through his house, sampled the meat on his table, examined the discipline and the uniforms of his attendants, but an energetic queen, accustomed to open bazaars and inspect markets, could cover more than this in a morning. If afterwards, as we read, she was quite exhausted, it may have been because she hurried, or the season may have been warm.

On the other hand, her acquaintance with Solomon's grandeur may have been gradual and thorough, and her enervating admiration may have gone less to superficial things than to the furnishings of his mind. Frankly, we don't know.

At the end, according to the legend, he and she exchanged articles of value, as was then proper between host and guest, but over and above these courtesies he gave her all her desire, whatsoever she asked. Here, as with those famous questions, we are left in the dark. What was her desire?

Those who call themselves romantic yet favor always the biological interpretation, say she asked Solomon for a child, and he was polite about it, and when she returned eastward she carried home a young prince, to be born patriotically on Ethiopian soil. The romantic are convinced he was a great man when he grew up. Several of my friends think he was their direct ancestor.

But if she wanted the child, she must have wanted Solomon still more, and if she had wanted Solomon she wouldn't have gone home. Moreover, if the suppressed questions were really a sample of her conversation, would she have cared to perpetuate a temperament so fastidious as his? Again we don't know. Maybe she would!

Most of these perplexities vanish if we explain her visit by a more reasonable hypothesis, contained in three propositions——

First, she asked her conundrums in private, and what has been handed down is the invention of baffled talebearers.

Second, she had a child, but not by Solomon.

Third, she went home because she was no longer enjoying herself.

As a matter of fact, her visit got off on the wrong foot. She arrived with her caravan only an hour or so after Hiram came back from that conference in Tyre, and Solomon had him in the study, hoping for some miraculous system of payment which would discharge the debt while they all were alive, and yet would save the temper of the taxpayers. Hiram was not encouraging.

"He knows what you want," said he, pointing northward toward Phoenicia. "I told him you like his products but it isn't in you to settle for them, and he may as well charge it off against experience, unless he feels like sending the army down and taking over the country."

"Does he feel like it?" asked Solomon.

"Sometimes he does, sometimes he doesn't. As he said to me when I left, you might at least pay for the temple, since it has to do with religion."

"I'll pay every cent!" exclaimed Solomon. "Only, we're a poor people, as you see for yourself, and we can't be hurried. *You* suggested the extras! I said just a temple, but now you give me two new palaces and a fleet!"

The mention of the fleet roused in Hiram those traits of his mother which made him a good salesman.

"Before I left, one of the ships was well along. Suppose I rush work on it, and we run down to Ophir, and bring back a cargo of ivory! Enlarge your trade, and you'll wipe out the debt in no time!"

At that very moment, as Solomon was about to reassert his distrust of commercial ventures, Balkis rode in, and Bathsheba came hastily to organize a cordial welcome.

"You should be on the steps of the palace," she urged, as though Hiram weren't listening, "or better still, you could ride down the street and meet her at the city hall, but I fear there isn't time to send for your horse!"

In the excitement of receiving a queen—not a mere

princess but a queen—Bathsheba dropped the poise which was her accustomed cloak. Her son saw before him an efficient woman, for the moment hard-pressed. Not his mother now, but the domestic despot, who would give him a wife, then remove her, with a change of mind, and provide another.

"This visitor," he explained coldly, turning to Hiram, "is the brown woman—brown or perhaps black—for whom you have constructed separate barracks. Greet her on my behalf, if you will be so kind, escort her to whatever you have prepared, and suggest that she unpack and rest. I may look in later."

To his surprise, Hiram went to this task with cheerfulness, forgetting to salute Bathsheba on the way out.

"Are you mad?" she asked.

"Quite mad! I have found out what it is to be a king!"

"My son," she pleaded.

He waved her out of his room. "I am no longer your son! You have contrived a kind of battle, where we must face each other!"

It was a pleasure to throw down the challenge, even though he caught the danger in her eyes as she left him.

The next hour or so he spent in Magsala's room, somewhat to her surprise at that part of the day, and his conversation, as she noticed, was forced. He couldn't explain he was making sure of her safety against whatever his mother had in mind.

Meanwhile Hiram gathered a dozen of his better-appearing men, told them to put their shirts on, and hurried to the city gate, thankful for the luck which brought him so early under the eyes of this woman from whom he intended to win back what he had lost on Solomon.

She traveled with a picturesque train, less formidable than Benaiah had reported, but still a noteworthy procession. Her locomotion was by camels and by less expensive animals, herself on a camel, with her womenfolk strung out in a swaying line on other loose-legged creatures, and the baggage piled on donkeys. Alongside ran or walked the donkey-boys and the camel-drivers, shouting to the animals when necessary, which was all the time, and a fragment of the Ethiopian army straggled underfoot, wherever there was room. Hiram distinguished them from donkey-boys by the armor they carried—leather shields, broad-bladed spears, arrows and crooked knives. Their feet were sore but they bristled.

When they paused at the gate, Hiram stepped forward and inclined to the ground, the first time he had bent his head to anyone in Solomon's country. No doubt at all, which woman was the queen. Here Benaiah had not exaggerated—shining black eyes, straight black hair, large forehead, strong mouth, slightly thick, and the air of enjoying life but wanting her own way. Like Magsala she was born to power and carried her past with her, but obviously it was a different kind of past. Her manners might be explosive. Those she commanded were slaves.

"The king my master," said Hiram in a loud voice, getting off the ground and looking up at her, "the king is enveloped in grief! For weeks he has been unable to sleep, with your visit closing in on him, and now he should be kneeling here, in welcome and worship, but at the last moment what should happen but a tiresome council of state, where no vote can be taken unless he presides, so he sends me instead, wretched substitute that I am! Will you follow to the house he has prepared? When you are dusted off and ready for some quiet talk, I'm to let him know, and he'll dismiss the council, whether or not they're through for the day."

Balkis gazed down at the brass-worker with the red hair and the prominent muscles and the masculine voice, and he continued to look up at her, and she forgave the informality of the reception, and cared little how far the council prolonged their deliberations.

When he walked ahead to show the way, she admired the straightness of his back and the panther reach of his stride.

The citizens, of course, pressed through the streets and filled the square, for a good view, and the Tyrian workmen, for this once, let the temple build itself. In the crowd was Abishag, squeezing along adroitly, always near the royal camel. Hiram noticed her, and recalled the episode in the study when she rested on Solomon's lap, but the reminiscence could be but fleeting, with Balkis on his hands.

"This is your room," he announced, at the most ambitious end of the capacious shed. "My master the king says, will you please distribute your people as you wish."

The camel knelt and she got off, and stood a second rubbing the small of her back, in a gesture of engaging naturalness. From his handsome speech she concluded he was one of the princes, a prodigy of breeding who affected simplicity in his dress. If the king, now, were even more superb——!

At the door of the guest-chamber, to Hiram's disgust, waited Bathsheba, with another low bow.

"My son prostrates himself at your feet! That is, he will in a moment. As you may have heard, he is building a temple, and a problem of architecture which only he could solve——"

"Will you enter?" said Hiram quickly, offering a shoulder to lean on up the steps.

Bathsheba fixed on him her most determined eye. "Announce to the king, your master, that the queen is here! Set a guard around the house, and send the people away. She desires quiet."

He caught at her blunder, the pretense that he was a servant of hers, doing Benaiah's work! Very well. Wouldn't he like to guard that house, of all houses! Let Benaiah recover the post now, if he could!

He turned and waved off the crowd—except Abishag, who ignored the signal.

"That girl too!" said Bathsheba, missing nothing.

But later when Bathsheba was gone to see what really detained Solomon, Abishag wheedled out of Hiram the privilege of knocking at the brown queen's door. Just one knock. She had his permission after a brief whisper in his ear.

Expecting Solomon, Balkis opened the door herself.

"I bring a message," said the girl, slipping in. "We've only a moment! There's a plot!"

Balkis had on her afternoon gown, white, knotted at

the shoulders, without sleeves, and a dark red band over
her hair. Also she wore sandals and earrings. The thought
of ambush turned her ominously rigid, like a jungle creature at an unaccustomed sound.

"It's not against your life," Abishag added.

"Oh, it's not!" echoed Balkis. "How moderate!"
She used a deep contralto, disturbingly husky.

"They think you wish to marry their king, and that's
very well, because he has only one wife so far, and they're
not sure she's satisfactory, but they want a queen who can
recognize a king by his essential qualities. They fear you
couldn't pick him out unless he had his crown on. There's
been talk about you."

"Me?" The red showed under the brown skin.

"Nothing discreditable. Everyone agrees you're beautiful, but some think you're not intelligent."

Balkis needed time to store away these ideas as Abishag
fed them, but her face was settling into a grim mask.

"So they're playing a trick on you," continued the girl.
"When the king calls to pay his compliments, it won't be a
real king, but only a timid young man with a beard, and
if you are deceived, we'll all be amused. In this country
the sense of humor is broad. The true king you will of
course run into, but he's going around in disguise. In fact,
you may have noticed him already."

Balkis forgot her anger and smiled with delight.

"That tall person with red hair—the one who's to guard
me?"

Abishag clapped her hands. "You *are* quick! Of course!
His mother thought you'd never guess, if he kept patrolling

up and down. Now they'll insist it isn't so, but I've given you the hint, and you'll compare the two men for yourself."

For an instant Balkis couldn't trust her hope.

"Who are you? Why do you spoil their plan?"

Abishag lifted her small nose.

"It wasn't my plan and I didn't approve of it. I don't enjoy seeing a woman made ridiculous!"

Thereupon she excused herself and left by a side door, because Solomon was coming, set in motion at last by his mother's pushing.

For a moment he stopped with Hiram outside. In fact, he asked why Benaiah wasn't doing this work and why Hiram wasn't finishing the temple. His temper was not improved, nor his self-confidence increased, when he learned that Bathsheba had changed his watchmen.

With the voices sounding at the door, Balkis prepared to be intelligent, even acute, and when he entered and bowed majestically, she attacked before he could straighten up.

"Are you the one who pretends to be a king?"

As though his own conscience had spoken! He clutched the back of a chair, and stared at this sensuous but somber angel, mysteriously commissioned to pronounce judgment.

"It was my father's wish," he began, in feeble defense.

She laughed. "If he got you into this masquerade, he must be sorry now. Don't you feel absurd? A grown man like you, making believe!"

He would have sat down, had she not remained standing.

"Did you come to tell me this?" he asked.

The idea amused her. In a large way she was charming when she laughed. "Would I waste my time? These days and nights in the desert, just to prove I know more than you thought? I came to find a king. There is none in my country."

"Nor in this, perhaps," he agreed sadly. "They're scarce. My father was a great king, but with him the glory died."

His words, too sincere to misunderstand, restored her habitual good nature.

"I'm glad you don't keep on pretending. They probably forced you into it. Who are you?"

He didn't understand. "My name is Solomon."

Her brow puckered. "But he's the king!"

"I am he."

She was disappointed. "Don't begin that again! You know I see through it!"

He feared she was crazy. "If there's anything I can do to provide comfort during your stay, any special entertainment——"

"You may go," she commanded. "We need not meet a second time. When you report to whoever sent you, say you did your best, and with a stupid woman you might have succeeded!"

"If it comes to that," said Solomon, yielding ground to irritation, "we on our part merely assume that you are a queen. Are we too credulous?"

Balkis smiled. "I don't know about you, but the real king of this land behaves with admirable judgment. Of my welcome, aside from this one trick, I have no complaints."

Solomon stroked his beard. "There's an easy way to find out whether you *do* rule a country. Is there any difficulty about the taxes?"

Balkis smiled more broadly. "We hanged my father's tax-gatherer, but the new one has done no better. The treasury is full of cobwebs."

"Beyond question," said Solomon, "you are a true queen. Did you by chance suppose that I—I mean the real king—had better luck here?"

"I heard about the buildings," Balkis admitted frankly. "A temple, a palace, and a fleet."

"If you stay awhile," said Solomon drily, "you will hear of much more. Tomorrow morning, if you wish, I'll show you all our public projects."

She hesitated to give away her time. "Won't the king have some plans for the day?"

He humored her fantasy. "Well, you'll probably breakfast with his mother. His wife may attend. I expect to be there myself. Afterwards we may look over the city. Meanwhile, is there any special diet your attendants prefer?"

His willingness to leave her so soon sprang from his fear that she was demented. Her eagerness to see him go had reference to Hiram. Through the window she could watch the true king collecting additional guards; the original dozen were swelling to several score. If this bearded youth would now go out, perhaps Hiram would come in.

No sooner had Solomon carried away his bewilderment

than she changed her gown for something still more comfortable, and reclined patiently on the couch, a bright gleam in her black eyes, a smooth satisfaction on her brown face.

She was roused by the noise of anger. Without haste she strolled to the window and drew the curtain. Benaiah was shaking his fist in Hiram's face. Benaiah had with him another armed guard, the choice group who had escorted Solomon on the mule ride. Hiram's guard had now grown to a brigade.

"Who commands here?" shouted Benaiah.

"I do!" said Hiram, just as loud.

"By whose authority?"

"The queen's."

"The Egyptian? She has no authority."

"I mean the old one, the king's mother."

Benaiah put his hand on his sword. "You lie!"

Hiram laughed in his face, and deigned no other answer.

"Well," said Benaiah, thrusting out his jaw, "will you send these Tyrians back to work?"

"I might," said Hiram, "if the old lady told me to, and then again I might not."

Benaiah, having measured his chances against such a crowd, let the sword fall back into his scabbard.

"We'll see about this!"

As he marched off toward the palace in Solomon's track, the Tyrian brigade permitted themselves a disrespectful grin. Through the parted curtains Balkis watched Hiram standing at ease, a powerful figure, obviously a king. His disposing of Benaiah indicated the habit of command.

Letting the curtains fall together, she went back to the couch and waited, but after a moment her patience came to an end. From the open door she waved at Hiram an inviting brown arm, and once she had him inside she bolted the latch.

"It's no use being so elaborate," she said. "I know what you're trying to do!"

He would have been astonished at what he heard had he not been still more interested in what he saw. In her savage way she was a feast for the eye, a very generous feast, and though he might be mistaken, she seemed to be—seemed to be—no, he wasn't mistaken at all—she was making advances! This remote and exotic queen with whom he had hoped to establish, for the benefit of the Tyrian treasury, certain relations proper but commercial— this desirable woman, promptly upon her arrival in Solomon's kingdom, had gone mad. Not that he criticised that kind of madness, if she insisted.

As a matter of fact, she was the first woman he had met, in all his laborious years, who awoke in him a spontaneous sympathy. For the moment the calculating traits of his father died in him, also those traits of his mother which were acquisitive; only her zest for a full life remained. For the moment he forgot his intention to sell Phoenician exports to this queen. There was a mistake somewhere, of course—if she knew what she was about, would she be lifting to him this tell-tale, soul-spilling gaze? He wished he were sure she would! There might be a place in the east, a wide colorful world, where they two——

"Am I overbold?" she asked. "When you hesitate, I feel shame! Must a woman wait till the man speaks? Adorable, I crossed the desert to reach you! Every echo of your greatness from the lips of lonely travelers seemed to ask, 'What more must you hear, Balkis, before you will fly to me?'"

He was still puzzled, but the greatest mysteries call less for investigation than for gratitude. He was very grateful.

It wasn't till the decline of the afternoon sun that his thoughts regained their accustomed channels, and to come to one's self is sometimes tragic. Duty compelled him to see what the guard outside was up to. Gently he disentangled himself from her beautiful but detaining hands.

"I must have met you ages ago," she whispered. "Do you feel so about me?"

He didn't, but he had the sense to let the question rest.

"Now," she continued, "we have pushed off from land, on a magical voyage!"

Bad luck! His father suddenly possessed him.

"That reminds me," he said. "Shall I build you a fleet?"

In the palace, meanwhile, Solomon was consulting Magsala. Though he had started to find his mother, his feet led him to his wife, and he reflected on the circumstances, as momentous. That tall girl from Egypt was beginning to exert an influence. Abishag was a little on his conscience. It mattered to him whether his wife were happy. How admirably she had behaved since Bathsheba had grown hostile! Not a sign of fear, not a syllable of reproach! And no jealousy at all when this woman from

Ethiopia was announced, an avowed candidate for Magsala's place in the family, enjoying, though she didn't know it, Bathsheba's support! He ought to ask Bathsheba at once why she ordered Hiram to neglect the temple and police the visitor, but first he must tell Magsala that Balkis was harmless, having lost her wits.

His wife happened to be talking with her other maid, Tii, the short comfortable creature who had not yet spoken in Solomon's presence since she arrived from Egypt, and who so far as he knew had fallen in love with no labor leader.

"May we be alone?" he asked.

At the hint Tii disappeared behind the black and gold hangings of the inner door, and when she was out of hearing Magsala looked up, amused.

"You still remember me! She has failed!"

Rising above even an amiable facetiousnes, he portrayed in strong terms the wreck of the visitor's mind.

Magsala listened, now serious enough.

"I doubt if she's insane—someone has played a trick—it sounds like a plot—someone who will pretend he is you. Jeroboam, do you think?"

"Oh, no, he's run away. Besides——"

Solomon caressed his beard while he picked safe words.

"My mother is at the bottom of it! She ordered Hiram to stand guard at the guest-house, but that can't be a plot because she wants this person to marry me."

Magsala shook her head. "It's not your mother. More likely Jeroboam. Perhaps he slipped home when you didn't notice. If Ano came back, I could question her."

"She wouldn't have the impudence!"

Magsala smiled, this time he thought a little sadly.

"If Sheba failed to recognize a king, perhaps—you'll forgive my saying it?—perhaps that doesn't prove her demented. You're too gentle, my dear! Also, you permit others to live your life for you. Did she mean you ought to take your own part?"

Solomon was hurt. "To what do you refer?"

"To Jeroboam. Your enemy. A king would hunt him down."

"Benaiah——"

She struck her hands to her ears. "Oh, don't say that! Benaiah won't find him for you! Benaiah is in no danger! Jeroboam doesn't envy Benaiah!"

He was shocked at the possibility that she too, like Bathsheba, was bloody-minded.

"You think I ought to take some soldiers, and go kill him with my own hand?"

She shook her head. "The soldiers are not essential."

"But you think I should kill him?"

"He's your enemy—he may be hiding for you, behind a door, with a knife. My father says power belongs to the one who gets there first."

"But I don't want power!"

"But that's ridiculous, if you stay a king."

She made the points with no unkindness, and if they struck him as awkward, it was because he couldn't refute them. Balkis had said the same thing. He had said it himself, long ago. Well, he would try to get started, for Magsala's sake.

"I'll ask my mother about Hiram," he said, in a tone closer to resignation than to courage. "We can't have a divided command! Then I'll go look for Jeroboam."

Magsala smiled. "It's all the finer of you because you didn't wish to be king."

He shrugged his shoulders. "I begin to see my fate. Here I am, and it's either I rule them or they rule me."

He left the room with a sense that for the first time he had her confidence. He hoped he could impress his mother.

Benaiah had sought her out with no such self-distrust. Fresh from his hot words with Hiram, he had burst into the shadowy chamber where Bathsheba kept cool among her rose jars and her perfumes.

"That Tyrian fellow says——!" he began, but she raised a placid hand.

"You refer to the guard for the dark woman? I ordered him to take charge."

"But that's a public affront! He defied me!"

"Let me explain," said Bathsheba, beautifully patient. "My son, in a moment of irritation, ordered Hiram to greet the visitor on his behalf. That was an affront to me, which at another time I might have resented, but I saw in it an opportunity. The woman is simple and will give us no trouble. Hiram is vain, and this post will flatter him. So long as he is preoccupied, you and I can work freely."

The captain of the guard, calmer now, waited for her to explain further.

"I think," she continued, "we'll take Jeroboam first."

"Anytime you wish," answered Benaiah. "He's in

Gezer, as I thought, with the Egyptian girl. She embarrasses him, but he can't shake her off."

"Really in Gezer?" asked Bathsheba. "I expected him to hide among his own people."

"He's no fool," said Benaiah. "He knew you'd expect that. Gezer is on the edge of the Ephraimites."

"Can you deal with him there, or should we entice him home?"

"That depends," said Benaiah philosophically, "on whether the execution should be public, for an example."

"The quieter the better," said Bathsheba. "It's results we want. . . . Now, after Jeroboam, we ought to consider Magsala."

Benaiah was embarrassed.

"That's not so easy."

Bathsheba had the air of careful planning, as though she were ordering a banquet. "I think it had best be an accident. For that reason I wanted Hiram withdrawn from the temple. There is still some stonework to be put up, is there not?"

"They've got to the roof now."

"Something heavy," reflected Bathsheba, "might fall some day when she was walking under it."

Benaiah looked at her, a non-committal stare.

"Think it over," said Bathsheba. "Perhaps you can suggest a surer device. With those two difficulties solved, I can manage this dark woman myself."

"How about the Phoenician debt?" asked Benaiah. "There is still the tax, and the people may turn ugly."

"For that reason," said Bathsheba, "we must marry the

Queen of Sheba, whose country, I understand, is as yet undeveloped."

Benaiah shook his head, the higher economics being beyond his grasp. "I've heard they live in huts."

It was then that Solomon arrived, with the new courage Magsala had inspired. Displeased to find Benaiah talking with his mother, he vented his wrath on the captain.

"Who put Hiram in charge of that guard?"

"Don't be angry," said Bathsheba. "I might ask why you let Hiram receive your guests for you."

"We'll stick to the first question," said Solomon. "How did Hiram come to have that group of armed men?"

"As a favor to me," said his mother. "It's only temporary until Benaiah and you have found Jeroboam."

Solomon remembered what Magsala would have him say, what David would have said.

"The Queen of Sheba will breakfast with us tomorrow. You, my wife, and I, will be present. Benaiah will now come with me while I thank Hiram for his temporary aid. He and his men can go back to their work."

Bathsheba, trained by much experience, took the rebuke easily, and Benaiah followed the king, not displeased to have his authority restored, but when they came to the door of Sheba's guest-room, Hiram was still inside.

"How long has he been in there?" asked Solomon, of the nearest Tyrian.

"Quite a while," said the man.

"I'll summon him out," said Benaiah, stepping forward.

"On the contrary," said Solomon, with a portion of that insight for which he is famous, "it may be that Hiram is better occupied there than he would be anywhere else. Let us attend his convenience."

When Hiram emerged at last, shortly after that impulsive remark about the fleet, he found Solomon waiting rather stiffly, with Benaiah antagonistic, and enough of the palace guard to outnumber the Tyrians.

"Your courtesy to the visiting queen," said Solomon, "has my thanks. My mother sends you messages of special appreciation. You and your men are excused for the day."

For once Hiram failed to grasp the bearings of the incident, his mind at that moment being over-laden with personal affairs. He and his men retired, Benaiah set the guard for the night, and Solomon in deep thought proceeded to his study.

In the morning Balkis arrived at her breakfast appointment much beclouded with the swift complications of her visit. When Hiram had mentioned the fleet she had tried to understand a poetic metaphor, but evidently he had meant something else, or perhaps he regretted his flight of fine language. She lay awake much of the night remembering the speed with which he had tried to withdraw the remark. It was the one flaw in a perfect episode.

Then when she had gone to the door to ask him a question about it, the sentinels were a new set of men who knew nothing about her disguised king. This was a strange land!

The least he could do would be to greet her at dawn. In her wakeful reveries she had fancied a magnificent apparition, the king in his true colors, as it were, with his

crown on, or something of that sort, and a handsome ret-
inue. Since she had recognized his greatness under a workman's garments, wouldn't he be glad to do the dramatic
thing and pay spectacular tribute to their instinctive unity
of soul?

But nothing of the kind happened. A very ordinary
messenger said something to one of Benaiah's men, and
the soldier offered to show her where breakfast was ready.
Balkis wakened in a world which had lost its bloom.

In Bathsheba's room she recognized the beautiful but
somewhat cold woman who had welcomed her the day before, and there was another woman, calm but not cold,
more beautiful, perhaps, but with a threatening laugh in
her eyes. Balkis suspected the younger woman of laughing
at her. Whatever these people had contrived, the joke was
now overdrawn and a little cruel.

There was also the tall young man with the soft beard.
She was inclined to be sharp with him.

"What are you today?"

He drew himself up in what she interpreted as a de-
fensive attitude. "You have already met the queen, my
mother. This is the queen, my wife."

"Your wife?" asked Balkis, not to make sure, but to
embarrass him.

Bathsheba urged them towards the couches around the
table.

"The fruit is gathered especially for you. We rather
pride ourselves on this honey. You rested well last night,
I hope?"

"I lay awake," said Balkis, "thinking of the king, that wonderful man, your son."

Bathsheba and Magsala both looked at Solomon, then turned their eyes back to the frank visitor from Sheba.

"We loved each other," said Balkis, "at sight."

Bathsheba glanced again towards Solomon. "Did you?" For a brief second she hoped he had developed initiative.

"I refer," said Balkis, "to the tall man with red hair."

Bathsheba permitted astonishment to show in her face. "You don't mean the fellow who greeted you at the gate!"

Balkis smiled. "When will you desist from whatever it is you're doing? If he were, as you say, a mere fellow, you would not have sent him to welcome me. It's but fair to say that I was warned of the joke in advance, but even without that help I couldn't have been deceived."

The bewilderment on Bathsheba's face turned to a flush of anger.

"My own father," continued Balkis, helping herself to the honey, "had a strong sense of humor. Whenever there was a family reunion he prepared some laughable prank."

"My father," said Magsala graciously, "had the same habit."

Balkis welcomed the link between them. "Did he ever put gum on the cups so they'd stick to the table? My father loved that one!"

They might have drawn deeper from the well of memory if Benaiah had not interrupted—not only Benaiah, but Adoram and Hiram.

"As to the army," began Benaiah.

"As to the revenue," began Adoram.

"As to the cedar and other materials," began Hiram.

"This is no time for matters of state!" said Solomon, resentfully.

"It's a calamity of the first order," replied Benaiah.

Balkis fixed happy eyes on Hiram, expecting him now to be revealed in his true colors, but he paid no attention to her. He seemed more than distracted, positively infuriated. Benaiah's mention of a calamity rang an ominous note.

"There's a war started down at Gezer," continued the captain. "The town is besieged! Unless we can get there in time, it will be destroyed."

"One of the few," groaned Adoram, "which still pay taxes."

"It's on the road up from Joppa," said Hiram, addressing Solomon, "and I left some of our goods there with a handful of my men to watch them! I hold you and your government responsible!"

His goods! *His* men! As though he were an outsider! Balkis felt the universe wobbling.

"We'll go to the rescue at once," said Solomon, already on his feet. "Every fighting man you can collect, Benaiah, and perhaps Hiram will join us with some of his Phoenicians!"

"But we have no enemies!" exclaimed Bathsheba. "I doubt this story."

Benaiah faced her. "Two citizens escaped before the Egyptians closed in."

"Egyptians?" challenged Magsala.

Benaiah faced around. "It's your father, Madam, that's trying to burn the city down."

They all had their eyes on her as she sat there pale as a sheet. For the moment they didn't notice Balkis, who would have turned pale if she could.

Chapter VII

In the town of Gezer, Jeroboam and Ano were sitting
down to their evening meal with Rezon, the local shoemaker, in whose hut they temporarily lodged. Since Jeroboam was known to be the tax-gatherer, the hospitality
was offered, so to speak, under compulsion, and since the
tax-gatherer might ask more if he saw evidence of comfort, the food was meager. Rezon fed them that evening
a bit of dry fish, seasoned with sour oil. For Ano this was
plenty; to be with Jeroboam, that large spirit, was feast
enough. He, however, had long ago sharpened his general
solicitude for mankind to a point where he was particular
about what he ate. At the moment, therefore, when the
Egyptian chariots descended upon them he happened to
be out of temper.

Rezon was young, shoemaker by birth rather than by
taste. Like Jeroboam he had a philosophy for improving
the world, but his was practical, and he avoided oratory.
It seemed to him futile to envy another's wealth. Why
not just take it?

Gezer was hardly the best place to employ such wisdom, for there was practically nothing to take. Trade was
feeble, except when the Phoenicians came through, on
their way up to Solomon's new buildings, but the Phoenicians were themselves grasping, and slippery besides. All

trade, Rezon held, was in essence predatory, and you shouldn't prey on your fellows unless you are certain of success.

The neighbors kept flocks outside the town walls, and sold to each other the wool and the meat. At the end of the year they were all poor. Rezon thought out for himself the fundamental difficulty of agriculture. You must have a market. And by market he understood correctly, in his primitive way, someone who will always buy from you, and not insist on selling in return.

Shoemaking is conducive to meditation. Rezon dreamed of a nation somewhere, altogether savage and uninformed, who might be setting their bare feet every day on veins of gold, without knowing the value of their territory. If you could go to them and say, "As many pairs of shoes as you wish for as many handfuls of that negligible yellow stone,"—well, that *would* be trade!

But he doubted if any people were so savage. If they were, they might not enjoy shoes. The more he thought of commerce, the less he admired its mystical uncertainties and its degrading subterfuges. He hoped some day to be a bandit.

Otherwise he was a pacifist. He had once joined a small military expedition in hope of plunder. He needed someone to keep house for him, and in the general division he intended to ask for a cook. He permitted himself to imagine a beautiful cook, a girl of his own age, as good as a wife and more docile. Among the captives there were three such paragons, but they went, as was just, to the mayor of Gezer, who led the expedition, to the chief of the commissary, and to one of the aldermen, if I may permit myself modern terms for eternal types. Rezon, being a novice, drew a woman of his mother's age, the sad creature who on the evening I speak of was serving the dry fish. Rezon held that war as such, public war, is a total loss.

"Why don't you give us lamb once in a while?" asked Jeroboam bluntly. "I saw immense flocks close to the wall this afternoon."

"The shepherds," explained Rezon, "have driven them in since we heard of the marauding strangers southward, but that hasn't brought down the price of meat. On the contrary."

"The fish," said Ano, "is excellent."

"It is not," contradicted Jeroboam. "I wouldn't ask even Solomon to eat it!"

"But it isn't Rezon's fault," pleaded Ano, "if he gives us the best he has."

"There you are!" said Jeroboam. "The toiler has a right to bread, but this is what he gets! Have you ever thought of rebelling?"

"Against what?" asked the shoemaker.

"That king of ours, of course! The sluggard!"

"You might be a spy, now, teasing me into folly."

"I'm not a spy," said Jeroboam, "and I don't like this fish. Let's start from there!"

"Under the old king," remarked Rezon, "we were no better off. I wouldn't blame the king. This fish, as you say, is vile, but haven't you noticed, the better kinds of fish refuse to be caught?"

"Ah, now," cut in Jeroboam, seeing a crack in the thought, "you wouldn't lay it down that the better kinds of men refuse to be poor?"

"But I would," said Rezon. "Just that!"

"Then you're not one of the better kind!"

"Not yet."

"Nonsense! Every man should have a fair chance!"

"King David," said Rezon, "was a shepherd, but he got on. We've a number of shepherds at this minute, huddled under the town wall, as you said, and shepherds they'll be. What's a fair chance? Can you give them all the same wit or the same age? Some get the prizes just because they're older than others. Can you level that out?"

"If I could, would you help?"

Rezon eyed him prudently. "You're a tax-gatherer."

"What of it?"

"The work is petty," said Rezon. "There, I've said what I mean, and you must stay friendly. A bit of silver here, a nibble of gold there, and none of it for yourself! That is, you daren't take much."

"My task," said Jeroboam in his deepest tones, "was put upon me, but I use it to free my people."

"From what?" persisted Rezon.

There was a clatter in the street outside, a rush of animals, with shouting. They left the table, and the old cook followed them, frightened.

"The sheep," observed Ano, "must have slipped through the city gate."

"It's an attack," explained Rezon calmly. "The marauders have arrived." He called to a neighbor several doors away. "Who is it this time?"

The neighbor was wringing his hands. "It's the end of us! The chariots of Egypt! They're setting fire to the wall!"

"In that case," said Rezon, still calm, facing his guests, "there's a way to slip out, at the other end of town, through an old tunnel. I've kept it to myself for a moment like this."

"Where could we go?" asked Jeroboam, on his guard.

"To Jerusalem," said Rezon. "The Egyptians will stop short of that."

"I shall stay here," said Jeroboam stiffly, thinking of his fate if Benaiah laid hands on him. "Should there be a siege, I might aid your people in the defense."

"Man, there *is* a siege, and against these fighters our walls are cobweb. Stay here and goodbye to you!"

"I don't know what the Egyptians want," interposed Ano, greatly troubled, "but they are not cruel. If the town is captured, we'll explain who we are."

Rezon was going around the room, putting in his pockets a few instruments of his craft, and other odds and ends. He also took from the cupboard a loaf of bread, which until then his guests had not seen. He was unhurried, quite unembarrassed.

"Who said they were cruel?" he asked. "They're great people. This town will be theirs in a few hours, but whatever they want, as you say, they'll be disappointed. Our tax-gatherer will have his throat cut, and you will have a half-Egyptian child. I shan't wait to see it happen."

If she told him she was Egyptian, it might make Jeroboam, in the crisis, still less popular. "Won't you stay," she asked, "to help your own people?"

He raised his eyebrows. "My people know the Egyptians wish to kill or mistreat them. From a curious sense of obligation, shared by many men and women, they will first irritate the invader by vain opposition, and then submit to the unpleasant consequences. Poets will sing of them when they are dead."

He was at the door. "If you were wise——"

The old cook, in a great tremble, was getting her shawl around her shoulders.

"Not you," said he. "When they come, don't hide. Stand at the door where they can see you. You'll be safe."

With that he picked his way among the cattle in the street.

"If there's fighting at the gate," said Jeroboam, drawing a deep breath, "I should be there."

"Let's go together!" said Ano.

He knitted his thoughtful brow. "Would it be possible," he suggested, "for you to approach your Egyptian friends, explain who you are, and persuade them to go elsewhere?"

She turned white. "I'm supposed to be with Magsala. They wouldn't like my running away. They might even——"

In the street there was a louder noise, a panicky wail or bellow from the animals, and when they ran to the door, several sheep and one cow were dropped to the dust, with war-arrows sticking in them.

"Evidently," said Jeroboam, "the streets are unsafe. For the present we should remain here."

While the words were yet on his lips, a shepherd began driving the unhappy creatures into the hut.

"Here, you," called Jeroboam, "this isn't a stable!"

"It had better be," said the man. "You'll be glad of meat if the siege lasts!"

"But there isn't room for them and us!"

"Move out!" said the fellow. "We can spare a tax-gatherer, but not a cow."

"I think," said Ano, "I'd like to see what's happening at the gate. The smell here is terrific."

Though they invited the cook to follow them, she declined. By clinging to the walls, they avoided the long battle-shafts, and found at length the excited group behind the wooden barrier, through which smoke was leaking.

"They've built a fire against it," a frightened Canaanite explained, "and when it's burned through, we're lost."

"Why don't you put the fire out?" asked Jeroboam, helpful.

"How?" asked the man.

"How's it usually done?" asked Jeroboam. "It must have happened before."

"They're a savage folk, with no mercy at all," groaned the man. "One of our shepherds, a friend of mine, was caught outside the gate. They stuck a spear up through him, and he's wriggling on it now, out in front, if you look over the wall."

Ano clasped his arm. "Don't look!"

Jeroboam was rather pale, but his voice was still sonorous. "Perhaps we could make a sally and drive them off. Who will follow me?"

The Canaanite didn't answer, in fact he stepped away, and Jeroboam let the inquiry drop.

"What is the fight about?" asked Ano. "This town must have done something terrible, to make my people so angry!"

Jeroboam called the man back. "How did it start?"

The citizen of Gezer was in no mood for historical surveys. "You're foolish!" he exclaimed. "How does lightning start, or any other pestilence!"

Then he walked out of earshot, nearer the smoking gate.

"I didn't like that shoemaker," said Ano, still seeking excuse for the attack.

"They seem to have no weapons of consequence," remarked Jeroboam critically. "Without serviceable arms a sally would of course be unprofitable. On the other hand, if they wait till the gate burns through—and you can see flame now, as well as smoke——"

He spoke in his magisterial tone, but Ano felt he was shaken by their evident fate. It seemed right that even he should be fearful. The Egyptians were shooting too many arrows for the defenders to show their heads above the wall, the fire was eating swiftly in, and the townsmen pressed close to the arch they must defend when the wood was consumed. They had swords, short and curved, light archery, miscellaneous spears, but the Egyptian host, Ano foresaw, would blast them. How pathetic to crowd forward, honor-bound to face their destruction!

"You will be safer in yonder porch," said Jeroboam.

"The gate is ready to fall. Stand quiet beside me, and since we shall make no resistance, we may perhaps escape the first punishments."

When the fire had done its work, and only the hinges stood out from the sides of the arch, the Egyptians shot their arrows through, to clear the street while the embers were cooling. Ano saw the man with whom they had talked, now lying with a dart in his throat.

"I can't bear it!" she cried, clinging to Jeroboam.

There was a loud shout from the Egyptians as the chariots came through the gate, scattering the last groups or herding them down the street, the chariots two by two, with marksmen at the driver's side, pulling a busy bowstring.

"The worst will be at the other end of town," said Jeroboam. "I'm glad we're spared that."

Since Gezer was a small place, the string of chariots came at last to a stop, for lack of streets to fill. A goodnatured man descended just in front of them.

"That's the king, Magsala's father," whispered Ano. "I hope he doesn't see me."

The good-natured man was surrounded at once by officers from the nearest chariots.

"Captain," he called, "the army behaves very well! I don't recall any maneuvers carried out more smartly!"

The captain bowed to the compliment, and the king looked back at the smoking embers.

"You might put that fire out—we want as little damage as possible. Let the men have the run of the town, to celebrate; then if you start the captives toward Jerusalem, you can get there some time tomorrow. It's cool marching after dark. Ten chariots will be sufficient. I'll stay with the rest to mend the wall, and put on a new gate, and generally clean up."

The captain bowed again.

"Tell my daughter home-matters demand my attention, but next time I'll stop for a real visit."

Looking around the square, he noticed Jeroboam and Ano.

"Take the bystanders along—tell her the whole town is hers!"

Through the night Jeroboam and Ano trudged between chariots, with the angry women of Gezer and a few men.

In the palace at Jerusalem Magsala, having just heard from Benaiah that her father was on the warpath, sat facing the reproachful eyes of the household.

"I don't believe it!" she said quietly. "He had no cause to do such a thing."

"The news," insisted Benaiah, "came from witnesses."

"They are mistaken," she answered. "They couldn't see my father burn the city. He didn't burn it."

Benaiah turned to Solomon. "Shall we have the men in?"

"If my wife says the report is false, it's false. We shan't call out the army. The Tyrians can resume their progress with the temple."

Magsala smiled her thanks.

"Even though it's not true, I'd like to hear what those messengers say."

Solomon glanced boldly at his mother, then at Benaiah.

"If my wife cares to listen, let the talebearers repeat their story! Afterward I'll cut off their heads!"

Benaiah was starting for the door when he caught the last words. He paused, then went out more slowly. The Queen of Sheba glanced from Solomon, whose firmness gave her unexpected pleasure, to Hiram. He too was firm, and angry besides.

"One of the messengers," said he, in a challenging tone, "is a Canaanite, and what becomes of his head I don't care, but the other is mine, a Tyrian, left there to watch my goods!"

Balkis lowered her gaze and shivered.

"Both heads," repeated Solomon, "if they lie about my wife's father!"

"We'll see!" said Hiram.

"We will!" echoed Solomon.

"When you ordered the temple," said Hiram, striking one hand upon the other, "you promised——"

"I've forgotten what I promised!" said the king, the veins standing in his forehead. "I've forgotten your wood, your brass, your gold, and the price you put on them! I've forgotten the temple! I stand in my own house, my mind is on my wife, and who speaks ill of her is a dead man!"

At that climax Benaiah led in Rezon the shoemaker, with a Phoenician carpenter who had a dirty rag around his arm.

"Wounded, are you?" asked Solomon.

"A rusty nail," said the Phoenician, pinching the wound affectionately. "I scratched it a week ago, on the cellar stairs."

"Did you hear what I was saying when you came in?"

"You mentioned a dead man."

"I spoke of those who breathe a syllable against my wife or any of her family! Now let's have the frank truth! You've come from Gezer?"

The Phoenician pointed toward Rezon. "He told me to run."

"There were too many animals in the street," said Rezon humbly, "sheep, goats, cows and what not, and an occasional arrow from some invisible source would fall on one of the creatures. Had I stayed, it might have fallen on me."

Benaiah shook a fist at him. "When you told us, you said Egyptian arrows!"

"I was afraid you were getting that part of it wrong," said Rezon. "The arrows were extremely well-fashioned, and those of my townsmen who have traveled thought they might have been imported from Egypt, where so many things are excellent. Who shot the arrows, however, I wouldn't venture to say."

Benaiah pressed him closer. "Wasn't the King of Egypt there, burning the walls down?"

Rezon raised a correcting finger. "Not the king! That I never said! The more hysterical did mention Egyptians, because of the impression the arrows made, but no one referred to the king."

Benaiah put an impatient hand on his shoulder.

"Step back," ordered Solomon. "We don't wish him to speak under compulsion."

"He'll be saying next there wasn't a siege at all!"

"Siege?" asked Rezon. "Who said siege?"

"You did!"

"You don't hear well," said the shoemaker. "How could I describe a siege when I never saw one in my life? There were those cattle in the street, with an occasional arrow, so I came here."

"Benaiah," said Solomon, "let these two men rest in jail till I question them again. They must not be harmed. Feed them well."

Hiram stepped forward. "I claim my man!"

"Out of jail," said Solomon, "he's yours. In jail he's mine."

Benaiah took the prisoners away, with Hiram behind, muttering.

The Queen of Sheba watched Solomon with sad, admiring eyes.

"My wife and I," said he, "will show you our temple, if you care to walk. It's not worth the trouble to get out a camel for so short a distance, but we have a mule."

Balkis preferred to walk, so they left Bathsheba, inscrutable, by the breakfast table.

Balkis on one side of him, Magsala on the other, and Tii to carry a fan.

"Yesterday," said Balkis, "I made a mistake which now covers me with confusion. I under-estimated your greatness!"

"The temple," said Solomon, "is the spacious building to the right, the one where the roof is half on."

"A few minutes ago," said Balkis, "while you were disposing so firmly of the scandal about the King of Egypt,

I saw for the first time the majestic side of your character."

"Shall I drop behind?" asked Magsala. "The path is narrow—barely room for two."

"If it's barely," said Solomon, "then there's room enough." He waved a hand for Sheba's benefit. "The porch, as you observe, is impressive. You can't see the pillars from here, because they're inside."

"Who built it?" asked Balkis.

"We did—with some aid from Hiram and his men."

"Who," asked Balkis, "may Hiram be?"

"I'd like to know," said Solomon. "He's a competent brass-worker, who has risen by his industry. He is said to be the left-handed son of a king. In his own right, as you may have noticed, he is a nuisance. He tries to sell you things."

"A fleet?" asked Balkis.

"I do happen to be building a few ships," admitted Solomon. "At least, so I'm told."

Certain now that Hiram meant actual boats rather than anything metaphorical, Balkis walked in subdued silence.

"We'll go up yonder incline," said Solomon, "where the workmen are wheeling miscellaneous objects."

"But in any case," exclaimed Balkis, "he's a king's son!"

"Who?"

"The one who's helping you."

"Oh, to be sure! I dare say the rumor has something in it."

The workmen stood aside and they balanced themselves up the narrow plank, Solomon first, to be sure it would hold, then Balkis, the guest, slightly out of breath, then Magsala, cool and graceful, then Tii with the fan.

"How beautiful it is!" said Magsala, gazing up at the pillars and the dark shining walls. "You've done wonders since I saw it first!"

"A little every day—it comes on."

Balkis was awestruck. "To think of a temple of solid gold!"

"Only on the surface," corrected Solomon modestly. "It's cedar underneath."

"Even then," said Balkis politely.

He was eager to maintain the impression. "There's to be a partition of golden chains at that end—the chains are on the way."

"You mean, they *were!*"

The royal group, at the sound of the not-too-respectful voice, found Hiram at their elbow, in working costume, a tattered cloth around his middle.

"The gold chains got as far as Gezer, my man tells me. Now they may be on the road to Egypt. Cut my head off for suggesting it!"

The men inside the temple listened for the king's answer, and it was as awkward a problem as Solomon had yet wrestled with. Personal combat with Hiram was not practical, and if it were, there would remain the necessary explanations with Hiram's father. And the debts.

"Let the men go on with their work!"

To his relief, Hiram waved a hand and the hive got in motion again. Solomon pretended to watch, but he was thinking.

"Why, they're taking the gold off!" exclaimed Balkis.

They followed her finger, and saw the men prying loose a large sheet of it from the wall where the chains were to hang.

"Didn't that piece fit?" asked Solomon, to show he understood what an architect has to contend with.

"It isn't paid for," said Hiram, "and one of my men is in jail. We're taking the temple down."

"You're breaking the contract!"

"It's already broken!"

Solomon exercised his wits. "If we are calm, these differences can be adjusted."

"They're adjusted now," said Hiram, "and I never was calmer. We'll keep on removing our property until I get my man back. Then we'll stop all work till we're paid."

Solomon stood there perspiring with shame before Magsala and Balkis. His wife kept her quiet smile, her unshaken dignity, but her eyes were unusually bright. Balkis, for private reasons, was pleased.

"I'll release the man on parole," Solomon offered.

Hiram walked over to a cluster of his workers who had paused to dip a drink from a water-jar.

"Take that ladder," he commanded in an audible voice, "and begin on the roof. Lower it over the side."

"We might as well return to the palace," said Solomon, leading the way down the plank as fast as was convenient for the women. "I'll get hold of Benaiah."

He realized that his wife, or the Queen of Sheba, or Tii, following with the fan, might expect him to say something, but he was too exasperated. The silence, as they hurried along, became stifling.

"That's a powerful man," remarked Balkis, in a rich tone of satisfaction—also with the air of helping out.

"You admire him?" asked Magsala, equally content. "I thought you did."

"As to the quarrel itself," continued Balkis, still with the manners of a guest, "your husband was probably in the right, but that half-clothed workman has courage and an aptitude for command."

Solomon was not listening.

"It seems to me," said Magsala, "he must come of a superior family, though his occupation for the moment happens to be practical. At times he does suggest a regal origin."

She offered the idea as if no one had thought of it before, and Balkis showed pleasure. "If there's any king in a man, it will come out!"

Benaiah was waiting around the palace gate with his guard, and Solomon would have run to him if Bathsheba had not stood there too, deep in serious talk. Solomon approached firmly.

"You may remove that Tyrian from the jail, and deliver him to Hiram. We find he is essential to the temple building."

"What has happened, my son?" asked Bathsheba, recognizing a diplomatic veneer on the truth. But since Magsala and Balkis had caught up and were now beside him, he held to his formula.

"The man is needed."

"Do you mean," asked Bathsheba, "the temple can't be completed without him? In that case, you must get on without the temple. Your Tyrian prisoner is dead."

"Why," exclaimed Solomon, horrified, "he was here, only a while ago——!"

"Death takes no time," said Bathsheba. "The other prisoner killed him."

"That fellow Rezon," explained Benaiah, "the citizen of Gezer. I was reporting the affair to your mother, you being not here. We put them in one cell, to save attendants, and I ordered food for both—a meal is soothing when they first go in. No sooner did we turn our backs——"

"Why did you? Those were state prisoners!"

Benaiah resented the criticism. "We can't stare at them all day! The window bars are thick, and we thought we had removed his knife."

"Ah! You thought you had!"

"And we had!" insisted Benaiah, raising his voice.

"Don't shout," advised Solomon. "After you had taken every precaution, what happened?"

"When we looked again, the Tyrian was lying on the floor, the bars were cut through, and Rezon was gone."

"Being rascals, both of them," reflected Solomon, "they had a quarrel. I wish it had been the other way—if the Tyrian had only killed the fellow from Gezer!"

"We have discarded the quarrel theory," said Benaiah. "Rezon was about to travel, and he wanted a double portion of food."

For a moment Solomon held his beard with his right hand, midway in an idea.

"We might as well face it immediately," he groaned. "Ask Hiram to come to my study. Keep your men in the corridor while he and I are conferring. You and Adoram will attend me."

He would have said more, but Benaiah wasn't listening. Nor were the women. They had turned their heads to catch a rising clamor in the city streets. Bathsheba took Balkis by the arm.

"It sounds to me like a very irresponsible mob, perhaps Tyrians, perhaps our own people. We can protect you better indoors."

"I'll stay and see it," said Balkis. "At home I get these visits too. If they're armed, we ask them into the court-yard and drop hot water on them. Once they came in haste, with no weapons whatever, and all we had to do was to empty a box of snakes."

She was disappointed when it turned out not to be a protest march. The officer in the first chariot recognized Magsala, stepped down, bent his knee, then stood up straight and made an oration in the tongue she was born to. A short speech, but before it was finished she turned white with horror.

"My husband," she cried, "you should never have married me! I bring your ruin!"

"Is that what he said?" asked Solomon. "Kindly give us a rough translation."

"The two prisoners told the truth! My father burned Gezer! He offers me the shell of it for a wedding present, and he sends along the survivors, if you and I want any of them."

Solomon took it rather well, showing neither despair nor wrath. His eyes roamed over the prisoners, now being prodded into long rows behind the chariots.

"My friend Jeroboam is with us again," he remarked to Benaiah. "My dear," said he, turning to his wife, "isn't that disheveled creature your maid?"

The Egyptian officers were waiting for a word from him. He continued to think out loud.

"The city must be rebuilt. More taxes. No taxes from *that* city. Never again! Meanwhile I must feed these survivors. Some of the killed were Tyrians! Break this to Hiram!"

He took a grip on himself. "My dear, ask the officer to tell your father his gifts are magnificent, and we send our thanks. Offer the chariots something to eat and drink before they continue on their way. I assume they'll continue. As for Gezer, I'll rebuild it, and send these folk back, and you shall govern it as you choose."

Magsala looked at him with a quick smile, but his kingly ease gave pleasure to no one else.

"Who's going to feed these people?" asked Adoram. "We're short of rations as it is, what with your Tyrian friends and your guests from the south."

Solomon turned on the old man such withering wrath as hadn't been seen or heard since David's best days.

"Are my guests not welcome? Are they not as my own family? One more word of that sort, and I'll hang you to your front door! Your father, I suspect, was a scavenger! Your mother, I perceive, was nothing I could mention in this gathering! Your earlier ancestors ate pig! Not otherwise can I account for the wretchedness of your mind!"

He bowed to the Queen of Sheba, as though the outburst were his apology to the slight on southern guests who ate too much, but Balkis hadn't followed, being busy with the scene as a whole.

Adoram raised his hands to the side of his head, bowed, and stepped back where he wouldn't be so conspicuous. Benaiah whispered in Solomon's ear.

"You're not sending them all home, are you? Shan't we seize Jeroboam and the girl?"

Since the emergency had put him in the royal vein, Solomon needed but a second to remember what David would have done with an enemy in his power.

"Bring them before me!"

While Benaiah was fetching them, the king turned to the ladies at his elbow.

"Perhaps you would prefer to retire. The execution will be painful to watch."

"My son," asked Bathsheba, "do you intend to kill Jeroboam now?"

"Him and his paramour."

"Is this quite the occasion?"

"When else?"

"I detect," said his mother, "a certain confusion in your thought, which will not impress these captains in their chariots, nor these natives of Gezer, among whom Jeroboam had friends. Send him westward again with the others when you restore the town—under a strong escort, of course—and if an accident *should* happen to him on the way——"

"Ano," said Magsala, "was once my maid."

"I'm not pleading for the Egyptian girl," contradicted Bathsheba. "If Benaiah runs his sword through her now, there will be little adverse criticism."

Benaiah had the assistant tax-gatherer and the tall dark girl up before the king, Ano worried, Jeroboam defiant.

"My husband," pleaded Magsala, "give these people to me!"

Bathsheba laid aside her calmness. "At your peril!" she cried. "Every misery which falls on us comes from Egypt."

"Give them to me!" pleaded Magsala. "To punish or to enslave or to send away, as I may wish! Let my own life answer for them!"

"I object!" called Jeroboam in a loud voice, happy to seize the floor with so large an audience. "I prefer to die a simple champion of my people! Sell yourself, if you like, to the heathen, but don't sell me!"

"If you will permit," Magsala went on, "I'll ask the captain who brought this unexpected wedding gift to carry Ano and Jeroboam back to my father. He will understand the exchange of courtesies."

"I won't go!" said Jeroboam firmly. "I decline! I appeal to heaven!"

Solomon gave Benaiah a signal. "Load them on the chariot, and get them started off."

They had to tie Jeroboam, hand and foot, but Ano went quietly. As the procession saluted and moved away from the palace, the king turned to his household.

"The citizens of Gezer will be fed."

"How?" groaned Adoram desperately.

Solomon overlooked the question. He also ignored the Queen of Sheba. He had his eye on his mother.

"Let it be understood, from this day forth, my wife and I agree on all subjects! I will love her as my father loved you—that is, unreasonably but completely!"

Bathsheba was not offended. On the contrary, she smiled with graceful good nature as she bowed her head to his challenge. It was Magsala who seemed astonished, not having foreseen this adoration, certainly not expecting it to be precipitated by the catastrophe her father had contrived. Solomon took her hand—she noticed that his trembled slightly. But at that moment they heard angry sounds at the neck of the street through which Adoram was trying to lead away the weary pedestrians from Gezer.

"It's Hiram!" exclaimed Balkis.

It was—with most of his Tyrians at his back.

"What's this about that man of mine you put in jail? Has anything happened to him?"

The soul of David lived in his son that day. Courage came easy.

"He got killed. The Gezer shoemaker slew him, just before escaping. Also," continued Solomon, "the rumor they brought was correct. Gezer is taken, several of your men have been cut down or burned, your stores, whatever you may have left there, are doubtless destroyed, and though *you* may be sorry to hear it, I can't see that it matters much, one way or another!"

"This," shouted Hiram, "means war!"

"You may take down the temple and ship the fragments to where they came from," announced Solomon icily.

"From this moment, of course, we feel relieved from our contract to furnish you with food or water. You will kindly convey to your king and employer my readiness to negotiate any bill for anything you decide not to destroy."

"War!" shouted Hiram, too surprised to hit on a better answer.

"Not a bad solution," agreed Solomon. "In a patriotic cause my people are at their best. Tell your king that at the first offensive move I'll lighten the taxes, or perhaps remove them entirely. A good war, the winner to pay himself out of what is left!"

After Solomon had waved his household into the palace, and himself had followed, for once superb, Hiram stood in the courtyard, thinking, with his men waiting for an order. Balkis watched him.

Solomon intended to do some thinking too, and for that purpose retired to his study. When he opened the door, Abishag was sitting in the big chair, the one with the carved lion heads.

CHAPTER VIII

HIRAM stood thinking there in the courtyard, with his men waiting, and Balkis watching him. He did not notice Solomon's departure. He was busy revising his strategy, in view of new facts, in view also of the shaky condition of the Phoenician army, and of the economic crisis in Tyre. In the exchange of diplomatic bluff Solomon had accidentally come out ahead. The point now would be to keep him in ignorance of his success.

"If you have a free moment," said the Queen of Sheba, "we could talk comfortably in the inadequate quarters these queer people provided for me."

Hiram came out of his meditations, looked at her, gave his men the signal to break ranks. "That's all for the day. Get back to work—take off the east end of the roof!"

He and she walked side by side, leisurely and without words, and when they reached her room, he took a chair, as though he belonged in the place, and when she had fastened the latch, she stood before him, disarmingly frank.

"When I gave myself to you, I supposed you were the king in disguise."

He nodded. "I knew there was some mistake."

"But was there? You don't regret it, do you?"

"Me? Why should I?"

"From what I heard," continued Balkis, "I thought he

was a great man, but you seem to be what I am hoping for. The title isn't important—I've enough of that at home."

To these generous advances Hiram failed to respond. Once more he was making a rapid readjustment of his program.

She drew up another chair close to him. "Do you really wish to fight over that temple, or about the dead prisoner, or for what he owes you?"

"In principle I do," said Hiram, "but I can't. These folks have no regular troops, but our army is unreliable. They wouldn't march so far. They know the debt hasn't been paid, and there's nothing here to plunder."

His face was glum, but hers shone with satisfaction. "If you dismantle that building and take the fragments back to Tyre, they won't consider it a triumphant return, will they?"

"They will not!"

She smiled. "If I go home alone, the women in my palace will raise their eyes."

He looked straight at her.

"When we first met," she went on, "you spoke of a fleet."

"We're building ships for Solomon, on the eastern sea," he explained, "and one's ready for launching in a day or so."

"If you and a few of your men know how to sail it——" she suggested.

He stared again, with the caution of a good trader. "Just what do you propose?"

She rose and paced the floor. "*His* kingdom is going to

pieces. So is yours." She turned and met his gaze. "So, as a matter of fact, is mine. I came because I had to, and I might as well keep on traveling. We'll start off on the camels, and then we'll let the beasts continue by land, and you and I can take the boat?"

"Where to?"

"It's a large world," she reminded him, "and neither you nor I have seen much of it. Somewhere there's an island or a promising shore. I've always wanted to make a kingdom from the ground up and start it right. What we come from is old and worked out."

"The idea attracts me," he conceded, "but we can't found a kingdom, not just the two of us!"

"You'll bring a handful of your men," she insisted, "and we'll land where there are natives, enough slaves to do the work, enough girls for your sailors. We'll have a kingdom in no time!"

To hide his eagerness he knitted his brow, but his consent was already granted. "I like the simplicity of it! But they mustn't suspect, not Solomon nor my people. I'll slip off and make sure the boat is finished."

"And provisioned," Balkis advised.

He rubbed the back of his red head. "To be sure—food and water!"

"Don't worry!" she consoled him. "I once learned a bit of poetry, 'Set your foot on the right path, and one thing will lead to another.'"

At that moment, in Solomon's study, Abishag too was developing a schedule for a good life, but with less brilliant effect. Solomon had not been altogether glad to find her enthroned in his lion-headed seat, and to her wise counsel he offered a wilful resistance.

"Why are you here?" he asked, a bit ungraciously, if you consider the reasons for her previous visits.

"Your wife would say, my mission is to be helpful to the men of your house."

He detected sarcasm and was not pleased, but while he was feeling around for an answer, she got out of his chair.

"You sit down and I'll stand," she said, as though he were a member of the family, advanced in age. "It's been a hard day, hasn't it?"

Her solicitude brought on self-pity, and he mopped his brow. "Rather trying, but inevitable. To be wise yourself is not enough, so long as you have neighbors. I can't imagine what madness seized the King of Egypt!"

He was resting on the cushion she had yielded to him, and being at the moment too philosophical for courtesy, he permitted her to pull another chair over to the side of his desk.

Sad to say, his sharpness increased, the nearer she came.

"Did you have any particular errand?" he asked. "I'm in no mood for poetry."

If his coldness offended, she didn't show it, that is if you overlooked the slight sting with which she began. "We'll keep the poetry for the empty moments! I've three special errands, one about you, one about your wife, and one about me. Only a minute for each, since you're in a hurry. Which shall we take first?"

His interest freshened. "Have you a personal request?"

With graceful vigor she rubbed her nose, as though to prevent a sneeze. "Rezon, that shoemaker who broke out of jail——"

"And killed Hiram's man!"

"That's the one."

Solomon was annoyed. "I suppose you'll plead for him, as you did for Jeroboam!"

She was puzzled, then saw what the trouble was. "Oh, I'm taking your case first, not mine! Mine isn't of consequence, but you ought to know about Rezon. He's got six men with him, and they'll rob whoever rides in or out on the road to the east."

"Bandits, eh? Who are the six?"

"All friends of Jeroboam's—one of them a patient of the doctor's—you know, the doctor who lets me stay in his house."

Solomon flushed.

"His patients are thieves, are they?"

Abishag's voice became dangerously gentle. "They call themselves patriots. They have sworn to spoil only our enemies."

"But that's absurd!" exclaimed Solomon. "Our enemies won't walk obligingly down the highway, one by one! Besides, you can't say that every stranger is a villain!"

Abishag's hand on the desk began stroking his clenched fist. Because she was obviously absent-minded, he permitted the liberty. "This prejudice against strangers," he repeated, "is narrow."

The dark eyelashes lifted. "It's not against strangers. The people they're angry at live right here. You, first of all! Adoram next, because of the tax. Then your wife, because of Gezer."

Solomon stiffened. "Very kind of you to bring in my wife! That's your second errand, I take it!"

"Oh, no, I'm still talking about you! Assuming that you love her."

He considered the words. "How do you come by this information?"

"Town talk," she answered cheerfully. "Two of the six are those servants of Shimei's. They didn't like the work on the temple, and now they blame you, because if you had left the old man in peace, he would have caught them, and they could have been happy doing the housework."

Solomon struck his hand to his brow. "You had a special errand about my wife, not simply this passing reference?"

Abishag nodded. "The schoolboys."

"The what?" asked Solomon.

She explained carefully. "Rezon and the six are outside the city, but in every street you'll find some who admire Jeroboam. They're mostly boys at school, and against you they've no grudge, you being David's son, but they don't believe in war or taxes, so they've sworn not to study again till one of them has killed your wife."

He gave a start. "Why her? Why not me? Why not Adoram?"

She was pleased to agree. "I said they weren't thinking straight."

He stared, mouth open. "You talk with them?"

"With anybody. So would you, if you had curiosity!"

He inquired in another direction. "What war disturbs them? We are not at war!"

She shrugged, and tapped her fingers on the desk. "We might be, and they want to get a good start with the protest."

"I admit the taxes," he continued, "but that's on account of the temple. Why link the actual taxes with a merely possible war?"

Abishag smiled, and again he suspected sarcasm. "You always oppose war and something else, don't you? You can't be against war just by itself!"

From the desk he drew a strip of parchment intended for verse. With dignity he dipped a quill in ink.

"Their names?"

She laughed. "You never ask names in the dark! They wouldn't talk!"

"Are you telling me," asked Solomon, holding the pen in air, "that I don't know what's going on among my own people?"

"Exactly! No one knows less!"

Laying the pen down where it wouldn't blot, he stared at her, so perplexed that she felt sorry for him.

"It's not natural for you, of course, and I wish you didn't have to, but you *must,* if you hold your kingdom, or if you keep on living! Or if you're ever to live! I wouldn't call it life if I weren't awake."

She had a way always of making him feel a bit cheap— not the bashfulness which overcame him in Magsala's presence, but an inner and involuntary confession of weakness. Though Magsala was noble, he saw no reason why he shouldn't with time lift himself to the heights where her spirit walked, but Abishag's peculiar talent was not imitable; he couldn't name it. She was neither stately nor noble, but she had a victorious gift for seeming true. Herself true—not merely what she said.

Now she stirred in her chair, as though bringing the interview to an end.

"Those were the main things, the threat to you and the queen. May I speak about myself?"

He inclined his head.

"I want your advice. The doctor thinks he'd like to marry me."

If indifference had cloaked Solomon's manner, he came out of it promptly. "That old man?"

"My destiny," said Abishag, "seems not to be among the young."

"You forget," protested Solomon, "I proposed to you myself."

Abishag turned a clear eye on him. "You were *too* young!"

He reddened under the insult.

"I wouldn't call you ripe even now," she continued mercilessly. "Not yet! My opportunities are with the immature and the aged, with nothing in between."

Solomon tried to put down a rising anger. "In any case you will do what you please. You ask no advice. You are taking your revenge!"

She raised her eyebrows. "For what?"

"You didn't wish me to marry the Egyptian."

"Absurd!"

"I know what I know!"

She laughed. "I'm afraid that *is* your limit! You think I'm jealous. I wouldn't have married you for anything, at least not as you were! I did hope you'd take hold of things and grow up—but what difference does it make? I've managed to like you as you are."

Why had she prepared these insults? He didn't doubt they were planned.

"The doctor may speak any day now," she explained, "and I want to have the right answer ready."

"If he hasn't asked you," said Solomon, "we may assume for the present that he will do nothing foolish."

Abishag pretended to weigh this contribution to her problem.

"At first," she said, "I thought he was saving me up in case he needed the treatment your father had, but he continues quite sturdy, and of late I've watched the squint in his eyes—you know, when I wasn't looking. He's almost ready to say something."

"You *wish* to marry him?"

"Not wish—but perhaps I should. Every girl needs a husband, wouldn't you say? Something serious and reliable. Don't you think I ought to have children?"

Her apparent innocence was amazing. She was closing in on him with these questions, and though he tried to guess her ultimate intention, his mind wouldn't work fast enough.

"Of course if you don't put some order into your kingdom," she went on, "perhaps the children would be a mistake. I wanted your opinion about that to. Is this a good world for children to be born in?"

He cleared his throat. "As a matter of principle," he began, "I intend to be faithful to my wife."

"Well," said Abishag, "I'll expect the doctor to be faithful to me. From what I've seen of you both, I think he will excel."

"I was about to remark," continued Solomon, "though my wife is a great lady, and I grow fonder of her as time passes, I once felt for you an impulsive affection which I wish you had returned, but since you preferred your foot-loose existence, I can see the progress in your state which would result from marriage with the doctor."

"Then you advise me to?"

"I didn't say that," he contradicted hastily. Some of the impulsive affection to which he had just referred spurted up again. "My sentiments at this moment," he announced with warmth, "are difficult for me to analyze, but when I hear that you are the doctor's wife, I believe I shall be sorry."

Was this what she had come for? She rose with a smile. "Keep a sharp watch over the queen," she urged, moving toward the door, "and over yourself."

"Do you intend to marry him?"

She faced back with a comfortable smile. "Perhaps."

He couldn't tell whether he was sad or glad to see her go. The love that he might have pursued was not for him, and if she came again, he ought to send her away. For a moment he saw a rather panicky prospect of other visits from time to time, even after she married the doctor, long after his growing admiration for Magsala should reach what he hoped would be its full height. The charm of Abishag had an element uncertain and irresponsible; even when wedded to another man she might appear some day in a flimsy and tantalizing gown, just to make sure she could recapture her first lover. If she succeeded, it would be reprehensible.

Of course if she didn't marry the doctor he wouldn't feel so guilty about it. But even then!

Yet this wisdom, satisfying in its morality, pricked his conscience. Once more he remembered the heroic ways of his father, and asked what David in such a case would have done. He knew it was a form of self-excuse even to ask. If David had loved Magsala, then Magsala he would have had. The same with Abishag, if she had been the one preferred. Or if he had loved both, then he would have had two wives. Solomon feared that his attempt at single-minded devotion, though it might be an advance toward the higher life, was a relapse of courage.

To do these thoughts justice he got out of his street dress and slipped on his literary robe, the loose grey gown. With slow paces he circulated around the room.

This world, even to a king like himself, was, as he now learned, meaningless, a conglomeration of accidents. The impression was hard to escape that the older one grew, the less sense there would be in living. This drab principle was established by comparing modern times with the long ago when David was young, or even earlier, when Abraham was a great man. How simple life had been for

Abraham! Of course there was that difficulty between Sarah and Hagar, but Abraham had not permitted himself to be seriously disturbed, and in a short while it ironed out neatly. Moses too! There was a career for you! But with no effort on the part of Moses. Thrust upon him, it was! Anyone could choose the right path if the options were arranged in advance. Solomon tried to persuade himself that if he had been found in the bullrushes, he would have led his people by inescapable logic to the threshold of a promised land.

But his brain refused to obey his wish. Against his will he suspected what he was. Though he turned away his eyes, as it were, he perceived the terms on which life might be clear, or on which it might be muddled. The clearness had to be in you, not in the world outside. If someone dumped a load of bricks right in your path, and if you wanted to build a wall, the bricks would come handy, and you'd call them an act of Providence. But if you hadn't yet thought of a wall or of anything else, the bricks would be only a crude obstacle, and you'd have to walk around them. Abraham and Moses never said that life was altogether vain. Like David they had ideas in advance.

It was in the mood of his deepest humility that Solomon proceeded down the corridor to Magsala's room, not stopping to put off the philosophic robe. He went to her frankly for aid in constructing a synthetic purpose in life, since none had come by nature, and to his comfort she was ready.

"What your father has done," he began, "I won't judge, not until I hear his reasons. Between you and me he can bring no estrangement."

"He wouldn't wish to," said Magsala.

Solomon appealed frankly. "I need your help."

His trust brought a light in her eyes, but her voice was sad.

"So far, I haven't helped much," she said. "What your people think of me, I can guess."

She was wearing a blue robe, a soft thing for secluded hours in her room. Elsewhere she never displayed it, with one exception—because Bathsheba admired it, she remembered to put it on when she visited Solomon's mother. Noticing it now, he was touched by her willingness to please, even where she knew herself disliked.

"The moment calls for a firm hand," he confessed modestly, "and unless you guide me, I shall probably do the wrong thing. It isn't Gezer, it's the debt. If I could pay it off, your father might capture a Tyrian or two any day, and the Phoenicians would love me!"

She had her fingers to her chin for a second, thinking hard. "There's always a cure, if you'll cut to the bone. We must pay what we owe, then get rid of these costly workmen, and finish the temple ourselves."

He groaned. "Get rid of them! As though they'll ever go home!"

She was still feeling for the right handle. "You have cities toward the north—on the border?"

"A few. That is, a number, but nothing of importance. Villages."

"Have you seen them?"

"Adoram describes them in detail. Wretched places!"

She refused to be discouraged. "Of course! Frontier towns!"

He thought she was proposing an official visit, a tour of inspection, and he blushed for his indolence hitherto. "We could take Benaiah and go up. The roads are bad, but if we covered a small stretch each day——"

"No time to waste!" she interrupted. "Send Adoram to Tyre—don't trust that red brass-hammerer! Let King Hiram meet us on the ground and select what cities he wants!"

"*My* cities, are you talking of?"

"In payment for the temple—for everything, in full." She smiled. "A spot of land which you never saw, in exchange for peace of mind, with which also you are unacquainted."

Solomon held back. "How do you know he wants land?"

"They always do."

"If I'm correct," said the harassed monarch, "the people in those towns would rather belong to me than to him. Would it be quite friendly, do you think, to give them away?"

For an instant Magsala permitted herself to look bored. "If King Hiram brings an army down, they'll be his slaves. If you make the offer, they'll be subjects in good standing."

He explored again what seemed almost a forbidden prospect, the vision of an untroubled era in which even a king might enjoy leisure and meditation and domesticity and the exercise of verse composition. If Hiram accepted the border towns, if the Tyrians withdrew——

"The people wouldn't mind the taxes so much," urged Magsala, "if the money came back to them. They dislike handing it out to foreigners. You could explain that the faster the temple went up, the sooner the rate would come down."

"I'll talk it over with Adoram."

"Don't! Not with anybody! Send Adoram to Tyre—give him orders!"

He gazed with admiration and envy. "Some people have the gift to command! Or did your father teach it to you?"

She laughed. "Father says it's natural in women, but men learn it in self-defense."

Solomon's mind went back to old thoughts. "David was born with it, I think."

She wouldn't be convinced. "I suspect he learned it."

"Not from my mother," said Solomon. "Of course his early days may have hardened him, out there among the sheep, meeting bears and giants."

"In my country too," said Magsala sympathetically, "the best kings were shepherds."

His face lighted pleasantly at the coincidence. "Do you suppose it's too late for me to begin at the beginning, as it were—to go back in disguise perhaps, and tend a few flocks, and get the point of view?"

As he said the words he realized their shallow boyishness, and he expected her to smile, but she didn't.

"I had something of the sort planned for you if you'd agree. When King Hiram is out of the way, I wanted you to go off and look as us from a distance, and think over what you wish to be. You've been ruling too much from hour to hour."

The offer of a vacation was exhilarating, but he saw difficulties. "I can't leave you here alone."

"And I won't go with you! If you worry about me I shan't mind."

When she laughed, he was amazed at her beauty. He saw her beauty more plainly since he had gathered the idea she was fond of him.

"We'll send for Adoram at once," he said. "I'll just step out and call a guard. You're sure it won't make trouble with Hiram, using another messenger? He'll have to go on a Tyrian ship."

She was slightly indignant. "Not at all! You must send chariots the way my father travels—with no one's help! Haven't you chariots?"

"A few, I believe. I'll consult Benaiah."

She stamped her foot. "*Tell* Benaiah—don't consult him! If no chariot is ready, it's his fault! When my father asks for anything, it's ready. And tell Hiram yourself that Adoram is going. Fear no one!"

"I'll attend to it at once," said Solomon with his hand on the door, but not yet enthusiastic. "If I'm to meet the Phoenician on the border, you must come too."

"Oh, no—you men by yourselves."

Solomon raised his voice. "I'm not consulting you—I said you must come!"

When he left her she was smiling, and Tii, summoned by a golden bell, found her in admirable humor.

Solomon did not at once find Benaiah. Every woman in his household that day was engaged in supplying strategy for some man. Benaiah was with Solomon's mother re-

ceiving plain instruction in his patriotic duty, and the heavy
soldier with the scarred face was obviously in anguish.

"But I can't lift my hand against her!" he pleaded. "I
can't!"

Though Bathsheba kept her habitual calm, her eyes were
steel. "I've done all I could for you, and now you teach
me that my favor was thrown away on a coward! If I made
you captain of the army, I can put you down again where
you belong!"

He smote his hands together. "Command anything but
this! I will not strike at the queen!"

"How fantastic!" exclaimed Bathsheba, pretending to be
amused. "She too owes her place to me—I arranged the
marriage! It's ridiculously simple. Since she won't be my
friend, I must dispose of her."

"I can't see that," argued Benaiah. "If you were in
danger, I'd shield you."

"Stupid!" exclaimed Bathsheba. "Why wait till the danger is large? If she dislikes me, if he goes to her now for
advice, then now's the time, while her father has put her in
disgrace! I'll say you did it because you love your country.
Then if my son won't have Sheba, we'll give him Abishag,
and a quiet room to write poetry in. I promise to share
the throne with you."

Because she argued at length, Benaiah got back his courage. "It's not yours to share, and he won't have Sheba, and
you must deal with Hiram, and Abishag won't stay in a
quiet room. I doubt"—he dared say it to her face—"I
doubt if you know even as much about ruling as your son!"

She sprang to her feet, with no further pretense at

calmness. "You challenge me, do you? Snake! When I tell Solomon what I know——!"

"That should have been done earlier, if at all," said the man. "Now I have something to report on my own behalf. He'll be interested to know you've asked me for the second time to murder his wife."

"The second time?" Bathsheba repeated.

"I told him about the first," said Benaiah. "Don't look surprised—he didn't. I learned much about you from the way he took the news."

Bathsheba faced him, paralyzed, but not with terror. She was trying to calculate the date or the hour when Solomon had become aware of her treachery, and she was reviewing their recent conversations to recall whatever might have had for him, in view of Benaiah's information, a sinister meaning.

"You may go," she said. "We need not speak again. I add you to the list of my enemies who are all doomed."

He sauntered toward the door, his loquacity stimulated by the effort he had made to put himself right between her and the king. "It's bad to have too many enemies," he reflected. "You did best while I was your friend."

"You may go!"

It was then that Solomon found him, crossing the threshold.

"Oh, are you leaving? Come back a moment! I want my mother to hear this!"

"You may speak to Benaiah," said Bathsheba coldly, "in some other room. I have discovered him to be a malicious trouble-maker, not to say a liar. I have ordered him out!"

"And I," said Solomon, "have just ordered him in again. Come here, Benaiah, and shut that door firmly! Have you twenty chariots in good condition? . . . No, I don't mean that—I wish you to bring twenty chariots, in good condition, to the entrance of the palace within an hour. There will be, of course, the proper number of archers, spearmen, and the like. You, in person, will conduct Adoram overland to Tyre. The journey will take a week, will it not? I mean, it will certainly take a week. Leave someone here to prepare fifty chariots seven days hence to carry my wife and me to the border, where we will meet you and Adoram. King Hiram, I expect, will be there too."

He glanced at his mother to be sure she was listening, or, since there was no doubt of that, to ascertain the effect upon her.

"Be ready in an hour!"

Benaiah hesitated.

"Why don't you go?" asked Solomon.

"Your mother told you I am a trouble-maker."

"As it happens," said Solomon, "that observation didn't interest me."

"Perhaps I *am* a trouble-maker now," persisted Benaiah steadily, "but I think you need me around the palace. I'll send a good man with the first chariots, and another with the fifty—unless when you go to the border you take your mother along."

"You'll be ready in an hour," said Solomon. "As you go out, send Adoram to me!"

Benaiah showed no disposition to move.

"Upon my word!" cried Solomon, staring.

Benaiah pointed a finger at Bathsheba. "She's going to tell you things about me, some true, others not. I can tell about *her!* Will you listen to us both now?"

Perplexed though Solomon was, he caught in the man's tone a frankness without disrespect, an honest claim to fair play. Besides, his curiosity was aroused. He might have let Benaiah expose Bathsheba in full, but at that moment Adoram sought admittance, bringing with him by the wrist an ill-clad, sullen youth of eighteen or less, one of the working class.

"Ah," said Solomon, "I was about to send for you." He was aware of the boy. "What is this?"

"This," cried Adoram, "is an imitator of Jeroboam! I found him addressing his fellow students in the precinct where Shimei once lived. He was urging an insurrection, and I was patient until he suggested that you and the queen are, as it were, murderers at second hand, and your activities should be stopped. I seized him myself," continued the old tax-gatherer proudly.

"This apartment," said Solomon, "is not a police court!"

Adoram bowed. "Your mother will agree that the case was urgent."

Solomon, looking at the boy, marveled that his young muscles had permitted the fragile tax-collector to arrest him. Beyond doubt here was another ambitious martyr!

"Did you say those things about me?"

The boy thrust up a defiant chin. "I'll say them again! Unless you do to my throat what you did to Shimei's!"

Solomon glanced involuntarily at Benaiah, who had performed the actual cutting. About professional executions the captain had an easy conscience. Though he worried over Bathsheba's intentions, it was obvious that he remembered Shimei as a good job well done.

Solomon turned to the boy again. "When you suggest that some restraint should be put upon me and the queen, my wife, what have you in mind?"

The budding fanatic drew a long breath. "I defy you!"

"That, of course!" said Solomon, smiling. "Is it just defiance in general?"

"Unless you first stick a knife into me," said the boy, "I've sworn to stick one into you!"

"And into the queen?"

"Into the queen!"

Solomon considered the heroics too juvenile to be taken seriously. Had he seen his mother's face just then, he might have formed a different judgment. From her chair somewhat behind him, all of them facing toward the door, she was studying the boy with ominous acuteness.

Solomon lifted his hand in a gesture half of authority, half of resignation.

"You're a foolish young man," he said, "and someone should teach you the beginnings of a decent life. I shall have a word with you later. Meanwhile you may rest in jail."

Benaiah stepped forward.

"Give him to the guard outside the door," continued Solomon, "and return quickly."

They waited in awkward silence, Adoram, Solomon, Bathsheba.

"I thought it should be nipped in the bud," explained

the tax-gatherer, as though apologizing for invading a lady's room.

"You came at a fortunate moment," said Solomon. "I am sending you within the hour as my special ambassador to King Hiram."

He was explaining the purpose of the mission when Benaiah returned.

"You can't give away your cities!" cried the tax-gatherer. "There will be a revolt!"

"Perhaps," said Solomon icily, "you have heard too many liberal orators. Do you threaten me?"

The old man raised his hands in despair.

"It will be courteous, of course," continued the king, "to inform Hiram—the local Hiram—why I am sending this message through you. We'll speak to Hiram immediately. You may then retire to your house—I hope with some speed—and having made whatever preparations are necessary, you will return to the palace entrance, where the chariots will be waiting."

To these blunt orders the tax-collector listened with open mouth. In a daze he followed Solomon from the room, neither of them stopping to salute Bathsheba. Benaiah lingered, hesitating.

"You too, Benaiah!" called Solomon.

The captain bowed stiffly and went after them, leaving David's widow with a slight smile upon her face, the smile of victory with which long ago she had greeted the messenger who brought an invitation to come down off the roof.

The three men, having wasted precious minutes search-

ing around the temple, found Hiram coming away from his
conference with the Queen of Sheba. He was in an inex-
plicably courteous mood, and when Solomon said Adoram
was to carry certain financial proposals to Tyre, which proposals, being of a technical nature, would be most clearly
stated by an expert, Hiram answered that Tyre was at its
best at that season and the natives would be glad to see
Adoram, whose well-deserved fame had preceded him.
Since the chariot ride, however, would prove to the last
degree uncomfortable, Hiram offered a ship with a convoy
of honor.

Solomon vetoed the ship, but in his relief at meeting no
opposition from the brass-worker, he ventured to indicate
in outline his new plan for squaring accounts with Phoenicia, and again Hiram listened with unforeseen sympathy,
agreeing that territory was what the Phoenicians needed
more than anything else, and the border towns were un-
doubtedly of a choice quality.

Dazzled by the progressive success of his diplomacy,
Solomon then confided that he and the queen, accompanied
by Benaiah, would meet Adoram on his return and pick out
the cities to be handed over, and perhaps the King of Tyre
also would be there in person to validate the ceremony. At
this news Hiram's pleasure was amazing. He laughed outright.

Meanwhile in Bathsheba's room the schoolboy patriot
was standing once more in the presence of Solomon's
mother. The sullenness had begun to drop from him, his
eyes were on the beautiful woman.

"I had you brought back," she was saying, "not because

I can release you altogether from this injustice, but because I too am in a sense a prisoner. You and I love our country; that makes us strangely equal, doesn't it, though I was once a queen, and you haven't yet begun to live! Whenever we find an occasion, the guard will bring you to me, if only for a moment—perhaps during the day, perhaps at night. Will you trust me? Can I trust you?"

Chapter IX

In his palace at Memphis the King of Egypt was sipping a cool drink and trying to recall, for the benefit of his wife and his four unmarried daughters, some further incidents in the raid on Gezer. He and his chariots had returned in record speed, and having washed off the dust, he had inquired after the family health, and they had asked what happened, and he had said the army was his heart's delight and the town would be worth nothing to Magsala except as a toy, because the walls were an inferior kind of egg-shell, and his wife had asked how was Magsala and what was Solomon like, and he had confessed recklessly that he never went near his favorite child.

That was three days ago, and he was still explaining. "I told you, we had to build a new gate, and the place had been full of cattle. If I sent on the prisoners, with affectionate greetings from home, wasn't that surprise enough? Remember, I promised to come again and just visit!"

"Father's so interested in his old campaigning," said the youngest daughter, "he forgot to inspect his son-in-law."

Before this close approach to the fact, the King of Egypt took refuge in another sip of fruit juice. "I merely said I'd give her a wedding present. You women can't rise above gossip."

"We've had no letter from her," complained his wife, "not since the first one, and I've a feeling she's unhappy, or at least lonely, and the briefest glimpse of you would have cheered her, and then you could have seen for yourself whether the marriage was wise, and——"

"Suppose it isn't wise!" interrupted the experienced husband, grasping at a chance to leave personalities and discuss principles. "Suppose I had gone there and found the fellow ugly as a toad, companionable as a flea, witty as a pig, what could I have done?"

"You could have brought her home!" cried the queen, on the edge of tears for Magsala's hypothetical wretchedness. "You had the army out for exercise, and if you could burn a town you could rescue your daughter!"

The lord of the Nile raised his left hand, the right being occupied with the fruit-cup. "Wait a minute, wait a minute! I didn't say her husband is a blight on the human race, I said suppose! As a matter of fact, I'm told he's everything a girl could expect, and if I'd gone there now, I'd have interrupted them. On a honeymoon no parent is wanted, not even you, my dear."

"Who told you he's so fine?" asked the queen, getting the debate back where she could handle it.

"Everyone I spoke to," said the king, going the whole distance. "And if that favorable rumor has flowed as far as Gezer, you can imagine how strong it must be at its source."

"You ought," said the queen, "to be ashamed of yourself!"

"I'm not," said the king, leaning over to set down his empty cup. The effort caused him to grunt.

His self-content was oil to the dying flame. "How you can face us," the queen burst out, "is beyond me!"

He rose without haste, adjusted the skirts of his lounging robe, and gazed down with a smile into ten rebuking eyes. "These pin-pricks, my dear, the familiar welcome which you and the girls provide, are nothing to cause penitence, not even in a sensitive man like me. They are not criticism, they are the essence of the home."

Pleased with himself, he delayed his progress toward the door, that he might develop the theme. "Most human conversation has to do with the shortcomings of fathers and husbands. At this moment, in every house on earth, a woman is saying how she would have acted had she been in his place. If there's no man, the women take it out on each other, sisters especially, but they prefer a man whom they love. When we voluntarily set up a home, we're betting we can make peace once a day with an adverse opinion."

He felt he was in a strong position, but at that moment, unfortunately, the second detachment of chariots returned, the escort, with Ano and Jeroboam, and the clatter of horses in the courtyard brought him out of his philosophizing. The queen and the four daughters tried to keep up as he hurried down.

"Excellent!" he called to the captain, acknowledging the soldier's salute. "You made faster time than we did!"

"Ask him about Magsala," suggested the queen.

He lowered his voice. "Not here in public!"

"Who's that girl in the chariot?" asked the youngest daughter.

The captain approached, saluted again, and in the best military phrase explained that his two passengers were by way of a return gift, with the Princess Magsala's compliments, and the King of Egypt would of course dispose of them as he pleased, but first he should have a separate conversation with the girl, to whom a private message had been confided.

"Bring them over here," commanded the king, puzzled.

They had removed the ropes from Jeroboam's ankles and wrists as soon as they were well on the way south, and his resentment had had time to change into sullenness, and his sullenness, assisted by advice from Ano, had gone over into a new set of plans for his own advancement, but now, in the presence of majesty, he forgot common sense, and reverted to his natural manners. His stride would have been proud had it not been pompous.

"Why, it's Ano!" exclaimed the youngest daughter.

The other daughters and the queen also exclaimed.

"What's this?" asked the king.

"The princess," answered Ano, "sent me to express her very particular affection and her thanks for the delightful surprise."

The king turned to his wife. "Didn't I say she'd like it? A very handsome way of expressing her appreciation!" He beamed upon Ano. "We'll give you the best vacation you ever had, my child, and when you return to the princess——"

"I shan't return," said Ano. "She told me not to."

The women in the family drew closer and the king frowned.

"Is this the part I was to hear separately?"

Ano drew a deep breath. "My husband prefers to be introduced in public."

"Your husband?" repeated the king.

"She's gone and married a native!" whispered the youngest daughter.

"My husband," explained Ano in a firm voice, "is the leader of the most important tribe. Some of the other tribes think not, but they're jealous. He is the chief opposer of the king."

"The chief what?" asked Magsala's father.

"In that country," explained Ano, "everyone argues, and my husband does it better even than the king. So the princess thought we should live here a while."

The King of Egypt tried to understand but couldn't. The captain of the chariots wondered whether it was his duty to report the condition in which Jeroboam had been shipped out. Jeroboam, feeling that the time had come for an oration, took a step forward.

"If this is the proper authority before whom to register my protest——"

Ano pulled his sleeve. "They can't understand you! Besides, visitors don't make speeches here!"

Jeroboam darkened. "Translate for me! I will pause at the end of each paragraph. If this is the proper authority before whom to register my protest——"

"He says," began Ano reluctantly, "we had an easy journey and he thinks the country beautiful."

The queen touched the king's arm. "May I question her? Where did she learn his language?"

The king smiled. "He's her husband. Any language is inevitable if you're married to it."

"What's all this chatter?" inquired Jeroboam, much put out.

"They asked where I learned to translate."

"We will proceed," said Jeroboam. "If for the second time in the history of my people we must dwell among the injustices and under the tyrannies of Pharaoh——"

Ano interrupted desperately. "You mustn't say that!"

"I will say nothing else!" he insisted, raising his voice.

The King of Egypt thereupon lost his interest. "In honor of my daughter," said he, "whose special ambassadors you are, we shall set aside for your use the smaller guest room in the palace wing. If you need any entertainment or comfort, you've only to command us. My thanks to the soldiers, Captain! This audience is ended!"

The queen watched Ano, unmistakably engaged in pacifying her husband as they were led away, and the captain waited for a whisper in the king's ear, to set him right.

Later in the month the twenty chariots of King Solomon were bringing Adoram to the palace of King Hiram, in the citadel of Tyre. That is, not Adoram alone, but Benaiah and the escort of fighting men, two to each wagon. Solomon's chariots lacked the glitter of the Egyptian, since he was peaceful and dispensed with maneuvers, but as innocent conveniences of locomotion they could still function, covering the ground at an average of seven and a half miles per hour, if you count the horizontal distance and omit the holes in the road.

Adoram froze to the side of the car, speaking only when they paused for the midday meal, or put up dog-tents for the night. He had neither the muscles nor the bones for diplomatic missions.

When at last they reached the main portal and entered the town, they were stopped within a block by the police, and because there was no common ocabulary, both the embassy and the officers of the law used gestures, some of which could be taken in the wrong sense, and at once there was a clutter of bystanders, unwilling to move on because there might be a fight and if so they wished not to miss it, until the row disturbed King Hiram, who feared another bread riot. Coming in person, he was gratified to see that the mob was angry with someone else.

"What we need," he said, "is an interpreter," and the police, not having thought of it, said that was of course what they needed, so they brought from the jail an inaccurate person who had been cutting cedars in Lebanon, to preserve the balance of labor, that side-by-side arrangement which Jeroboam had originally suggested and which Solomon had put into the contract. This fellow, in happier times a baker, had swung his ax at the tree but had hit the Tyrian with which he was teamed. If he escaped hanging, it was because none of those familiar with his woodchopping could believe he had aimed at the Tyrian.

The baker, therefore, fetched blinking from his dungeon, listened to some of what Adoram was saying, and when King Hiram understood it was to be a debt conference, he took them up to that retreat in the tower where on a similar occasion he had received his son, Sheba's Hiram. That is, Adoram, Benaiah and the baker climbed to the circular room with the table and the hard benches and the window-slit toward the harbor. The chariots, the archers and the police waited uneasily at the foot of the stairs.

"This payment," began the host bluntly, "is overdue, but the fact that you bring it at all is one of the marvels of my reign. Which of you heads this committee?"

The baker confined his translation to the concluding question, not because he was delicate about the insolvency of his fellow-nationals, but because he could remember only the words which most recently sounded in his ears.

Adoram bowed sadly, and King Hiram faced in his direction. "I assume you computed the debt with the assistance of my agent. Just what is the final amount?"

Again the baker skipped all except the last, but here the last contained the meat.

Adoram lifted supplicating hands. "We have brought no money!"

The baker, having picked up his Phoenician from the impolite classes, added from force of habit a popular but derogatory epithet, which made Adoram seem to express contempt for the money he hadn't brought.

The veins in King Hiram's neck began to swell. "I knew it, I knew it!" he cried. "Robbers to the end! And in the name of religion!"

"What's he say?" inquired Adoram with as much privacy as was possible.

The baker clung to what he had heard twice. "He says he knew it."

"Ah, did he? That makes it easier for both sides. Instead of gold, tell him, we offer territory. Cities, I mean, not waste land. Inhabitants included."

At first King Hiram thought they were making a present of Jerusalem, which was more than he would have asked, but reasonable enough if Solomon wished to acknowledge the interest on the capital investment, the impairment of the mines and the Lebanon landscape, the deterioration of the workmen abroad, the decline of consuming power in the population at home. But Adoram kept after the baker till the idea of small cities came through—border towns, outposts.

"That's another matter," said King Hiram, with a trader's care to look disgusted. "Which towns? How many?"

Adoram saw the first gleam of hope. "Tell him twenty cities. Or perhaps you might say fifteen and go up later."

But here the interpreter faltered among the grammatical complications, and by good luck the tax-gatherer stopped him just in time from translating the promise of a higher bid.

"You'd better start off with ten."

The baker made it ten, in Phoenician. King Hiram snapped his thumb as though shooting marbles.

"Raise it to fifteen!" prompted Adoram, without waiting for a translation.

King Hiram yawned, and with offensive indifference got up and looked out the window.

"Say twenty now, and if he wants more, tell him he

should first see what they're like. Tell him we agree that a Tyrian village wouldn't be worth much, but one of ours is another matter."

The baker hesitated. "He'll ask how he's to know that!"

"By going there and using his eyes," said Adoram, gathering courage. "We wish an immediate answer. We expect him to come at once with Benaiah and me. You might add that Benaiah commands our army."

King Hiram, after several probings, drew from the baker this permission to look at the towns before he accepted them.

"But if they're no use to me?"

"One thing at a time!" retorted Adoram. "Tell him the worth of these particular cities is such that he may owe us something!"

King Hiram sent for his own chariots, and the two troupes started racing toward the border.

Almost at the same moment the other Hiram was disengaging himself from his temple tasks, and stealing through the back streets toward the barracks where lodged the Queen of Sheba. At sight of him she was prepared for sentiment, but he came on business.

"Get us two of your camels, and we'll find that ship now."

The prospect of recreation pleased her. Since Adoram had left for the north and the Egyptian invasion had blown over, Solomon's realm provided nothing more exciting than meals. Yet she pretended to be coy. "Not two by ourselves?"

"That's enough, if you know how to drive the animals," said the brass expert. "Do you?"

The Queen of Sheba admitted that she could steer a camel, control its gait, and persuade it to kneel at both ends of the trip.

"Perfect!" said Hiram. "Just you and I by ourselves!"

"Are we going far?" she asked hopefully.

"Very."

"But we'll be back before dark?"

"We shall not! This night we'll spend in the desert, tomorrow morning we'll reach the navy yard, by noon we'll be hoisting sail."

"But the sailors, and the food?"

He lowered his voice to explain, as though the sentry might listen at the keyhole. No sooner was his plan fully sketched than she kissed him, but he said they would have more time on the voyage, and the thing now was to be off before Solomon heard of it. So she wrapped herself in a thick white gown, with a yellow veil over her face, all but the eyes, and packed her comb and her jewels in a red handkerchief, and when ten minutes later he strolled up to where the camels were tethered, outside the gate, there she was sitting on the curb like a tired market woman, but really enthusiastic and impatient, so they chose the two camels with the longest legs, climbed up to the elevated saddles and got under way, with their necks swaying, toward the southeastern sands.

The camel at once produced on Hiram a stimulating effect, shaking up the philosophy in him, but interrupting all consecutive conclusions, what with the up-and-down of the back and the hither-and-yon of the shoulders. In his boyhood he had learned with agony that a ship can roll as well as pitch, but now he endured the subtlety of a camel's rhythmic contradictions. Balkis rode ahead, an attractive woman on the whole, but less attractive, temporarily, since he was too much in her power. He still enjoyed the liberty of shouting which path to take when they reached a cross-roads, but without her aid he could neither stop nor get down. Well, it wasn't her fault; he himself had suggested camels.

The roads were dusty, and Balkis's camel seemed not to lift its feet.

Now and then they met a countryman or a traveler, plodding toward the city. Once they slowed up to let a youth get by with sheep for the market. For the most part the fields were empty, but every so often they passed a man with bent shoulders who struck at the earth with a mattock, and sometimes a woman worked beside him with a hoe. Most of the women, Hiram thought, were old, but he couldn't be sure, with the camel so vibratory. Twice the woman seemed young and, under the dust, beautiful, but he couldn't be sure of that either.

Sentiment of a kind, which he hadn't expected, induced him to look back toward the retreating city, toward the massive walls with a dome or two showing above. He would have enjoyed a glimpse of the temple fabric, perhaps a gleam of gold on some pinnacle which he had put up and had not yet taken down. But the walls, from the angle of the camel, were too lofty.

He knew he was saying farewell to that kind of town

and to his old work, and the knowledge had a salty flavor, zest for adventure mingling with streaks of regret. Certain things were left behind which he would gladly have known more of. There were people in that city with whom he would have liked to talk. He remembered Abishag. Had there been a choice, he would have eloped with her instead of Balkis, but there must be something to elope on, and the Queen of Sheba had two camels. His thoughts could not get away from the beasts.

Next after Abishag he recalled Magsala. Were he visiting the city again, with complete leisure, he would give some study to that woman. Rather lucky to see that Egyptian squadron come in from Gezer! Did Solomon's wife expect it? Or was she really surprised? If she was warned in advance, the acting was superb. But to be innocent and still act so well would be unique! He was inclined to set a high value on any woman in this disordered world who refused to be startled out of her wits.

Well, he could be content, since fate so willed it, with the Queen of Sheba, and since so much of his past was broken, he would find out now the trick of doing nothing and letting others work. His dusky queen was also his camel driver. Not a bad beginning! Not a bad sort of woman, either! She probably knew how to cook. When they reached that island, or that remote shore, which she imagined, he would direct her affection toward the upkeep of the home. No more of this exploring! Children are the best anchor.

Only once did he think of King Hiram. His father would soon be talking with Adoram, perhaps would soon be inspecting the border villages. No use guessing what would happen next. If his father brought down the unreliable Tyrian army, mercenaries who hadn't been paid, Solomon's father-in-law would probably send up the Egyptian chariots. Without a fight, the debt would stand unchanged. With a fight, it would grow. His father, if he had sense, would run away! There were plenty of Queens of Sheba. Solomon, if he had sense, would run away! When the roof promises to fall, why not step from under?

After an hour or so, the motion of his steed got into his bones, and he relaxed to the eccentric swaying. His mind too rested upon the first coolness of approaching twilight, the nervous procession of thoughts slowed down, sensations took their place. Balkis and he were now on the edge of the desert, the roads narrowed to a trail, the sun was low, already the sky settled closer to earth, they were enveloped in infinite distance. A few green spots remained, islands in the sand, marked by palms or sycamores, but before long the dry reaches would be unbroken, and they would traverse the hypnotic emptiness until sunrise. Then they would smell salt air. There would be green spots again, a trail, at last a road. Then they would find the ship.

At sunset Balkis halted her camel and waited for him to catch up.

"We might as well eat here."

Though hungry, he glanced with some hesitation at the waving barrenness under their feet, reddened or shadowed where the light touched a rise or missed a hollow. "A while ago," he suggested, "there was a tree."

But her camel was already kneeling, and his beast obeyed

the signal and sank. He stretched his stiff legs and gazed around. Balkis, happily without false reticence, was massaging her back, repeating the gesture which had caught his attention when she descended at Solomon's. Not to be too fine in manners, he began rubbing back to life the same parts of his body.

From the camel's harness she removed a small carpet, spread it on the sand, sat down cross-legged. "There's food in the bags—and bring the water bottle."

Though he had imagined a world in which others would work, it seemed no moment to establish the system. He explored the saddlebags, found another carpet on his own camel, unfastened the two water skins. These creatures were provisioned like ships, for emergency sailings. Biscuits, dry dates, raisins——

By the time he fetched her supper, she had eased her clothing informally, laid aside the yellow veil, unfastened the gown to enjoy the air from throat to waist.

"What a relief to be free!" she cried, sniffing at a biscuit which might or might not have turned sour. He thought she referred to garments, but she meant liberty of soul.

"If I had to be queen again in my own country, I'd kill myself!"

Hiram was trying a dry date. "What's wrong with it? You never told me."

"Worked out, like tired soil. It happens everywhere. You can't enjoy a kingdom unless you build it yourself— do the first plowing. Then you plant what you like, and whatever you plant grows. But if the land's old you spend your days trying to save it, and you can't choose the disease your people expect you to cure. Of course the wise thing is to move over on young soil and begin again, as we're doing, but your people insist on your staying, so they can be angry with somebody at the end."

He was gratified by the spread of her thought. "But why did you visit Solomon?"

She laughed. "Wasn't that a good excuse to travel? Your people are always delighted if you meet another monarch. Isn't it absurd? I expected to go back and tell them Solomon was the wisest man on earth, and he and I lost our hearts to each other, and he was so rich, I was ashamed of the basketful of pearls I had brought for him, and he covered me with such amazing jewels—your handiwork, my dear!—that two merchants counting for a week couldn't add up their value, and I, considering the repute of my country, made a gesture which put him in his place! Instead of bringing the marvels home, I gave them to the poor. If I had told that fable to my people, they would have been puffed up for half a year."

"That," said Hiram, "explains the visit in principle, but why Solomon?"

She laughed again. "I thought it was my destiny! And now," she added, "I'm sure it was!"

The sudden love in her eyes was more than flattering, and Hiram would have paid a compliment in turn, had he shared her theory of fate, but since he was committed to freedom of the will, he pressed on toward further information.

"You don't mean that no kingdom at all will last?"

"They last too long! We prop them, we say prayers, we water them with tears, instead of letting them wither naturally at summer's end. We won't admit there'll be another spring."

He munched a raisin judicially. "After all, if we had what we want, we'd make an effort to keep it. The next spring, to use your phrase, might be different."

"Impossible! It's never a different apple-tree—when the heifer grows up, it will give it's mother's milk!"

He turned the idea in his mind, not gravely arrested by it, but willing to master her opinions, since they were to live together. The dusk was falling. He noticed the grace of her small hand, the softness of her rather stout arm, as she felt the chill and drew her robe across her breast.

"Kingdoms and all possessions," she concluded, "are no more than the jewels in my handkerchief."

"Oh—in your handkerchief?" he exclaimed, surprised and interested.

"The ones I intended for Solomon. The only real treasures, I always say, are in body and mind, health and brains, our bare selves. That's why you are a king."

He knew she was smiling in the dark, and once again he avoided the threat of sentiment. "We should be riding on—the night is short."

An hour more they traveled, aiming by the stars, calling to each other at intervals, but mostly dozing in the saddles, dulled by the monotonous swaying. Then Hiram roused suddenly, as the camel in front of him came to a stop, and when he drew close Balkis pointed, whispering, "If we get down, they may not see us!"

It was a cluster of dark bodies hurrying to head them off.

"Men on horses! Robbers!"

Her camel folded up on the ground, and his promptly did the same, but they had been seen minutes before, and the horsemen wheeled like swallows. A dozen men with spears and war arrows, circled around the camels in no time!

"Search them!" The voice sounded so familiar that for a second Hiram thought Solomon was pursuing.

"I'll save you the trouble! No workman of yours ever had money on his person, and the knife in my belt was a gift from my father!"

"What's this?" The voice wasn't Solomon's, after all, nor Benaiah's. Hiram began over again, plaintively.

"I've a small and inexpensive knife in my belt, there's a biscuit or two in the saddles, my wife has a comb in her handkerchief, and I dare say a needle and a bit of thread. That's our wealth. We're a simple couple, seeking work in the new shipyard."

Rezon, the shoemaker, laughed. "Your wife, eh? Pretty employment *she'll* find in a shipyard! Where'd you steal the camels?"

"They're mine," said Balkis, off her guard.

"Yet he said you were poor! Get down, men—search them!"

While the brigands were running their hands over Hiram in the dark, Rezon was puzzling out the accent, the two different accents.

"You are Solomon's people?"

"We are," said Hiram, "and this interference with the king's servants on·the public highway——"

"You're a liar!" interrupted Rezon. "You're a foreigner! I know you both! Great Moses, what a find! Here, men, let me see this woman! A light!"

When he pulled the yellow veil from head and shoulders, the skin showed brown in the torch-flare.

"It's the thief from Tyre and the drab from Sheba! Right in our hands! So may all our enemies perish!"

"You are not thinking of violence, are you?" asked Hiram with admirable composure.

"In half an hour," replied Rezon, equally polite, "you will both be dead. We have sworn to discourage the wrong kind of visitors. Four of my men will hold you down by ankles and wrists, and I personally will operate with the knife, with your own knife, if you keep it sharp. Or we may do the woman first, to let you see the method."

"But this assumes," argued Hiram, "that we are the people you suppose. As a matter of fact, we are not! On the other hand, I have no difficulty in recognizing you! As a good citizen, unfortunately unemployed at the time, I was standing in the crowd when King Solomon sent you off to jail with that disreputable Tyrian. Had you not been preoccupied, you would recall I shouted encouragement to you. Our meeting now proves that my wishes counted for something."

Rezon was not deceived by these transparent wrigglings, but his men were, and a bandit leader must bend with the mood of his followers. They were Jeroboam's converts, sincere fanatics, respecting the name of justice, which they considered the right label for their maraudings. Even in the day no one of them could have picked out Hiram or Balkis.

"It's too dark—wait till morning!"

"And have Benaiah after us!" said Rezon. "Now or never! I know what we've caught!"

They held back only a moment more. When he waved a peremptory hand, four of them seized the woman, the rest keeping a grip on the man.

"If you still doubt what I told you," continued Hiram, with unshaken nerves, "you could send a fast horse back to the city."

"For Benaiah to hang the rider?" asked Rezon.

"I'm supposing you have a friend outside the walls. Most patriots have. Now, if the Tyrian and the queen are still there, then I know who I am better than you do, but if he and she have left town on two camels, then the coincidence will be fatal, and there's no contesting the will of God. I appeal to you all as honest men!"

"Let me ride!" said the fellow who had hold of Balkis's right arm.

"I suppose that's what you all want!" said Rezon in disgust.

"It is!" they answered.

So the fellow galloped off into the darkness, and they settled down to wait, with Hiram haltered to a stake in the sand, and Balkis likewise, some yards away, and one man assigned to watch the camels, and another to guard the horses, and the remaining nine in a circle under the stars, talking in low voices.

The rope that held Hiram to the stake went around his neck, and it was so short he couldn't sit up, or otherwise get a purchase to pry himself free. He tried, of course, then he stretched out patiently and racked his brains.

The rider would return by dawn, unless the horse dropped dead.

The rider would doubtless bring the truth.

If Balkis and he were still there——

These were the main points in his problem, all three simple ideas, but stiff as iron. He leaned on one or the other, to make it bend, but it wouldn't. The rider would surely come back with the news that the Queen of Sheba and the Tyrian had disappeared, and when Rezon's men heard the words, Balkis and he *would* disappear!

If he could think of a way to get loose! If he could free Balkis! If he could recover the camels! But merely to tabulate these steps in escape was to choke your courage. That group in the circle over there would be on their horses in a second! They were quiet now, resting on the sand, but they doubtless had ears as keen as an antelope's.

Balkis was quiet too. He raised his head slightly and strained his eyes. They had taken her over there to the right. Was she, like him, groping for a plan, or had she abandoned hope? She had let him do all the talking, but he wouldn't hold that against her. Except the Egyptian queen, he had never known a woman who kept her faculties in sudden danger.

Lying with his head to the ground, he thought he heard the galloping of a horse, and then he woke up and realized with some horror that he had wasted a moment in sleep. One of the horses over there really was stamping. If he could think how to get Balkis on a horse, or two horses, one for each——

When he fell asleep again and began to dream, he knew he was dreaming, and agonized to break through the trance. He was at home in Tyre, walking in the garden which his father reserved for himself, but which you could slip into when the king was somewhere else, if you gave the gardener a bribe. Now he was at the gate with Magsala, the inscrutable princess from Egypt, and by a miracle there were two coins in his pocket, and he explained proudly how he could purchase for her the sight of incomparable roses, and immediately they were inside, skipping the gardener and the vulgar palm-greasing, and the flower-beds were at their height of bloom, but unfortunately they met Rezon in one of the alleys, strolling as if he owned the place, and Rezon asked him for a password, and when he couldn't guess the right formula, Rezon wondered if Magsala could hold Hiram down while the knife was being used, and she, ever so friendly and a little sad, feared she wasn't strong enough but she would try, and when her lovely fingers closed on his wrist——

In the sudden blackness he was lost, but Balkis whispered, shaking him again, "Get up quietly—hold my hand!"

Someone had cut the rope. He stumbled after her toward the spot where the camels were guarded, too dazed to ask how they could mount and ride, but answering by instinct the thinnest hope. She was amazingly sure of the path, as though she had been there before, and she knew where the man was lying asleep who had been set to watch the camels. She pointed at the shadow and put both hands to her throat, by way of advice.

The hint called into action all the fierce energy which had slumbered since he mounted the camel. He fell on the limp guard so suddenly that the wretch was choking before he woke, and the fingers of the brass-worker on his wind-pipe shut out the least whimper. By the time Balkis had the camels on their feet the admirer of Jeroboam was unconscious. Hiram gave him a parting squeeze, Balkis persuaded his camel to kneel again for the belated cargo, and they sped into the black night.

Every moment Hiram expected the hoofbeats behind them, but there was no pursuit. For an hour, a long hour, they hurried in silence, and then he called to her desperately. She waited till his camel was alongside, and they could move off together.

"What is wrong?" he called. "Won't they come after us?"

She laughed—in the darkness he found the laugh flippant. "They won't—we are safe!"

And safe they were, as it turned out. By sunrise they found the trail to the ships, and meanwhile no bandit made his appearance. She had, in some mysterious way, invented a rescue for them both! He should have admired this achievement, but most unreasonably it worried him. A managing woman, with ability!

Shortly after the dawn they smelled salt air, and knew they were safe. He asked her to stop for food, but his real need was to solve the night's puzzle.

"You cut the rope and freed me," he granted, "and for that I am your servant always! But who untied you?"

"Rezon," she answered simply.

He thought it over. "But I don't understand!"

"You would if you knew Rezon," said she. "What a rascal! When the other men were asleep, he came over to where I was spread out on the sand."

"And what happened?" asked Hiram, a bit thick in the throat.

"He's the least honest man I ever met," said Balkis.

"How did you get loose?" asked Hiram.

"He's the sort of person," said Balkis, "who accepts a bribe."

In the cool morning there was sweat on Hiram's brow. "Then you bought our freedom? I owe my life to your sacrifice?"

"If you insist on putting it that way. I bought my life, and he threw yours in."

Hiram turned faint. "I'd rather be dead!"

"How foolish!" said she, with an easy conscience. "What would I do with the pearls, if I lost you?"

"Pearls!" said he.

"I gave him everything in my handkerchief except the comb, and I swore I wouldn't tell the other men he had them."

"Did you," asked Hiram, moistening his lips, "did you

throw in, as you would say, anything else besides the pearls?"

She stared at him. "What else had I?"

Shortly afterwards they came in sight of the ship, and she clapped her hands, having the tricks of a child when she was pleased. He wondered why, against the evidence, he found himself painfully in love with her.

CHAPTER X

AT HIRAM's vanishing the Tyrians in Solomon's city became restless, and the natives too were uneasy. The Queen of Sheba they considered no great loss, merely one more barnacle removed from the ship of state, but the brassworker was ballast.

Solomon, rising to the emergency, took charge of the working squads in person, with Magsala beside him, and persuaded the goldsmiths to put back what they had been taking off. The temple ceased to disintegrate and gradually resumed its shape, but the common folk suspected there might be a further revision when Hiram returned.

Then Solomon put a lieutenant in authority over the town, an earnest youth without experience, and the fifty chariots bore king and queen northward, on an errand not explained to the public, who of course fell into a gully of gossip and guessing, everyone spilling his mind at street corners, and no one tamed by the flimsiest acquaintance with the facts.

It was in this shaky period that the doctor asked Abishag to be his wife. The incident is but a footnote to the main flood of events, and the official record therefore omits it, yet on its merits it deserves mention.

He made the proposal, not under the moon nor at any hour when the resistance of the sentimental is supposed to be low, but after breakfast on a bright morning, as he was starting the round of his patients. He was standing in the doorway, to be precise, with his bag in one hand and his hat in the other, and she was clearing the table. It is supposed that the sight of her at that domestic task detained him momentarily.

"My age is out of proportion," he admitted, "but knowing you wouldn't waste yourself on one of this ineffective younger generation, and believing myself good for several years more, and having developed for you an affection which is beyond the fatherly——"

"You've been extremely kind," she interrupted, to help him on, "and I couldn't repay you, not if I had three lives and married you in all of them, but let's be sure what you're asking for. Is it love, or is it just me?"

He was a little hurt. "I hold you in the deepest respect, as you've reason to observe! It's marriage!"

She seemed cheerful and interested. "I was afraid that was it! Well, I'll go so far as this—if I were to make that mistake with anybody, you'd be one of the nicest to make it with. And such a comfortable way to thank you for not having bothered me before!"

When he looked still sadder, she hastened to apply balm. "Plenty of others would have given me a home, but you asked nothing. Don't think I'm not grateful!"

He didn't care much for this kind of encouragement. "Naturally, men being what they are—a girl in your detached condition—and so charming—you must be annoyed daily."

"I'm not. It's never really unpleasant and you can always say no. One man," she added, "insisted on a legal ceremony."

The doctor faltered. "You—you already have a husband?"

"Oh, I declined."

He breathed freely. "It must have been someone you didn't love."

"On the contrary, the only one I'll ever want!"

He was stunned. "I beg your pardon—I'd no idea——"

She finished with the table, he watching her.

"If you could not accept him, for any cause, and if you wish an established home, if you now can see your way to take my devotion——"

She came over toward him. "Do you want me on such crippled terms?"

His trouble was too strong for him. "Who was the man?"

She shook her head. "You shouldn't ask."

"I know I shouldn't!"

"After all, there's nothing dishonorable about it," she reflected. "It's the king."

"Not Solomon!" he gasped.

"Himself."

The doctor stepped back into the room, put down hat and bag, straightened up, faced the implications.

"If you have at any time belonged to the king, you naturally couldn't marry me."

She nodded.

"Do I understand," he continued, "you do belong to him?"

"Belong?" she repeated. "The word isn't clear. I'd do anything for him."

The doctor held on to the back of a chair. "Did you— what *have* you done for him?"

"You seem to be asking," said Abishag, "whether he has yet taken liberties."

"I must know!" cried her tortured suitor. "The king might properly resent my innocent desire for you, if he has already——"

Abishag, reaching up, silenced and pleased him by covering his mouth with her hand. "I wouldn't hurt you—and he hasn't yet done me the slightest harm."

"Then," said the doctor, "I renew my request, but in a different form. Whether I marry you, is for you to say, but if you say no, you will, I hope, seek another home. Your proximity has become—that is——"

"Am I tantalizing? Then I'd better go. Perhaps I could find employment with a near-sighted person——"

"Take a month," advised the doctor, picking up his hat. "Think it over from all sides for thirty days. Then we marry or we part friends."

Though she had tossed back at his elderly sentiment light answers in a flippant tone, she watched him now as he walked up the rudely paved street, and her thoughts, to judge by the shadow on her face, were of an awkward melancholy. It was some time before she resumed her housework.

Meanwhile, in the sparsely populated district toward the extreme north, the fifty chariots, with Solomon and Magsala in them, had reached the border, and the first of the

villages had been appraised by its hereditary owner, before
King Hiram and his Tyrians joined them. Benaiah and
Adoram arrived last, because the horses felt the terrific
trip, up there and back, and besides, Solomon's chariots
were fitted with obsolete wheels, much too small.

The village which he inspected before Hiram got there,
brought to Solomon's mind Abishag's saying, that he
didn't know how his people lived. Yet with this squalor
thrust under his eyes, he embraced his ignorance as an
excuse.

"If it were less far from me," he explained, "I could
have the place swept out occasionally, as you would a careful stable, but how can I keep up with the habits of these
folk on the edge of space?"

Magsala paused to look into a doorway, a one-family
room. Because of the high sun, the family happened all
to be at home—a man, two women, six children, and several hundred flies. The children came forward out of the
gloom to stare at her.

"In Egypt too," she confessed in a low voice, as they
strolled on, "we have some bad spots, and father always
says you can count on the first good sickness to sweep them
away, but that seems cruel. I suppose I'm too tender."

"They eat and they sleep," said Solomon, still thinking
of his own subjects, "and they furnish duplicates of themselves, but they never wash. I can't understand that."

Magsala caught him up a bit sharply. "Have they water? I saw only one well, and that a mile away!"

"They should dig another," said Solomon firmly, "or
else move to where the present well is!"

"Move?" she asked. "These wretched folk build new houses?"

"Well, am I to blame?" he retorted. "Should I be digging wells?"

"Not for these now," she answered gently, "not if King Hiram will undertake the water supply. But perhaps you have other towns you ought to visit."

"And furnish water?"

"Perhaps."

Her quiet advice was doubly irritating, since he could find nothing wrong with it.

"People are what they are, and they get what they desire!"

"Has that been your history?" asked Magsala.

"It will be!"

Then Magsala laughed and said she was glad, and he was about to ask wherein the humor lay, and why had she forced on him this plan of giving away his dirtiest towns, when King Hiram rode in and blocked the street from the other end, and he and Solomon got down and told each other who they were and asked how-are-you, without waiting for a reply, and Solomon said this was his wife, and Hiram glanced at her absent-mindedly, and went on about the temple.

"Our work satisfied you, didn't it?"

"Well enough, but it's going better recently, since I took charge."

"Of what? The building?"

"Only while your man is away. As you may know, he disappeared with the Queen of Sheba."

King Hiram clenched a fist, then remembering he was in society, loosened his fingers again and wiggled them. "That alters the case entirely! Your ambassador didn't inform me of this fault on our side."

"We can walk as we talk," said Solomon, glad of firm ground, "and your chariots might as well back out, so we can hurry to the next town while the day is young."

King Hiram strode along past his own escort, lined one by one through the narrow street. Solomon had switched his thoughts from the debts to the possible ambitions of his son.

"She wouldn't go far with him if she knew who he was!"

"Who wouldn't?" asked Solomon, knowing the answer but wishing to increase the embarrassment.

"That queen what's-her-name!"

Solomon pressed his advantage. "She is of a brown color and primitive in her temperament, but I understand extremely wealthy. Her kindness was originally directed toward me, her visit having for object alliances of one kind or another, but your representative, I'm bound to confess, diverted her good will in the direction of Tyre. Though the loss is mine, I admire the skill with which he cut me out."

"He's a rascal!" cried King Hiram.

"Oh, I wouldn't say that," Solomon interrupted. "Of course, if the Queen of Sheba and I had decided to cooperate, I should now be paying you the debt in cash, but it comes to the same thing, he'll get it directly from her."

King Hiram was frantic. "Not a penny will I see! He's a thief! He'll take it all!"

At the end of the village where the street no longer confined them, Magsala stepped forward. "You don't mean he's untrustworthy?"

Solomon regretted her entry into a discussion which he had so skilfully begun. King Hiram looked her over as though her presence were a surprise. "Madam, he was a liar from birth!"

"I can't believe it," she answered pleasantly. "I prefer to think it was the demoralising influence of our country, because if he had always shown those evil traits, you wouldn't have sent him to build our temple."

Solomon withdrew the regret. He liked "our temple." She was throwing in her lot with him, and the King of Tyre was caught in a neat perplexity.

"But whenever the fault began," Magsala continued, "if he *is* unreliable, I can understand more easily the excessive cost of the work. My husband and I noticed that the bill was several times too large."

Under the impartial sun King Hiram mopped his brow, puzzling how to restore his agent's reputation just enough to preserve the debt.

"Shall we get into our chariots now?" suggested Solomon, repressing his satisfaction. "The next town is only a brisk gallop away."

Across the sand they kept the cars within conversational distance.

"Had he progressed with the fleet?"

"A boat or two," called back Solomon. "I haven't seen them myself, but they're well along."

The King of Tyre fell silent, trying to recall his geography, if by chance his unreliable offspring should find a passage into the main sea, and spoil trade with the Iberians.

The dwellers in the second village, as poverty-stricken as those in the first, were grouped outside their huts in timid welcome, and to Solomon's amazement they had marshalled a row of horsemen.

"I didn't know they were armed!" he whispered to Magsala.

"It's Adoram waiting for us."

King Hiram ignored Adoram, Benaiah and the twenty chariots.

"Who now directs the work on the temple?"

"I do," replied Solomon, "and I may say we get on excellently."

"I'll send you an expert," said King Hiram.

"None is needed," countered Solomon firmly. "Here is my treasurer, with whom you have already conferred, and if we drive rapidly through this and the adjacent towns, you may balance the account to suit yourself."

King Hiram recognized Adoram. "Why didn't he tell me about this running away with a queen?"

"It occurred after he left," explained Solomon. "Now if you'll examine the condition of my people in this district, you'll see the installation is as yet no more than elementary, but the emplacement could hardly be improved, right on the border, in the inevitable path of whatever may develop between us. Once the debt is adjusted, Adoram tells me, trade will open up."

Adoram, shattered by chariot travel, heard himself quoted but let it go, and it made little difference after all, because King Hiram was at last measuring the property, peering into the houses, discovering the congestion of males, females, children and insects. Besides, the odor of this hamlet was special.

King Hiram drove through the main street rapidly, as Solomon had urged, but coming out on the other side, he drew a positive rein.

"Brother," he sighed, "what city is this you're giving me?"

"Do you want the name of it?" asked Solomon. "Or do you inquire about the total number?"

Adoram interrupted. "I told him we could go as high as twenty."

"My question," said Hiram, with cold precision, "referred to the type or kind. When your ambassador offered cities, I assumed something you or I could live in, but these—these pens—are——"

In spite of his indignation, he chose the word carefully, and since it was a Phoenician word, it wouldn't mean anything to you, but it is usually translated freely as "undesirable," and literally it is equivalent to "overrun with vermin."

"Well," said Solomon, mildly set back, "if you don't want them——"

"I do not!"

"That's all right. We just thought you might like to settle the debt this way, but if you're in no hurry——"

"Tax your people and pay up!" shouted Hiram, forgetting himself through weariness and disappointment.

"I will consider what is best for us and fair for you,"
said Solomon, "and what we ultimately do will depend."

Magsala touched his arm. "Don't forget, my dear, if the
cities aren't enough, my father expects to be consulted."

Hiram was alert. "The King of Egypt? I trade with him."

"I know that," said Magsala.

"But Egypt is at the other end of the world! Even if you
sent a messenger today——"

"My father visits the neighborhood from time to time,"
said Magsala. "He likes to do his army exercises on our
land."

The King of Tyre pursued his eloping son with mental
curses. "Not to have told me this!"

From the circle behind Adoram, Benaiah now stepped
out and stood respectfully in Solomon's presence. "Start
now and we'll reach a good well before dark."

"Ah yes," agreed Solomon. "We will start now."

"Then," exclaimed Hiram, "I came down here for nothing!"

Solomon bowed. "You forget you came to meet me, and
though you did not expect it, you have had the privilege of
looking upon my queen."

Hiram couldn't think of a thing to say, offhand, so they
drove south again, seventy chariots in all, and the Tyrians
stood rooted in their tracks until Hiram remarked they
might as well go through the villages, so long as they were

there, and perhaps one or two settlements would turn out to be better, since nothing could be worse.

At the well that evening, when they paused for supper, Magsala told Solomon she saw in him the beginnings of a great man.

"You carried yourself admirably—no one could be firmer or more adroit."

"But I was amazed," he said, "at that possible aid from your father. I hadn't heard of it."

"Neither has he, but he'll do what I ask."

"That's one thing I can't get used to, we shouldn't get used to it," he pondered.

"Asking for help?"

"Saying what isn't so, even with an adversary like Hiram."

"You mean it was wrong to scare him, mentioning father?"

"I did some pretending myself," admitted Solomon tactfully. "I resort to that trick more and more. Is it possible to govern and yet remain honest?"

She smiled wisely. "To be honest, or to govern, you must make good your threats. You will now decide just how much you can pay, and that will be your final offer. For my part, I'll see that father knows all about Hiram. We shall have told the truth."

"Perhaps it was the form I object to," said the reluctant ruler. "I don't like threats. And my impulsive statement as to the Queen of Sheba was of course fabricated. I am really ignorant of her finances, as I am of her personal intentions toward me."

Magsala took this confession demurely. "There you *would* have to guess, but since she ran away, it's all history now, a mere matter of opinion."

In Memphis the King of Egypt had been inquiring into Solomon and his family, as interpreted by the opinions of Jeroboam. Day by day, with Ano's assistance, supplemented by comments from the chariot captain, he pieced fragments together, until David lived in his thought, heroic and popular, Bathsheba ambitious and vindictive, and Solomon ignorant and literary. The news that his son-in-law wrote poetry was a shock.

The picture would have unveiled less gradually if Ano had felt it wise to expose her husband as a hater of his own people. Her translations were progressive. In the first version Bathsheba's womanly charm was stressed, Solomon's inexperience was noted, and certain qualifications of David's fame were postponed. It was fully a week before Magsala's father learned how lucky David was to die when he did, and how merciful it would have been had he died sooner, because the old man was of the primitive type, an individualist, absolutely without social conscience.

Jeroboam's social ideal had to be fed out even more gently than the short-comings of the royal household, but here Ano in the end was faithful, though she knew the danger. It would not please the King of Egypt to hear that a monarch holds office only during good behavior, the subjects to say whether it's good. Nor would he hold it against Solomon that many who dwelt within sight of the costly temple lacked food. The toilers in the Nile Valley, under the shadow of more majestic shrines, bred like gnats, shrunk up in a dry spell or shriveled in a cold wind, but there was always another swarm to take their place. Ano conveyed at last a strong hint that in Solomon's land, which was the home of strange attitudes, the working class objected to shrinking up or shriveling—in fact, might at any moment refuse in this respect to carry on the Egyptian tradition. Jeroboam, she explained, believed it more foresighted to guide the workers than to oppose them, because they were in the majority and were finding it out, and if you took charge of their grievances, you could get them to keep on working just the same, only under another theory.

Though this may have been close to Jeroboam's actual thought, it was far from her own aspirations for the under-privileged, but like Solomon she was learning what modi-fication of the truth is imposed by the exigences of govern-ment in a practical world.

From all this information the King of Egypt drew con-clusions and formed plans which may be considered nat-ural if we remember that he was a veteran where Solomon and Ano were novices. The conclusions were, first, that Solomon was a failure, and second, that Jeroboam was a rascal. Here was news, but the accomplished ruler, like the successful parent, is never surprised. The plans there-fore were, first, to keep Jeroboam in Egypt as Magsala wished, out of mischief, at least for the present, and second, to groom him for a helpful career in case Solomon lost con-trol or was deposed or was assassinated. The King of Egypt wasn't sure what method the northern people used to retire their rulers, but he didn't wish his daughter to be retired.

If Jeroboam could manage the working class without their knowing it, perhaps Jeroboam could be headed in the right path without feeling the guiding hand.

The King of Egypt expounded the strategy to his wife one evening, or later than evening, to be precise, for they had already made preparations for sleep, and the conversation was in tones muffled and relaxed, from pillow to pillow.

In fact, he was sleepier than she was, and if his authority at home had been as absolute as it was abroad, he would have done no talking at that moment, but the queen ran her finger lightly down his spine to ascertain whether he was awake, and when he turned over in self-defense she asked why he had ceased to be fond of her, and he knew he had a real conference on his hands.

"Fond of you?" he murmured. "Adore you! Same as I always have!"

"You've changed," she sighed. "I try not to notice it."

"What have I done this time?" he asked, resigned.

"You once loved Magsala," said she, making it sound like a rebuke.

"Still do," he protested lazily. "You too. All the family."

"I worry about the girls," she said, "the four."

He groaned. "They seem all right to me."

She pressed hard on the reproachful note. "There was a day when you would have cared!"

He was roused to strike back. "I wanted a son, of course, but that wasn't your fault, nor mine, and I never held it

against them. I don't see how they could be improved on,
as girls go. What are you nagging about?"

"They're not married," said the queen.

"That's natural, isn't it, when they're young? All in
good time."

"They're not young!"

"So? I thought they were."

"You're heartless!" she snapped, and turned her back to
him, but when his breathing threatened a relapse into slum-
ber, she faced around again.

"Do you know who Jeroboam is?"

He recognized the target she had been aiming at. "Why
didn't you ask that in the first place? I shall try him out on
a small pyramid. Ano says he has a gift for handling workmen."

"Did she tell you he's a spy? Solomon sent him to watch
us."

"Magsala sent him," her husband corrected. "Solomon
and he don't get on."

The queen was frankly contemptuous. "I was sure you'd
believe that fiction, but you're the only one who does! Solomon wants to know which towns you'll burn next."

"See here," he exclaimed, "this nonsense tries my patience! If you don't like what I do, say so! You once were
able to say it without bringing Solomon in!"

"I once thought you had your wits," she retorted. "Now
you permit this man to roam up and down, gathering his
reports——"

"Ano translates for him, remember!"

"Does she? Some of your men understand his tongue!"

"Don't move the subject around so!" commanded the king. "No doubt we can check up on what *he* says, but so long as *our* words remain incomprehensible——"

"But do they?" put in the queen. "Your men are whispering about Ano's translations. He says one thing and she turns it into something else. Those two are playing a game."

To give himself the color of confidence, the king raised his head and adjusted the pillow, but inwardly he was disturbed.

"Your error is ingenious," he began at last, "and if I had only a partial acquaintance with the facts, your interpretation of them would be convincing. But Jeroboam is Solomon's enemy, not his spy. He also exerts a stimulating influence upon the ignorant, by means of oratory. I shall ascertain, as I say, what speed he can make on a pyramid. If the workmen were entertained, perhaps they'd move their feet."

"You'll employ your son-in-law's enemy?"

"Now you begin to get the picture," said the king. "That's it!"

"Then the man you married your daughter to——"

"Is, as you feared, a disappointment," said the king, cutting in. "You read his character correctly. A weakling; but then, your insight is always remarkable."

"Poor Magsala!" said the queen, obviously mollified.

"My plan is approximately this," explained the king. "I'll build up Jeroboam at once. He's to be the hope of the oppressed. At the same time we'll give him the larger guest-room and we'll ask him to dinner. That will teach him the full range of social sympathy. Then when our son-in-law abdicates——"

"Who thinks he will?"

"It can be arranged," said the king, pushing on. "I will then take over the entire country, striking at the crisis, before they guess we are coming. Magsala will of course represent me on the throne. Jeroboam will be her chief adviser."

"Does Magsala want all this?"

"Want it? Does she want me to furnish safety, prestige, power? If she doesn't want it, she's hard to please!"

"Of course," said his wife gently, "but her ambitions used to be simpler. I think she'd be happy if you just went to see her once in a while."

"Oh, that again!" said he, irritated. "I promised a visit—now don't wear me out!"

"If you went soon, my dear, you could learn whether Solomon really will give up his throne, whether Jeroboam really is his foe, whether Magsala sent him to us, or whether——"

"I'm going shortly," said the king, "but not tonight. Shall we catch a wink or two of sleep? Don't be surprised if I appear surly tomorrow. I always need eight hours!"

Thus do our parents, beyond their intention, influence us; thus, in far distant parts of the ancient world, Solomon's father and his mother projected through him the conflicting logic of their tireless personalities. David, who thought he had taken a farewell of life, urged from his grave the building of the temple, the dealings with King Hiram and the other Hiram, the raising of the taxes, the desperate offer of the twenty cities; Bathsheba, playing the successful widow, brought about the apparition of Magsala, and the sack of Gezer, and the insubordination of her own son. Between them they provided cause for Sheba's visit and for her hasty departure; also for the disloyalty of Jeroboam and Ano, with possible consequences yet to emerge from Egypt.

And David in a sense was responsible for Abishag.

All this time, while the chariot conference was in session on the northern boundary, while the King of Egypt was analysing Jeroboam and placating his wife, while Sheba in her simple way was saving the skin of her brass-worker, Abishag was making up her mind about the doctor, how to get out of marrying him when the thirty days should pass. His proposal shocked her, not because it was unforeseen, but because when it came it sounded like a stroke of fate, a deep bell closing the hours. When she watched his elderly person retreating up the street that morning, her melancholy had little to do with him, but much with herself. Her hour had come to an end. Never again could she knock on Solomon's door, thirsting for his love, thankful for his quaint poems, if at the moment he had nothing else to offer. She had suddenly grown old. The doctor's amiable wish to domesticate her had chilled her heart with a shadow. All very well to live joyously, to accept the casual gifts of destiny and not ask for the main things, but there really are main things, and when you know you can't have them——

To knock at Solomon's door again, with no hope of his love, would be cheap!

In his absence now, in the safe emptiness of the city, she would visit the places where he had talked with her, or where she had seen him—the mound of stone and soil near the temple, where he had come in the night to hear Jeroboam's tirade; the plank from the ground to the building, along which he had helped his wife, his happy wife, that first day after the wedding; even the room where David died.

Her love was woman's love, fatal but not self-deceiving. She knew how men, whether Solomon or the doctor, set up for themselves a schedule of perfections, and gaze in your eyes, smother your lips, feel around your body, to make sure you illustrate their idea; and if you don't, as you probably won't, they leave you with regret, or perhaps forgive your inadequacy, and continue their blessed search. For herself, she saw all of Solomon's shortcomings, yet she could love him forever. A very ordinary man—except that he was hers.

The thought of him was most tender and most pain-starting when she climbed the palace tower and stole down the steps to the sheltered sentinel-post, the balcony where one starry night she had confessed her readiness to stay forever in his arms, if there were a forever in mortal bliss, but she knew there wasn't, and though he put ridicule on her lack of faith, she had told only the truth. That was before the princess had appeared from Egypt, when he still believed he could marry the girl he wanted, forgetting how his mother would finish off whoever wasn't the right girl.

If happiness cannot last, why risk at all the tantalising undertow which for a second drowns us in deep water, then breaks us on the rocky shore? So she would have said when she lay curled over David's fainting heartbeat, or even when

she had walked to the young king's room, at his first call.
But now there was debate in the town of Hiram and Balkis,
who had left kingdoms behind them and had run away,
and the heads of settled families, after much cautious beard-
stroking, glanced at each other and admitted a wistful
beauty in the escapade. Their wives disagreed, but without conviction. Hiram and Balkis, they held, would come to
a bad end. Abishag wished that Solomon had forced upon
her a dream no less wild, though no less fleeting.

If she paid frequent visits to the sentinel-station, it was
because the city was full of the doctor, and of young men
on street corners, and of neighborly women who thought
they could have cured David, had they been chosen. The
niche in the tower wall gave her solitude. That is, until the
evening before the chariots returned. Solitude, like other
joy, is brief. Walking across the tower-top and starting
down the stairs, she recognized the sugared absurdities of
the love-sick. Some boy and girl learning from the moon.

Abishag stood motionless, not wishing to listen, but
caught by the bubbles which to the mad seem a satisfying
utterance. When she and Solomon talked, did it sound like
this?

"My most beautiful!"

"My hope, my hero!"

"My queen!"

"My hero, heaven-sent!"

"My unbelievable!"

"My——"

If they paused, it was for a kiss, or for breath. Abishag
leaned her head back against the tower wall, and waited.

"I should have gone to my death poor, had you not pitied me!"

"To death?"

"My loveliness, you know!"

The pause this time, Abishag, was for thought. She leaned closer to them.

"Death!" The woman caressed the word. "Why not, after all? The cold hand will touch me tomorrow, or another day, but soon. I almost see the dark form, face-covered."

"Not for you, not for you!"

"Dear boy, I am old!"

"Not old!"

"But the king is my son, and there was another before him, and long ago——"

"You destroy me, say no more!"

"I would make it easier for you—to go."

Now the silence was troubled, and when the woman spoke again, she pleaded.

"Had I left you in the prison-cell, you would have ended in filth, among the rats, forgotten. Now you have the air, and light, and afterward remembrance."

"Now I have you!"

She tried eagerly to break off the thought of her.

"When Sisera came down from his chariot and fled away on his feet to the tent of Jael, she said Turn in, my lord, turn in, as though she knew not our enemy, and when he turned in she made him a bed and brought a bottle of milk and a dish of butter, as though he had been a friend, and when he was fast asleep she took a nail and a hammer and went softly and smote the nail through his head and fastened it into the ground, so he died."

"But did she have to die too?"

"She might have died, she was ready! If she lived a while longer, she did nothing again so brave. Samson was happier—I should have named him first. He said, Let me die with the Philistines! So he bowed himself with all his might, and the house fell upon all the people in it, and he killed more in his death than in the battles he came home from."

The boy was still reluctant.

"You wish me then, when I have thrust the knife into her, to turn it upon myself?"

"Was it not your own thought?"

He faltered. "It was—until you——"

"Ah, must I take back my faith, and regret the gift?"

The pause was for a tragic kiss, an agonised embrace. Then the boy made a sad little effort to speak like a man.

"I have not seen the king's wife, the Egyptian. How shall I know her?"

The woman became cheerful.

"That also I have planned for you. When I bid her come to my room, at the end of the day, she puts on a blue robe, thinking to please me, because I once praised it. Now, when the moment is here, I will bring you from the prison to a hidden corner outside my door, and then I will send for her, and you have only to watch for the blue robe."

"And after I have struck, I must——?"

The woman lost patience.

"No coward ever loved me before! I am soiled!"

"Ah, my beautiful! I will die! I will die!"

"To what refuge would you flee? At that hour the palace doors are locked!"

"Speak of it no more, my Queen! My knife in the blue robe—then my blood for you!"

While his devotion was collecting its reward, Abishag crept across the tower again, and down to the palace, and past the guard who remembered that Solomon had once sent for her, and so slowly home to the doctor's door.

Chapter XI

WHEN the seventy chariots drove in from the border conference, Magsala and Benaiah were the only two still fresh after the rough journey. Adoram showed his years, Solomon showed impatience, the horses were fagged, but the captain with the scarred face looked neither better nor worse than when he set out, and the queen had managed even without Tii's ministrations to keep herself dainty. She had on her best black wig, the one with the gold band around the forehead, holding the precious stone in the middle, and she wore a brown linen cloth which couldn't be spoiled by dust, and her skin was a smooth dark ivory, and her eyes were shining. She had had her own way.

That is, she had forced King Hiram's hand in the matter of debts and territory, and having seen him, she wasn't afraid of him. Moreover, she had pushed her husband into heroic boasts and resolutions from which he could not very well back out.

And he knew he couldn't. The longer they rode on the way home, the more clearly he saw he had done right but wasn't likely to enjoy it. By the crumbling of his Phoenician alliance he was left with his kingdom to himself, but he foresaw the inconveniences of isolation. He had publicly declared his ability to finish the temple.

Well, he'd have to do it. The emphasis would now be laid on his people exclusively, on their skill and on their willingness to work, and the mouths of the Jeroboam party would be stopped, theoretically, but also, since all labor would be done on the ground, there would be a unanimous request for prompt pay, which would involve more revenue, which would imply more taxes, which would reopen the complaining mouths.

Whichever way you approach the mystery of work and trade, of buying and selling, you come at last, he feared, to a blank balance of poverty. If you leave other folk alone and work for yourself, you have to pay yourself. He, for instance, must now invent a magic to extract from his people enough to make them think they were getting high wages when he handed it back. But then, if he kept on sending wheat to Tyre and if King Hiram sent him cedars, after a hundred years they'd be where they were now, except for the race between cedars and wheat, which could grow faster. The only advantage of exchange, so far as he could see, was that you postponed the judgment day, and you might be dead before the reckoning was called.

The cedars grew of themselves, being a gift from God, but the wheat must be planted, and if you planted enough, you'd have something left over after you were fed. Solomon perceived here the sole promise of a beneficent surplus. Unless you added poetry. There was a resemblance between poetry and wheat. By toil you could bring out of nature, out of the earth, something which wasn't there before, and the harder you worked the more you'd bring out. In that case you'd be a farmer. Or you could skim from human nature a beautiful wisdom which hadn't previously been collected. In that case you'd be a poet.

But there again, you fetch up against a puzzle. If the farmer produces more than he can eat, he ought to get rich. But he doesn't. Poets too.

These reflections, depressing at any time and difficult in a chariot, rendered the trip home a grievous ordeal. Even without pen and parchment, Solomon seized the essence of it in concentrated phrases, which he would develop later, if ever the privilege of versifying were his again. As to trade, foreign or domestic, he would say something like this, that he looked on all the works which his hands had wrought, and behold, all was vanity and vexation of spirit, and there was no profit under the sun. That would stand for the farmer. As to the wisdom which you make into poetry, and which no one, not even Abishag, really cares to listen to, he would try this formula; the wise man's eyes are in his head, the fool walketh in darkness, and I've noticed they both come to the same end.

He would have shared his discouragements with Magsala, but for once she refused to sympathise. Farmers and poets were nothing to be so gloomy about, and if you brooded too much on commerce she was quite sure you would become vulgar. In economic argument, like most women, she was a bit simple; she thought you'd better pay as you go, and if you couldn't pay you'd better not go, and when he said that would mean abandoning the temple, she replied with unexpected flippancy that the

god of Solomon's people had by definition passed a large
section of eternity without a home to dwell in, and this
particular house, being so small, would even when complete be only a symbol, not an adequate enclosure for a
deity, and perhaps with the universe to gaze on, high
hills, vast deserts, unmeasured sea, all girdled about with
stars and moon and sun—perhaps with so many distrac-
tions Jehovah wouldn't notice the temple if it were built,
and wouldn't miss it if it weren't.

Solomon, having harkened to this balm for his melancholy, conceded that his wife had in her the germ of
magnificence, yet he was sorry that at that critical moment
she must remind him of her heathen origin. Though she
was willing to learn, she would never catch the idiom of
his ancestral faith.

It was without enthusiasm, therefore, that he addressed
the populace on his return. Magsala wished him to make
the speech, and he recognised the propriety of an announcement in some form, but his instinct would have
been for a later moment, after an interval of rest and
meditation, and whatever message should at last formulate
itself, he would have let Benaiah or Adoram say the
words. But she thought he should speak for himself,
because when you have a good voice your enemies can't
pay so much attention to what you say, and she also advised the spot where Jeroboam had made his night-time
harangue.

When the city watchman, therefore, saw the dust of
the chariots, and the people came running into the streets
to cheer their king on general principles, as you would
anybody who had been away, Magsala said now was the

time, and the pilot chariot, the one which goes ahead for assassins, if such should occur, to shoot at, turned abruptly to the right and drew rein not at the palace door but beside the temple.

His subjects came running pell-mell, as soon as the car had stopped, and he would have begun at once with his hands on the chariot-rail, leaning as from a pulpit, but Magsala thought it looked better if he set his feet on the ground and conferred with them eye to eye. So he got down, and she stood by the rail, just behind and above him, listening.

"The days of trouble," he said, "through which you and I have passed, are over. In all frankness, my friends, I bring you this news. We have carried out the program of the king my father. I will not conceal from you that the burden has been heavy. From time to time I have called upon you for more support, financial or moral, and doubtless I shall need to call again. But I appreciate the loyalty upon which I may count."

The crowd withheld their applause till they knew what he was up to, which wouldn't appear so early in any good speech.

"I have just terminated some very interesting talks with that accomplished friend of yours and mine, the King of Tyre. As a result of certain new understandings the work on the temple will be completed entirely by ourselves."

A spontaneous cheer, shortened by caution.

"The Phoenician friends who have so happily labored by our side, will now go home, to inaugurate several enterprises in a larger field."

The applause lasted ten seconds, at least.

"They go with our thanks and our good wishes."

Perfunctory hand-clapping, and some one laughed.

"No more wheat will leave the country. You who do the work, will receive all the wages. You who raise the food, will eat it!"

He hadn't meant to promise quite so much, but with the faces in front of him it was hard to hold back. The prolonged shouts of the delighted crowd gave him a moment to reflect.

"The necessary works upon which we are engaged, such as the temple, can be finished with comparative comfort if we proceed upon an intelligent program, so much to be accomplished each year. I would suggest five years, which is easy to remember, and we might allow ourselves a margin of two. The temple in seven years! Let that be our goal and our inspiration."

Applause respectful but moderate.

"By distributing the work over so leisurely a period, we can also spread out the taxes. Of course, as I don't need to tell you, this program will cost heavily. But when the requests for revenue are divided among so many years, you will I trust find the weight easily bearable. In the sixth year, as I now estimate, or in the eighth, we shall have reestablished the good aspects of the life to which our fathers were accustomed, and we shall have mended the few natural shortcomings."

When he drove off to the palace, they cheered, not because he had threatened higher taxes, but because he was driving off. Once indoors, he went to Magsala's room. His mother had neglected to greet them.

"Well, how was it?"

"A splendid speech! Just what I hoped!"

"I promised too much."

"Not at all! Most of them didn't really listen, and if they did, you can say they heard you wrong."

He sat on the bed and put his hand to his brow. "I'm awfully tired!"

She sat beside him. "I saw that while you were speaking. You know, I've an idea! You remember what we talked of once, about your going back to the place where your father kept the sheep? The place is still there, isn't it?"

"No doubt, but I've no training with sheep."

"You could learn. Now, here's my plan! You go back there in disguise, live as nearly as possible the way your father lived when he was a boy, be free of these worries, think of your own life, of David, of your poems, and I hope of me! Then come home and start the way your father would!"

She saw the brightening of his eyes—she was pleased that his thought turned promptly back to her.

"If I go, you will be alone. I must watch the danger here."

"You mean your mother?"

His eyes clouded again. "I can't believe that of her, but if anything should happen while I was absent——"

"Nothing will. Benaiah is here, and I trust him. He's her man, but he'd rather be yours. I think he begins to approve of me."

Solomon rose with a new interest. "I'll talk with him,

and if I decide it's safe, I may go.   I've always wanted to see the flocks at Bethlehem."

As he went toward his own room, down the corridor, he passed Abishag, standing close to the wall, waiting. He supposed she was waiting for him.

"We're glad you're home again," she said.   "That was a fine speech."

"Ah, you heard it?"

"Of course!"

Jealousy bit him, more sharply because he blamed himself for not having picked her out of the crowd.

"Did the doctor hear it too?"

She smiled.   "The doctor was by my side.   We both thought it excellent."

Rather than discuss the doctor in public, he turned rudely and walked on, but he intended to send for her at some better time.   Perhaps after he had visited the shepherds of Bethlehem, and had renewed the sanity of his opinions.

The Queen of Sheba knew little about ships, and the boat which Hiram appropriated for their eloping was an astonishment to her and a delight.   It stood fairly high in the water, considering its modest length, and the mast, hewn from Lebanon cedar, touched, as she remarked, the heavens.

"When the sail is up," she asked, "won't it turn over?"

"In a good wind it would," he explained, "but in that case we take the sail down."

"Do you always get it down in time?"

"Some don't," said he, "but I haven't drowned yet.

We don't fear wind. The real peril is in a leak. You see, there must be a mast to hold the sail, and the mast is useless if it isn't high, and if it's high, like the one we've got here, it leans this way and that and sooner or later it spreads the planks apart."

"What do you do then?" asked Balkis.

"You swim for a while. Most people think it a misfortune to go to sea at all. But you needn't worry," he added. "We're the best builders in the world. Our ships last, on the average, two and one-third voyages. We always make them over after the second voyage."

She admired the arrangements for the oarsmen, in case there should be no wind. They could sit on oak benches just below the deck, in the middle part of the vessel, and their feet fitted into holes in the planks in front of them, so they wouldn't lose their balance, and they doubled up to push the oar forward, and then leaned back in a long curve, like a tight-strung bow, to draw the blade through the water, and since the deck shaded them from the sun, it was humane toil and comfortable. For greater ease they put off the last stitch of clothing, and it was a beautiful sight, that brown bending and stretching, not an ounce of fat, all the muscles coming through the skin. Hiram was too accustomed to it, but when they were making for deep water, outside the harbor, where the wind would begin, she went below to watch. Hiram persuaded her, in fact commanded, to climb the ladder again and enjoy the sacks he had spread for cushions on the high shelf at the end, where the steersman clung to his paddle-rudder.

On that shelf Hiram and she were to eat and sleep,

wake and take their exercise, unless a storm should force
them below. She wished to move around and investi-
gate, but he said positively you mustn't invade the men's
quarters, not on a ship, because it interrupts their work.
She admired his wide knowledge and his willingness to
teach her the best ship manners.

How he persuaded the sailors to come along, she
couldn't imagine, especially since neither he nor she knew
where they were going. The source of his authority was
perplexing. They merely rode in on their camels, he
asked if the boat was finished, said launch it, and it was
launched, counted off twenty men, sent them aboard,
picked out a twenty-first to steer, ferried Balkis from the
shore on a skiff and pushed her up the side, followed at
her heels, tied the skiff to the stern, told the steersman to
get going, and straightway the oarsmen began their bending and leaning. That was all. The boat held food and
water, but who supplied them? And do sailors put the
food on first, before they launch the ship?

Discovering for herself that you move faster if you
accept the direction of the breeze, she wanted Hiram
always to sail with the wind, to make the best time. When
he said the wind changes and you wouldn't be sure where
you'd land, and frequently the wind goes the wrong way,
she asked if it made any real difference where they landed,
and he replied that every man on board knew how to
steer by the stars, a cryptic reply which seemed to evade
her question.

She would have thought it prudent to steer within sight
of land, in case of misfortune and because they were look-

ing for a territory in which to set up their kingdom, but Hiram made for open water, preserving, as he explained, an equal distance from both sides of the gulf. She wondered why he called it a gulf when they were already tossing in the center of a green unsteadiness creased with foam, which stretched to the edge of the sky, but he said the sea would come later, and meanwhile they would strike a rock if they didn't stick to a safe channel. By the end of the first day the glimpse of a good rock would have been welcome.

The night had its own surprises, not the stars, which were less wonderful than in the desert, but the shimmery gleam of the waters, the silence of the crew, and Hiram's care of her, which was at the same time a sort of neglect. The wind was behind them, the ship didn't rock, the rowers could leave their benches. All but the steersman were asleep. Hiram was asleep too, curled up close beside her. He might at least have stayed awake and talked.

Had it been in her disposition to foresee trouble, she could have regretted the impulses which one by one and in their total had reduced her to whatever discipline he chose to apply. Evidently he intended from now on to do what he liked and she must obey his arbitrary will, especially on shipboard. He slept profoundly. She could hear his breathing, and even in starlight she fancied she could see the slow heave of his body. Once she rose softly to be kind to weary muscles and to watch the water churning along the side, but the steersman cleared his throat, and Hiram sprang up, unreasonably vexed with her. Had the steersman been further away, she would have demanded at least the pretence of liberty. But ever since she had saved him from Rezon, he had been unpleasantly possessive, easily angered.

In the last part of the night she slept, and at dawn she found herself again. He was relieving the helmsman, who had gone below to prepare breakfast.

"You really can steer it!" she exclaimed. "I thought you were only boasting."

With that she went over to him and laid her hand beside his on the steering oar.

"We made good time last night," he confided, ignoring the mixed compliment.

"Shall we reach an attractive shore today?"

"We're going to Ophir."

"Why, that's a city!" she cried out. "Aren't we landing in some vacant spot where there are natives, and where we can establish——"

"No savage shores for me!" said the brass-worker. "I prefer cities, and Ophir is one town I haven't visited."

"You said we'd find some island or some untouched shore——"

"*You* said it, you mean. I've always had Ophir in mind."

The steersman returned for a moment with hard bread and raisins, and then went below again for his morning's nap. Hiram ate with his arm over the long oar, leaning right or left, with his eyes fixed ahead. Balkis munched the food, watching him.

"I'm not to be queen, then?"

"You're to be my wife and the title doesn't matter. Didn't you agree to that?"

She finished eating and brushed off her hands. "Are you angry?"

"Why should I be?"

"I don't know. Maybe you're sorry I gave the jewels to Rezon."

"They were your jewels."

She revived the first question in another form. "I thought you were to be king somewhere."

"Perhaps I am."

"But you can't be king in Ophir—they must have one already!"

He gave an irritated pull on the steering oar. "See here, whatever I've done, it's been at your request, remember! You invented that throne for me, you proposed in the first place, though you admitted it was bold, you asked me to go off with you and start over again in a fresh country!"

She challenged him. "Will you swear you didn't think of all those things yourself?"

"Of course I thought of them, but you put the ideas into words!"

"Wasn't that all right?"

"Not if it made you think you're managing this journey, or me!"

Her dignity, even in the wind on the exposed deck, was impressive. "As you just implied, I owe you much, and I'd rather not owe you more. It was gracious to welcome me at the city gate, and to give me for a while your attention. Thanks for protecting me across the desert, and for receiving me on your boat! Now if you'll stop somewhere and put me off, I need impose upon you no longer."

"I don't see any place to stop."

"But as soon as there is."

"Have the goodness not to begin this kind of talk again!" said he. "I overlook it now because you're not used to boats, and the pitching may have disturbed your judgment, and besides, you've suffered hardship on land, as I know, and perhaps more than I know, but there's a limit! You're my woman, I'm fond of you, and so long as you do what I wish, I shan't thrash you!"

"Thrash me?"

"Those were my words. Have you never been thrashed?"

"Not yet, I must confess!" gasped the Queen of Sheba.

"I thought so! My mother used to say——"

"Your mother? Poor soul!"

"She wasn't. I never met a person who understood men better. If she hadn't died so early, I'd have learned everything."

Balkis gazed over the sunlit waves and pretended to nurse her pride, but Hiram showed no sign of repentance, and her curiosity was roused.

"You were about to quote some saying of your mother's?"

"I was, but on second thought I won't."

"As you please."

She walked to the port side and turned her back on him.

"See that white speck on the horizon?" he called. She didn't reply.

"It's another ship," he explained cheerfully. "We'll pass several every day now, as we get out of the gulf. Why don't you move a sack over there and sit down?"

Ten minutes later she was standing beside him again, helping on the oar.

"Was it men your mother taught you to understand, or women?"

"Men."

"What was it you were going to tell me she said?"

"Oh—she said if a man knew himself, he needn't bother about the women, because they'd follow along."

"That's what she said, was it? And do you know yourself?"

"I think I've got a clue."

She laughed, then she stroked his large brown hand. "What's the clue?"

"It wouldn't do you any good," he explained. "It's a guide for men only."

"What is it?" she pleaded.

The corners of his lips turned up as he chose discreet words. "Let's see—I wonder if I can say it—man must attend to nature's one great lesson, as my mother used to say, only he's usually too busy to notice the deep meanings. That's about it."

She clung to him. "What's the one great lesson? Hasn't a woman anything to do with it?"

He grinned. "She's in the picture, all right, but he's the one who learns."

"I think," she said, "you expect to tell me sooner or later, and it might as well be now."

"You mayn't like it—it will sound raw."

"Tell me!"

He looked straight at her, unmistakably serious. "Well, there's a moment when even an ordinary man is a god—a short moment, but sample enough of what grandeur might be. You know what I mean?"

She pretended she couldn't guess.

"Why," he explained awkwardly, "when two people are loving each other—it's that second—that flash of glory at the end—the universe comes apart—you feel as though you were riding the lightning, driving the stars. It's probably not quite the same for the woman, but I'm talking about the man. Some say it's just an impulse of the body, some say it's the call of children asking to be born, but my mother said it's a plain hint from nature, how a man should be master in his own house and everywhere else. She thought it pathetic that nature must repeat the hint so often, because men don't pay attention."

Balkis wrinkled her forehead. "I don't see how it helps in the more humdrum duties of life."

"Why, this way—if you remember your godlike confidence in that brief illumination, then you can be confident again when you sail ships or build temples or welcome queens to strange cities or ride camels or face your enemies."

"Or thrash your wife," added Balkis.

"Exactly! If you've once been capable of lofty flight, you needn't be content with the ground."

"If I understand," she mused, "the man must first realise that as a lover he is a god. He must grasp this truth all by himself. Then when he buys fish in the market, let us say, he will recall how he felt when he felt like a god, and perhaps buy the fish cheaper, or at any rate be masterful in his bargaining."

He knew she was taking revenge for his firm handling of her. He could afford to smile. "I told you the lesson was for men."

"I wonder," she inquired, "what Rezon's mother taught him!"

Then she lay down on the sacks, in a sudden weariness, and pretended to sleep, and all that day he avoided speech with her.

In the night they ran into a storm, a gust which left in its trail a heavy sea. Balkis found the lurching of the ship pleasurable, on the whole. By relaxing on the sack-cushions and by avoiding the instinctive effort to prevent the boat from rolling, she derived benefit from this cradle-motion and slept soundly. But when the light got in her eyes and woke her up, she saw the swaying of the tall mast, shaken from side to side by the rocking hull. She looked nervously for Hiram.

"He's below," said the steersman, "stopping a leak."

She caught the sound of a minor chant coming up from the crew. She had heard the like at funerals.

"That," said the steersman, "is the crew at the pumps."

In a sense, she wasn't frightened; the danger did not interfere with the steady aim of her black eyes, the friendly receptive line of her soft lips, the serene depth of her husky voice. She preferred not to drown, of course, but in her this sentiment, like any other, provoked constructive action.

She descended the scanty ladder to the space below, the level where the oarsmen sat, but instead of rowing now they were pulling at something up in the front end of the ship, under Hiram's vigorous direction, and as they pulled they gave that groan she had noticed. The purpose, she could see, was to secure unanimity in the pull. It didn't look like a pump, the helmsman hadn't heard accurately, she would just step forward along that raised plank between the benches, and whatever they were doing, perhaps they'd be glad of another pair of willing arms.

When Hiram glanced back to be sure the chain was coming clear, he saw the Queen of Sheba between two of his men, heaving away as though in a tug-of-war.

"Get out of that! Get up on deck!"

She decided not to obey, because no matter how godlike a man happens to be feeling, he shouldn't use that tone in public.

They were lifting a long chain from a dark hole where it had been stored, and as they pulled it out, they laid it in convenient loops so it wouldn't tangle.

"If you want to be useful," called Hiram, more in the way of a suggestion, "you and those men on each side of you might start it up the ladder."

As soon as they had it on deck, they carried it forward, and by a miracle of agility let it down on one side of the thrashing bow and drew it up again on the other, and then they played it out and hauled along toward the center near the mast, as though they wanted the vessel to skip the rope.

"What's it for?" she inquired at Hiram's energetic elbow. Since he neglected to answer, she asked again.

"If we live, I'll tell you!"

"I'm alive now," she reminded him.

"Six men on the windlass!" he shouted. "The rest of you back to the pumps!"

Like monkeys they slid down the ladder, all but the six, who began walking round and round, two to a bar.

"Oh, I see!" she exclaimed. "You're tying the boat together!"

"It may be too late," said Hiram, calmer now that he had done all he could. "We leak like a sieve."

Then he went below to watch the pumping, and she returned to the sacks and asked the man at the rudder how fast a sinking boat sinks, and either he didn't know or he was discouraged or deaf. She passed the next hour comparing the nearest waves with the rolling deck, to estimate whether the leak was winning or the pump, and now she guessed one and now the other, but mostly it was the leak.

When she first saw a fixed dark object stretching along the water, over to the right, she was so dulled with the vigil that she took it for an additional and unnecessary storm-shape, and let her glance turn away. Then her mind caught up with her eyes. Then she wondered if you could have a mirage in rough weather. Then she beckoned to the sad helmsman and pointed.

This time she got an answer out of him.

"Land!" he called.   "Below there—land!"

They dropped the pump and came up for a look, some a leap or two ahead of Hiram.

"That means we needn't drown, not today," he said. "We'll anchor to leeward and get off in the skiff—that is, if we don't hit a rock."

She had grown accustomed now to his avoidance of optimism.   It harmonised with his understatement of affection, as when he addressed her before the men.   But he and she had saved the ship, he with the chain, she with the island.   She was content with the augury.

A bleak solitude the island proved, a waste of rock and sour soil, inhabitable only by sea-birds, yet there was fresh water on it, springing from remote foundations.   Balkis explored the lonely coast next day in quiet weather, while the men filled casks or tinkered with the cracked ship. Hiram had to go look for her when they were ready to move on.

"Why not stay here?" she urged.

He offered the least of the objections.   "The men would rebel."

"But do we need the men?"

He was bored.   "We'd starve in a week."

"I wanted an island," she sighed.

"Let's hurry along," said he.   "If we can reach a town, we'll go ashore and stay there.   You don't know!   You were nearly done for!"

Approaching the ship, she noticed the chain still in place.   "Haven't they taken it off yet?   I should think it would drag in the water and hold us back!"

He laughed, not politely, and pushed her up the side once more, then went below to be sure the men had rigged the extra pump. Putting out again they could hear the swash of water in the hold.

For once he showed unchecked delight when two days later they sighted land toward the east, and in a few hours made out a handsome settlement with shining roofs.

"There we are!" he cried. "Lay on the oars, men! A lively port, and shore leave for all!"

"It may be just a village," said Balkis, picking up the caution he had dropped. She hoped for just a village.

"It's a great city, I tell you!"

He happened to be right. One by one the minarets rose up clear, the walls of a harbor, the shipping along the docks, the colored awnings which shaded bazaars. Hiram chose a dock close to the shore, so that if the boat should go down, it would rest on immediate mud. Loafers in number watched them lasso the dock and make fast.

"They ought to help," commented Balkis.

"Just as well they didn't," said Hiram. "I've nothing to pay them with." He faced his eager crew. "Four at a time on shore. Take turns. The others get at the leak again. Lean her over and work on the hull."

They grumbled at the meager holiday and the continued toil, but he sauntered up to the high shelf beside the steering gear, and surveyed the town.

"What place is this?" he called. One of the loafers went so far as to put a hand to his ear.

"What place?" called Hiram, a bit louder.

"He doesn't know your language," said Balkis. She

raised her hands and made a trumpet for her lips, and the fellow understood. Even Hiram got the answer.

"Well, Ophir is what I thought of," he said, "but now we've arrived, I've nothing to trade with—no wares, no gold! You were right about the island."

Pleased to be vindicated, she drew from her bosom or from an adjacent fold of clothing a large jewel. "Trade with this!"

He held it in his hand, turned it over, looked at her. "I thought you gave them all to Rezon!"

She displayed her happy white teeth. "He thought I did too, but I wouldn't give him all. I saved something for you."

Though obviously kind in intention, her words troubled him. He was still meditative when she had got into her white gown, with the yellow veil over her face, and they were walking toward the markets of Ophir. Being so thoughtful, he didn't notice the hard looks his tired men sent after him.

The marvels of those fabulous streets made him soon forget. As he remarked to Balkis, you might wander here for a lifetime and see but half.

He noticed the ivory first of all, because you couldn't miss the tusks, standing in rows for the buyers to examine, monstrous head-teeth, but Balkis preferred the counters on the fringe of this market, where the ivory was worked up into combs and spoons, necklaces, boxes, rings. She had an interest, he discovered, in rings. With some difficulty he drew her away, promising better bargains further on.

The bird-emporium came next, a world of feathers, squawks, queer odors. He and she both stopped willingly, charmed by the riot. There were peacocks of course, a city staple, but parrots were more numerous and to Hiram's wonder more beautiful. He had known only the common green, but on that particular day Ophir entertained a consignment of grey parrots which the experts pronounced memorable—grey parrots with scarlet tails, and with a wide assortment of experience among human beings, deceitfully innocent creatures who live as long as elephants and, like them, forget nothing. Moreover, as Hiram had heard and now could test for himself, they speak not with the nasal rasp of the green imitator, but with whatever precise variation of elegance or vulgarity they've had to listen to, through layers of changeful fortune.

One rich-plumed marvel must have visited Tyre, for he broke into highly idiomatic comments which could be identified almost to the hour and the spot. Hiram told Balkis who it was the bird was swearing at, and in what street he might have lived. From the same beak, a moment after, Balkis heard a haughty lady in the tongue of Sheba, and laughed, recognising, she said, a friend of her mother's whom she didn't like. She was fingering her jewel, but he quickly remarked that though this was more attractive than an ivory ring, they couldn't yet afford to invest in sentiment.

They moved on to quiet and perfume, to a clean section where rose essence was sold, and musk, and the breath of lilies. The men who offered the precious flasks had long black beards and wore white robes, white hoods, flowing

sleeves—silent men, not disposed to call out for cus-
tomers, like the fellows who tended the birds or the hunt-
ers who brought in the ivory. Perfume was a still thing,
pleading for itself. Hiram felt respectful but out of
place, and Balkis agreed that these were luxuries, though
if he had not pulled gently on her arm she would have
stayed longer.

In every street there was music—music by itself or music
with dancing, and here and there they came on acrobats.
The music was persistent, like bagpipes, helped out with
drums, and the tune wavered high, sometimes less shrill
but always a little mad. The purpose, Hiram gathered,
was to produce excitement rather than pleasure. Men of
mature years made these noises, and apparently the pro-
fession was honorable.

The dancing consisted of waving the hands and turning
around. Once they saw a man dance, but usually it was
a girl, bundled up with many garments, only the eyes, the
hands, the feet bare. You were to watch these eloquent
spots. The hands bent, lifted, fell, the fingers stuck out
or folded up. Hiram suspected a meaning but it escaped
him. The eyes opened and closed, squinted and glared,
glanced up, down, sideways, and the feet served to whirl
the dancer like a top. The music went best with the
whirling, Hiram thought, but Balkis said she had better
dancers at home, and this was an old style, too much
technique, too little nature.

The acrobats were what she liked. To Hiram's perplexity, she gave them too the name of dancers, and perhaps they were the new school who in time would succeed

the whirlers. They operated on a carpet spread in the middle of the street, stopping progress, and they were accompanied by a flute. Flute-players, like pipers, were elderly men. Acrobats were of two sorts—fat girls with little clothing, or thin boys and girls who wore the same kind of tunic and trouser, so that, what with the thinness, they couldn't be told apart.

The stout acrobats kept the head and the feet still and moved everything between. This was the art Balkis approved. The thin acrobats seemed to Hiram more subtle, and though what they did might be a novelty, it implied generations of devoted practice. They could spin several plates at once on the end of canes; with a cane in each hand they could turn a slow somersault and the plates wouldn't fall; or with the hands so engaged they could bend backwards, feet on ground, till the head touched the feet, and in this incredible posture, they could drink a cup of water upside down. When one performance ended, Hiram kept his eye out for another.

Here and there among the street-shows there were vendors of candy, sweet soft messes; there were bakers, handing bread directly from oven to mouth; there were shoe-makers, ready with a new slipper, if you had walked till you came through; there were donkeys staggering under leather bottles, from which the driver poured sugared drinks.

Hiram and Balkis strolled on, bewildered and inspired, till they chanced on the slave-market. The merchandise stood in an open space, the bidders formed in a circle, the auctioneer with reverence called attention to the good

points in God's chief handiwork. A doubtful customer
might ask the slave to walk a few steps, or to jump over a
hurdle, to estimate grace or agility, but most of the buyers
appraised at sight. Two thickset youths were sold for
farm-work, one woman for the kitchen, a lame boy because he was cheap.

Just as Hiram was turning away, they brought on a
girl, not dark like Balkis, nor even like Magsala or
Abishag or his own mother, but creamy white, with golden
hair. The bidding was instantaneous and determined.
He glanced at Balkis; she was studying the girl through
and through.

"You were once accustomed to servants," said he, "and
the change to my poverty may be too abrupt. This girl
could wait on you. Though I know little of such things,
I fancy she is worth the jewel."

Balkis took him by the arm and started him off. "You
fancy so, do you? What I don't need, most of all, is that
girl!"

From her vehemence he drew a compliment, and his
good humor rose still higher in the next street, when they
came on an austere man who covered his bald head with
a black cap, and carried a tray in front of him, held up by
straps over the shoulders. In the tray were precious
stones, set in rings of gold. It amused Hiram to see
Balkis come to a halt, fascinated.

"Is this what you need most?"

She refused to be teased. "That jewel," she said pointing, "is like mine!"

"Yours is finer."

"But the gold makes it seem brighter."

He feared she was about to throw away their fortune. "You can buy more with the jewel by itself!"

"I could wear it, and enjoy the sight, and then if ever we had to sell——"

"You should say, if ever we want to eat! We have nothing else! If we're to trade with the natives in that island of yours——"

"I'll ask the man what the value is, anyway."

She had the jewel out before he could stop her, and she and the black-capped tray-holder were talking like lightning in a tongue he couldn't understand, and the man was holding her jewel this way and that in the sun——

There was so much noise in all the streets, how was he to know this extra shouting meant something special? When the runner struck him between the shoulders with a staff, he turned to strike back, and there was the king of the city on his white horse, with the chamberlain carrying the pink umbrella over the royal head, and all good people scurrying to the house-walls, to let the procession go by.

Hiram and Balkis, not having scurried, were hustled, and the king observed the commotion. He was a grand Arab, beautiful as the ivory that had made him rich, his black eyes gleaming under a snowy turban, his beard fresh-oiled. He gazed down from his steed, at first indifferent, then pleased. Hiram wondered what was giving such pleasure, then followed the king's look. It was Balkis. She had folded back her yellow veil, even in that second, and she was returning the friendly smile.

Hiram thought the king was about to stop, but he moved on at last, merely turning for another view of the handsome woman. The crowd surged into the street again.

"We'll get out of here! Back to the ship!"

"My jewel!" she cried.

"It's nothing to stop for now!"

"Where's that man with my jewel?"

Since she called so loud and the passers-by paused to learn her trouble, he returned with her the few steps they had been pushed, but the man with the tray was gone. They searched through all the streets. Hiram reflected that the jewel must have been genuine.

"Shall we find the ship now?" he ventured, when there were no more streets.

"I hate this city!" she wept. "I never wanted to come here!"

He consoled her with his humility. "I dislike it myself. If ever I desired to dwell here, I was a fool!"

So she resigned herself to the loss, and was behaving handsomely, in the circumstances, by the time they reached the dock.

"Where's the boat?" he asked, as though she could tell him.

It was resting on the mud, and he could see the mast, of course, but he missed the hull, which was just below the street level. The chain had been removed, since in a port like this it had commercial value, and the men had also taken the great oars. Doubtless the pumps were gone. If they had left any food, it was under the deck, and the deck was awash.

The skiff swung safe at the end of its rope.

"Why didn't they steal that?" asked Hiram bitterly. "And the sacks! They've spared you something to sit on!"

"Don't take it so hard," said Balkis. "I can live without the jewel, and it wasn't a very good boat."

In a tall rage he splashed down on the shelf by the rudder, unfastened the tow-line, brought the skiff to the dock, threw in the sacks.

"Come on!"

When she hesitated, he grasped her arm.

"Be careful," she cried, "I'll fall in the water!"

For a moment he held her poised, ready, as she said, to fall.

"Did Rezon have from you anything beside the jewels?"

She smiled broadly. "I'll never tell, and you'll think he did! You'll be following me always, to find out!"

He threw her into the skiff and started rowing the length of the harbor, out beyond the city, eastward along the coast, looking for an island refuge or an unspoiled shore.

Chapter XII

When Magsala asked Solomon why he didn't seize the quiet interval and visit the region where his father had once tended sheep, he said that on second thoughts he could find no justification for such a pleasure-trip.

"Here I am with the taxes and a restless people, problems the like of which not even my father had to face, and they call for study. The day of mere courage has gone by. There are no more giants. I don't need a sling-shot, I need knowledge."

She leaned back in the long settee, in the cool of her room, under the window, and clasped her hands over her stately head.

"Not a sling, but whatever belongs to you, your poetry perhaps."

"Poetry? How would that help?"

"Does a poet ask? My dear! We had a poet in Egypt, three thousand years ago, who wrote—if I can remember —it's a famous passage—oh, this is it; we may busy ourselves with people, or we may busy ourselves with ideas, but in the end we busy ourselves with people."

Solomon stood beside her, walked up and down, came back to admire those companionable eyes.

"Very fine!" he concluded. "I wish I could study it in the original."

"My translation was rough," she admitted, "but that's the sense."

"To be frank," said he, "I don't quite get it."

"Why, everything depends on the person you are. Men may agree with your thoughts, but if they remain friends it's because they like *you!* Let others learn about taxes and such matters; you can employ their knowledge. For yourself, see to it you're a man your people will admire! It's a simple rule for all kings."

"What kind of man?"

She was amused at him. "Yourself, my dear—you can't be anything else, but unluckily you can fall short of that. You think your father became a wonderful ruler because he first watched the flocks, day and night, and so had leisure to learn the beautiful outside of the world— mountains, brooks, trees, stars—till life sang through him. You think if you made the same approach, you'd come at the same power. Since you think so, I say you ought never to forgive yourself if you don't hurry down there and try it."

He was eager to be convinced, but it seemed more in- telligent to give in slowly.

"I doubt if everything depends on the person, aside from his ideas. A man might appear like nothing at all and yet be wise."

"In that case," she laughed, "someone else will get credit for the wisdom, someone who was charming or magnificent, and therefore easy to remember."

He took the theory under consideration. "Really, I'd rather be remembered for my brains."

Her lips almost smiled, but she spared him. "It can't be done, my dear! Earn a name for wisdom, and they'll call you wise, but they'll hand on the story of some brave thing you did, or the splendor of your house, or your manners in public, or even the number of horses in your stable. Ask them to repeat one sage idea, and they will have forgotten. That father of yours, for example, a king above kings—already they mention chiefly the giant and the pebble."

"I don't want it to be that way!"

"It's the way men are," she insisted, "and I like it! Wisdom may be shared or handed on, but power is yourself."

So he went to Bethlehem, in search of power. Benaiah took him most of the journey in a chariot, they two alone, and set him down within easy distance of the sheep-covered hills, and told him where to find the farmers, from one of whom he would ask employment. Benaiah had secured for him a suitable costume, a wretched shirt, breeches belted around his middle, a crude staff. Under the belt he hid a small purse, against need, and in the purse, besides gold, he had packed a bit of parchment and a colored chalk, against inspiration, but in all else he was a poor man, to the life. For complete disguise Benaiah had warned him not to wash. His feet were naked.

To face the world thus, after the softness of his youth, was at once a soul-lifting adventure. The sound of the chariot rattling back to the stable was a blessing to his ears. The sun bathing him, the air touching his body— why had he let this freedom go unused? And why did men, with this privilege, complain? Jeroboam was a fraud! The common folk couldn't really be unhappy. He who works with his hands and walks barefoot, even though he lacks possessions, or because he lacks them, can breathe health and peace, and at night, his weariness being wholesome, he can sleep.

The sap of poetry, he observed with thankfulness, was already flowing. As he hurried along the road, he composed. A short thing, to be recorded when convenient.

> The sleep of a working man is sweet,
> Whether he eat little or much.

He liked the rhythm, and the thought had unity, but perhaps the end was feeble. The last words should sustain what went before, and you couldn't rest a poem on hunger. Why not reverse the lines?

> Whether he eat little or much,
> The sleep of a working man is sweet.

The hunger still got in the way. Why not distribute the thought over a wider area, dilute it perhaps? Or establish a contrast which would put even hunger in a favorable light? Ah, that would do it!

> The sleep of a working man is sweet,
> Whether he eat little or much,
> But the abundance of the rich
> Will not suffer him to sleep.

He said it out loud to fasten it down. One of his best things! So far as he was concerned, the second two lines weren't strictly true; he usually slept from one end of the night to the other. But the poem might be taken relatively. His sleep would be still sounder as soon as he became a working man.

Before night, however, he learned to his amazement how difficult it is to get at your work. Apparently you could be born to a throne but not to a job. A ragged fellow told him so, outside the door of a hut, the first he stopped at.

"I've sheep, to be sure, but you look little like a man who could buy any."

"Not buy but tend them," explained Solomon. "I'm a shepherd."

"And who isn't?" said the fellow. "Especially if you come from the city, as I wouldn't swear you don't. When they starve yonder, with the sort of king we have, they drop down here and call themselves shepherds. One for every sheep, if we took them all on!"

"Try me for a day and a night!"

"Listen to this," said the fellow, "we let the children do it, now the weather is pleasant, and there aren't enough flocks for the large families we have. If you were familiar with sheep, you wouldn't be asking, a grown man like you!"

Of course David had been very young—Solomon was discouraged when he recalled how young. With diminished spirits he inquired of the next house, and the next, and had the same answer. No one hired a shepherd in that country—they all gave the task to the youngest and least useful, and they all had many children.

At the last door Solomon begged the favor of a bed, and since it was a charitable home, they let him sleep in the yard on straw. Perhaps because he hadn't yet worked, he didn't sleep well.

Since there was no hope of employment, and therefore no inspiration for poetry, he decided to shorten his visit, but before he departed from the neighborhood he wished to look at the very field in which David, Jesse's youngest son, once filled the duties which the local children still monopolised.

"Just over the far hill it was," said the man who provided straw. "You go straight to the southeast a mile, then turn left."

"Northeast!" corrected his wife from the inside of the hovel. "Didn't my uncle, of the same age, have the nearest flock to him? He's told me many a time!"

"Me too," replied the husband, "and it was a good story up to twenty years ago, when his memory gave out. Now, my own father's elder brother was in the army the day the lad ran at Goliath——"

"But that wouldn't be here!"

"Did I say it was? I'm explaining to this wayfarer how my father's elder brother knew better than your uncle just where the flocks were when David came up for a look at the camp and resolved to run at the giant."

Solomon abandoned them to their history, and tried southeast with a turn to the left, but since the road was harder on the feet today than it had been yesterday, he soon perceived the folly of investing effort in random explorations. Turning, he plodded back toward the little

city itself, trusting fragments of his father's talk, vaguely
recalled. There was a well which gave the best water on
earth. It was near a gate. Solomon skirted the walls
looking for the well, and he found two. In each case the
proud citizens swore theirs was the authentic one. He
drank from both and went on.

To the east the land fell away in a series of orchards,
rich with many kinds of fruit but chiefly olives, and under
the trees he saw a group of children with three goats. He
walked faster. Below spread the plains, squared off in
wheat-plantings, or left open for grazing. He caught
sight of creatures in groups, slow-moving. The flocks!
There was the pasture he looked for! Whether a little
more this way or that, north or south, did it matter? That
landscape from some angle had filled his father's eyes!

Stirred deep, he walked from flock to flock, creeping
up behind the lads to observe them at their happy work.
He expected a youthful vigilance, shot through with
heroic promise. That is, he expected too much. These
were no Davids. Their habit, it seemed, was to stretch out
under a cypress or an olive tree and doze, with the crook
resting on their legs. By way of variation, two boys were
busy with a game, tossing a knife. Solomon concluded
that at least one flock was watching itself.

Though he pushed on, his ardor flagged, and he asked
himself what he was seeking. The past was not here, nor
was his future. Noon approached, the sun grew hot, he
was hungry. "Whether he eat little or much"—he was
in no mood to compose poetry!

Yet he chanced on one pleasant picture, worth storing

up—a boy and a girl sitting in the shade of a rock, eating fruit. As he came near, the boy was singing, between bites.

"Did you find that fruit in yonder orchards?"

The boy nodded, his mouth being full.

"Would I be permitted to feed myself from the same place?"

Simply, without hesitation, the boy counted off a third of what remained in his basket, and handed it over. Not a handsome child, not clean, not—if one judged by the features—full-witted, but Solomon sat down and ate.

At that moment he felt as little a king as on the day when he rode the mule, yet here on the plains his humility was neither timid nor baffled, as it had been during his progress through the city streets, while watching the back of Benaiah's head and the mule's ears. In a short time he had come far. The dirty boy and the awkward girl were kind to the stranger within their gate. The rock-shadow was the gate; he didn't mind being the stranger. They were themselves, as Magsala would say, perfect according to their ability, and there was justice in the gift of food and in his acceptance of it, since they were at home in their world, as he was not yet in his.

Was it ungenerous to notice, even while he honored these children, that the life of a shepherd no longer prepared you for wisdom, valor, conquest? One look at that boy, and you'd know he'd remain as he was, unless he shrunk to something less admirable. A dull animal, with good manners, as you might rate a dog of medium quality.

Perhaps it wasn't the shepherd's life that made David become David!

Nor any other occupation!

Perhaps you must be David to start with!

We may say that at the stroke of this truth Solomon's education was complete. Here began the full flow of that wisdom with which his name, as Magsala foresaw, is now somewhat loosely associated. We need not stop to argue against those busy commentators who would assign to other pens his best poems and his meatiest aphorisms. Magsala foresaw this also. But the point is, he loved his father and wished to imitate his greatness, and here among the flocks he discovered the only way. Magsala had told him, but here he learned it for himself.

He would have returned to the palace forthwith, if the boy hadn't resumed his singing. A ballad of the people, evidently, one of those interminable things which can be laid down anywhere without loss and taken up again when the throat needs exercise. As the boy mumbled them, the words were not clear, and he sang certain lines twice, either because he was recalling what came next, or because he was rolling a special beauty under his tongue. The tune clung to four notes. Solomon wondered if his father had encountered this droning——

His heart all but stopped its beat—the boy sang his own name!

> King Solomon made himself,
> Made himself a chariot,
> A chariot,
> Made himself a chariot,
> Of the wood of Lebanon!

"Who taught you to sing that, boy?"

"Me? I always sing it."

"Who wrote it?"

The child was bewildered. "Wrote it?"

"Do you know what it means?"

The boy stared with honest eyes. "It's pretty."

Solomon stared back. "Go on—sing the rest!"

"Do you like it?"

"I don't know yet—let's hear it all!"

Perhaps he had frightened the child, or perhaps the poem had got mixed up ages ago, but the sequence was erratic. Anyway, it had nothing to do with Solomon, the name just happened in; there was no criticism of his government, Jeroboam wasn't the author. The mangled plot concerned someone in an advanced state of love, two people, and they were putting rhapsody into verse, an achievement which Solomon had found impossible, and though you weren't clear always as to who was speaking, the man or the woman, they both spoke so well that instead of wishing the language could match the passion, as you do with most loves and most poems, you caught yourself wishing here that some passion, at some time, might be worthy of these fire-touched words.

To come upon beauty, anywhere! But to receive the gift of it from this stolid boy, with the awkward girl lying on her stomach, elbows propping up chin, eyes glued on the singer——! Solomon hoped she didn't think the boy was describing her.

Tell me always, my love,
My soul's love,
Where your flock will rest
At noon!
Why should I lose my way
And find another flock
Not yours?

How beautiful you are, my love,
Ah, how beautiful!
Your eyes are doves' eyes,
Your teeth are white
As the shorn lambs
Fresh from the washing!
Your lips are a scarlet thread,
Your neck is an ivory tower,
Your breasts are two young roes
Feeding on lilies!

You are mine, mine only!
My garden enclosed,
A spring shut up,
A fountain sealed!

For a while Solomon paid no more heed to what the
boy sang. His mind was going back over this praise of
beauty, cherishing the pictures, envying the boldness, the
vigor, the happy confidence of the unknown poet. Nobody could make such verses who had not himself adored
a superb woman! Solomon was convinced of that, just on
a first hearing. What full-hearted desire, expressed on
such a soul-respecting plane!

That is, his contemplation of ideal beauty in a work of

art slipped off promptly into two questions, both about people, as Magsala would have noticed. He wondered who composed the poem and who was the superb woman. He also wondered whether she were still alive, and in case she were, and if they should ever meet, whether his own literary talent could furnish a tribute even approximating this one.

The boy had got on to that section of the ballad where the heroine has her turn, explaining to the hero the ultimate reach of her devotion. Solomon paid attention again. He hadn't expected the woman to say anything.

> He called me his garden!
> Ah, my beloved,
> Come to your garden,
> Come soon!
>
> As I lay on my bed sleeping
> I dreamt of him,
> My heart dreamt,
> My heart heard him knocking at the door!
> Is not this he whom you long for?
> Cried my heart.
> Rise up! Will you keep him waiting?
> He pleads, Open, my love,
> Hasten,
> On my head is the dew,
> On my hair the drops of the night!
>
> I rose to let him in,
> For joy my hand tingled
> On the handles of the lock,
> But when I opened, he was gone!

Whither have you withdrawn,
Ah, beloved?
Whither?

I call, but he gives me no answer.
It is my voice calling,
My voice, beloved!

He gives me no answer!
Those in the house say,
Call not so loud, he is gone,
If indeed he ever was here!

The watchmen about the city
Say, Peace, daughter, call no more,
He will not return!

Friend, which way do you go?
You might find him, I think!
Tell him from me, I charge you,
If ever you find him,
Tell him I am sick with love!

It was this passage which determined Solomon not to go home till he could repeat the ballad for Magsala's benefit. Since she had quoted an Egyptian poet, he'd like to lay before her this masterpiece of insight, the work of his people. By masterpiece, he meant the woman's declaration; the earlier section, however fine, paled before this revealing of the heart, or rather of the methods by which words can indicate the heart.

When he should say the lines over for Magsala, having first memorised them, he would explain that in order to convey absolute passion you must underline the poem with despair, even when you handle happy passion, because any emotion, even happiness, when carried to an extreme, becomes painful, a gratifying pain but still an ache.

He intended to remind her further that when you are in love you frequently dream of the object, and in the dream the object—that is, the person loved—evades you, and you experience an agony of frustrated longing, which continues for days after you've waked up. Now, if a poet can imitate the dream in this respect, and convey the sentiment of tragic longing, the result will be to express, as it were, unutterable love, which is what most poets wish to do.

And here it was all accomplished in a ballad, picked up in a field! The woman dreamt the man knocked at the door, and when she got up he wasn't there, because it was a dream—or perhaps it wasn't, perhaps her calling to him was the dream; you could take it either way; if it wasn't a dream, would the city watchmen be in position to tell her whether the lover would or would not return? In either case, the yearning of the woman, calling through the streets and even stopping a stranger, produces a pleasurable pain in those who listen to the poem, and this pain makes them feel in their own persons that the woman was very much in love.

He'd ask Magsala if she could match that with Egyptian parallels.

It was his plan to leave the children for a while, walk here and there through the plain, and as if by accident happen on them again in the late afternoon, when the heat would be relenting, and perhaps the boy would feel like singing the ballad several times, and somewhat more slowly. Perhaps also there were other boys who knew other poems and in idle moments chanted them. If one could gather all that material, it would be a mirror of David's people, perhaps, or even of other people, though that would be secondary.

But in the afternoon the boy was out of temper and no more singing could be wrung from him. He had the impudence to pretend he hadn't sung in the morning. Solomon walked back toward the city and begged another straw bed and passed another sleepless night, though weariness was heavy on him. The poem kept him awake. He couldn't remember it! He probably couldn't learn it, not short of a dozen repetitions! If he hoped to take it back with him, he must write it down.

At dawn the farmer whose guest he had been gave him food and hurried him away—a grudging man who was hospitable only because he feared not to be.

"Why don't you work," he inquired, "instead of living on those poorer than yourself?"

"I have sought work in vain."

"Not here you haven't!" retorted the fellow. "Take that spade and help with the ditch I'm putting behind my cowshed. The drain is backing up."

"I am a shepherd," explained Solomon.

"Even at that, you have arms, haven't you?"

"I've a special reason for seeking employment among the flocks."

"You're a tramp!" shouted the man. "They always

have an excuse! You looking for work? Step off now before I lay my staff on your shoulders!"

This rough start of the day, though it wounded his pride, may have roused in him more of what Magsala wished to develop. He could have rebuked the farmer, he could have broken the astounding news that he was the king, but that course would have been final; the last possibility of playing shepherd would have been sacrificed. Besides—suppose the farmer didn't believe he was king? How would he get a message to Benaiah or to his mother, to furnish evidence? Suppose—it wouldn't happen, of course—but suppose Benaiah said he *wasn't* king?

For a moment he chilled at the thought, then an admirable anger, a novel courage warmed him; he would do what his father had done, he would fight his way up!

He was in the farmer's courtyard again, to the fellow's disgust.

"What can we give you now, Handsome One?"

"Your spade!" shouted Solomon back. "Where's that ditch?"

The farmer showed him where the trench began, offering a few instructions, and Solomon laid aside the rags of his shirt and bent to the toil. The farmer let him manage the task alone, and by noon it was finished; also, the skin had vanished from the underside of Solomon's hands.

"Is it what you wanted?"

"Not what I wanted, but more than I hoped for from a vagabond. Step into the kitchen and take your pay in a dish of soup."

Solomon wanted the soup, but he covered himself again

and stalked forth on the road, the farmer gaping after
him.

On his way through the orchards, he helped himself to
fruit on the ground, with an apprehension, odd in a king,
lest the owner might rise up and shout, but the stillness
of midday was unbroken and the fruit remained sweet.
He even carried something in his hands, for the boy and
the girl.

At sight of the modest gift the boy agreed to sing once
more, but when Solomon took out his parchment, the bar-
gain was promptly repudiated. Parchment and chalk
were, it seemed, instruments of evil; the marks Solomon
was making would doubtless break one's health or snap
a bone! The boy whitened under the dirt, shouted to his
flocks, began moving off. It didn't help to offer him gold,
and Solomon knew the mistake the moment he stumbled
into it. The boy ran.

Not till another morning could the poem be written
down, and then only because Solomon crept up on all
fours and hid behind a tree while the boy was singing, and
still again, only because the boy had nothing else to sing
and went over the ballad several times. He sang it so
much because the awkward girl liked to hear it. Now
that they supposed themselves alone, she asked for one
more rendering, and her cunning was beyond her looks,
for she praised not the poem but the boy's thin voice. So
the ballad was captured.

It had been hard to win, and Solomon had come to love
it! The kind of poem he would have written, had the gift
been his! Now that he had it safe, he changed his mind,

he wouldn't lecture Magsala about it; it was too beautiful.
Perhaps one ought not to talk of beauty; the ache that
comes up in your heart is criticism enough. But Magsala
would enjoy learning the verses, he was sure. They might
spend unforgettable hours learning them together.

He didn't ask whether she would consider his development complete; he had forgotten his development. Living
with this poem, these days, he had forgotten himself. His
head was full of verses which sang to each other, and he
liked to listen.

> Who is this that comes up from
>   the wilderness,
> Leaning upon her beloved?
> Set me as a seal upon your heart,
> As a seal upon your arm!
> Many waters cannot quench love.

If he walked fast, he would reach the palace in another
day.

The very evening of his triumph, a few hours after he
had rescued the great song from its lowly condition,
Abishag was huddled close to the wall of the corridor,
watching toward Bathsheba's door.

Several times now she had stolen into the palace and
occupied that station, during the minutes when the keeper
of the jail was having his rapid supper. The coincidence
was remarked by more than one of the guards.

From where she stood she could see what persons called
upon the king's mother, from which circumstance the
guards nursed the theory that Abishag was a spy for Solo-

mon, a theory easily proved by the quickness with which she would call upon him after his return.

On this particular evening, they noticed, she seemed weary; that cheerfulness of hers faded unless you spoke to her, and it died again with her smile, when she stopped speaking.

Spy or not, they knew the king was fond of her. If she wished to stand for a minute there in the shadow against the wall, it was her affair—and perhaps it was the king's. They let her stay, but they watched.

Only a minute, that night. Then they saw the jailer, who should have been at his supper, leading to Bath-sheba's door the boy who admired Jeroboam and wished to kill somebody. The Queen-mother was no doubt examining him again.

No sooner had the boy been led to Bathsheba, than the jailer came out alone and returned to his post. The guards made a note of this circumstance. One of them took courage in hand and knocked on the door, and asked Solomon's mother if anything was amiss, and she was singularly pleasant and said all was well. Her room, except for herself, was empty. The guard came out puzzled. Abishag, he noticed, was gone. The other guard said she had walked with a lagging step to Magsala's apartment.

"We have seen little of each other," said Solomon's wife, "though we promised a cordial rivalry. You still love him, I suppose."

"I still do."

"It has seemed to me best to put no obstacle in his path or yours. I have fought you fairly because that was the surest way to win."

"You have won," said Abishag. "He loves you."

Magsala looked at her. "Why did you come here?"

Abishag imitated her challenging tone. "Why did you let me in?"

"You excite my curiosity."

"Well, you excite mine."

Magsala frowned. "For you that is not a good reason."

Abishag tilted her head. "If you're so particular, I can supply another. You'll be pleased to learn that I'm going away. Out of the city, I mean. I shan't return."

Magsala did not relax her suspicion of this cheerful mischief.

"It's not easy for a girl to travel—with whom do you go?"

Abishag put on a maidenly embarrassment, clasping her hands and gazing at the floor.

"That's the queer part of it, and I'm glad the king isn't at home, because he says the best women don't travel at all, but the fact is, I'm going by myself!"

"Where?"

"I'm just going to wander, one place after another."

"It doesn't sound respectable."

"It isn't!"

Magsala laughed, as though it were useless to contend with the brazen.

"You'd like to make me feel sorry, almost penitent, as though the fault were mine!"

"That's it," said Abishag cheerfully. "I'd like to wring your heart, for revenge."

"You're incredible! Also, you may go! A happy journey!"

Abishag gazed deliberately toward the door, then toward the window, then toward the queen's bed. "I've a moment or two still," she said, "and I'd like to leave a particular message for the king. I might have given it to him myself, or left it for him in the hands of a nice man who is fond of me, but I thought it would be graceful to trust it with you. I suppose I *can* trust you?"

"I hope you can!"

"Can I trust you to tell him—I love him?"

"You have given proof—he knows it."

"Will you say I go because I don't wish him hurt?"

Magsala was struck by the phrase. "Who would hurt him?"

"I might," said Abishag, "if I didn't go."

"Very well, I'll give the message. May I say farewell now?"

Abishag stood with her head turned. "Did I hear some one at your door?"

"See who it is, Tii."

It was a servant bringing a request from Bathsheba that the queen her daughter should do her the honor——

"Bring my blue robe, Tii."

She was ever so little annoyed, seeing Abishag still there. "We have taken our farewells!"

"One favor, and I'll go. I want your blue robe."

"My blue robe?"

"For a remembrance, and because I never had a dress like that—— You see, I'm finding out whether you are generous!"

Magsala gazed at her, astounded, then turned away. "Give her the blue robe, Tii."

Abishag began putting it on, over the linen she was wearing.

"Do you dress in my room?" asked Magsala, weary rather than wrathful. "What an extraordinary person!"

"It's a bit long for me, isn't it?" asked Abishag, gazing down. "But temporarily I can hold it up."

She even paused to glance in Magsala's mirror.

"You wear the hood over your wig, don't you? I've always wanted to look like you."

The stately queen shook her head and laughed.

"Run along and be happy!"

With the blue robe about her, Abishag walked like Magsala herself toward the dark corner near Bathsheba's door where the knife was waiting.

THE END